# *The Sun Also Shines for me*

*A Pride and Prejudice sequel*

*Written by*

*Noe & Cindy*

Cover illustration
Noe

Edited by
Cindy

Also by Noe & Cindy:
## Mr Darcy falls in love

Based on Jane Austen's Pride and Prejudice

ISBN: **1500859141**
ISBN-13: **978-1500859145**

*This book is dedicated to everyone who loves to read <u>Pride and Prejudice</u> as much as we do.*

*We also dedicate it to the*
**middle child**
*in every family ...*
*The sun also shines for you.*

*We'd like to thank all of those who have read our book*
*Mr Darcy falls in love.*
*Your doing so encouraged us to continue writing, and for that we are very grateful.*

# Chapter One

Mary Bennet was inadvertently granted the position of middle child in her family of five sisters. Throughout her formative years, she was overshadowed by her two elder sisters and noisily obscured by the two younger. Like a plant reaching for the sunlight, she would attempt to come out, for she had her own wishes and dreams that would not be satisfied with simply continuing to be overshadowed as the middle child.

Such a thing is not unusual, as can be noted from this anonymous poem by an aristocrat, who obviously was such a child himself:

> *The child of the middle is often not seen.*
> *The first and last are those for whom*
> *The light has been.*
> *Leaving but little*
> *For the one in the middle.*
>
> *This light has not been taken by force*
> *Or stolen away by cunning.*
> *The middle child had no idea, of course,*
> *That a race to the light there was to be running.*

This is just the circumstance Mary has grown up with, everyone having come to know her only as the sister of her siblings. But marriage in the family, like a shifting in the earth's crust, has a way of bringing what was not in the light out for display. And it is often discovered that there is something well worth seeing that had been deeply hidden away.

The shifting in the Bennet family is here related by this bit of family history: the first to be married was the youngest sister, Lydia, who nearly brought the family to ruin by her scandalous elopement which had not resulted in a proper marriage. All was corrected, however, when the scoundrel she was involved with was made to marry her. It was not long after this that Jane and Elizabeth, the older sisters, were themselves married and starting their new lives with their very fine, and very rich, husbands.

To keep Kitty, sister number four, away from Lydia's bad influence and to refine her manners, Jane and Elizabeth had her spend most of her time with either of them, for they would take Kitty in hand in a way their mother would not, or could not—it is difficult to say which. But be that as it may, all this rearranging of the family landscape had its effect on our dear middle sister.

Mary, you see, was left at home under the management of her mother when all her sisters were gone. This challenged her more than the most complicated piano piece she had thus far taken up to learn, or even some new investigation of knowledge and ethics, for Mary had always been interested in becoming proficient at the piano and also delighted in furthering her knowledge by reading as much as she could on subjects to improve her mind and character. Mrs. Bennet, on the other hand, knew how to manage only one thing for an unmarried young lady, and that was how to find her a husband.

Initially, Mary took to this challenge with the same determination she had for her other more solitary pursuits. In an effort to groom her to be more appealing to a prospective partner, Mrs. Bennet would have Mary sit with her to receive visitors, who were more numerous now that the two eldest daughters were established with such distinguished gentlemen as Mr. Charles Bingley, formerly of Netherfield Park, and Mr. Fitzwilliam Darcy of Pemberley Estates.

In addition to this, her mother had been having more dinner parties and accepting all the invitations by every prominent person she could arrange to be included with. Mary understood the objective for all this socializing, although, since Mrs. Bennet quite often took these opportunities to broadcast how prosperous and gay things were for Jane and Elizabeth, she often felt her social education was really the secondary reason for these comings and goings. She was constantly being lectured by her mother about her powers of conversation after each visitor had left their home, though what she was really complaining about was Mary's choice of subject. On this point, dear Mary would wonder, "Why am I to be found fault with just because people in general choose to remain ignorant about matters that are of greater importance than balls and the latest gossip?"

More than a year of this had been enough for our heroine. There was a growing sense of restlessness in Mary, for though she had accepted her mother's tutelage on the ways of husband-getting in all sincerity, she felt a nagging desire for something more meaningful. The activities she was involved in with her mother paled in her estimation to the things she held of value and interest. Mary was finally moved to action by (of all things) something she had read in a book about birds: *The Beautiful Sunbirds of the Mekong River.* In the chapter, <u>Captured Light</u>, the author describes what happens when the sunbirds are caught in order to be sold to people who live in those places that consider themselves more civilized, who rationalize that they must have the beauty of nature brought to them on their own terms. *"After some time passes, the birds become accustomed to their captive state and, having been bent to the will of their captors, will no longer fly away to where their natural inclination so strongly urged upon them when they were first snatched."*

Young Miss Bennet considered how sad for such a thing to happen to those birds that were meant to be out spreading their wings, flying wherever they wished. Yes, there would be certain dangers and challenges in their natural habitat, but how just it was for the sunbirds to live free under that great luminary that gives their plumage such radiant colors! "Are birds the only ones to be thus affected?"—she certainly thought not.

So at last she said to her mother one day as Mrs. Bennet was talking of the next engagement she had arranged for Mary's benefit: "There is so much that is going on in the world that is infinitely more profound and interesting than husband-hunting, Mama! Have you any idea how much is happening beyond the confines of our home environment? I've read books on things such as expeditions into unknown lands and a growing understanding of science, not to mention the older books of poetry and expressions of wisdom."

"Pishposh," was her mother's response. "There you go with your books! Such things are of no use to ladies! What man would be interested in you for knowing such things?"

"Mama, these things hold an interest for *me*, and I thirst for such knowledge for my own sake."

"How can you say things like that, when you have seen how your sisters Jane and Lizzy have made such advantageous matches? Can you not see how fine a situation they now have because of the way I handled matters and helped them along? This nonsense of your not wanting to pursue a good match and simply hiding away in your unintelligible books must end *now*. You must go visit your sisters straightaway—after reminding yourself of how things are for them, you will change your view! I'll talk to your father immediately about sending you on your way."

Mary shook her head and repined as she went to her room to await what would come of her mother's talk with her father. There was at least some reason to hope, since her father did not have that same view of things as her mother. And such hope was not ill-founded, for even that anonymous aristocrat ended his verse this way:

> *Get by as best as you can, you child of the middle.*
> *For who you are will often not see the light*
> *When you are little.*
> *Take comfort, though, for someday it will be known . . .*
> *That, for you, the sun also shown.*

# Chapter Two

"My dear Mr. Bennet, I am concerned about Mary."

"And what is it that concerns you, madam, about our third daughter?"

"She seems not to understand the place of a lady. She talks nonsense, and I blame you for this! She follows your example of being occupied with books and learning, constantly having more interest in them than in people. Why, she doesn't even realize the way to improve herself is to follow the example of her sisters and make a good match! For heaven's sake, now that Jane has Bingley and Lizzy has Mr. Darcy, there is no reason for her not to entertain the hope of finding a man that is comfortably situated. She need only follow Kitty in this regard. We *must* send Mary to stay with Jane or Elizabeth for a time, for then she will see the sense of it ... but since Jane is out touring abroad, I suppose she must be sent to Lizzy, for I dare not postpone this action."

Mr. Bennet sighed. "Is it not enough that we have two daughters married to very rich men, and one married to a worthless fool? We have in this way covered all possible areas of the marital scene and, of course, Kitty will soon attract some fellow under the direction of Jane or Elizabeth. What possible need could there be in making Mary pursue such a course before she feels impelled to do so herself?" The head of the Bennet family did not want to concern himself with such matters, but complying with his wife's request was much preferred to having the subject canvassed time and again by her. Quickly considering the pleasure he took in being at Pemberley, he thus acquiesced, declaring, "Although, upon further reflection, I see your point, my dear. I shall take her to the Darcy estate myself, and in this way I will be able to express our concerns to Lizzy directly."

"Now you are being sensible, Mr. Bennet," cried his wife.

Mary, upon being informed of the plan by her father, was ready to comply, for the library at Pemberley was extensive. Being there also had the added benefit of not being where her mother was, for no one in the family had her mother's knack for badgering, so there would at least be some relief from that. She and her father made arrangements to leave by the end of the week, and soon that day arrived. With Mrs. Bennet's parting instructions firmly impressed upon them both, they made their departure.

Before they had been in the carriage for long, Mary abruptly posed this question to her father: "In your view of things, Papa, is it fair for women to have such limited prospects?"

Surprised by this strange query, he asked, "To what are you referring, Mary?"

"Well, only consider the sphere of women: we must spend our time when we are not married in contemplating how we may become so. When we are married, our sphere in some respects grows smaller by our being concerned with merely managing a household. As for those who do not marry, they are relegated to being inconvenient aunts who must trespass on the kindness of others. Or perhaps, if she has learned anything of worth, one may become a governess, which, of course, still has her in the domain of the home and family."

Mr. Bennet, who had grown accustomed to hearing Mary's opinions for the diverting bit of humor they would provide, found quite a difference in this speech. It had become so easy throughout their lives for him to categorize all his daughters as *silly*, without taking any time or interest in really getting to know them individually. Years of habit cannot be thrown off in a moment, however, and even though what Mary said expressed insight and a legitimate concern, his immediate response was said in his typical lightheartedly dismissive way: "So, the domestic scene holds little appeal to you, I see."

"I am not saying I would not want to get married at some point, but why is it that women must be confined to the domestic scene only?"

"There are those who say women do not have the capacity of going beyond that," her father replied.

Mary now said in a heightened tone, "Yes! And if I am not much mistaken, those that say it are *men*, and those who believe it are these very same men, along with women who see no other alternative than that which is placed before them. But Papa, our time is like no other, since more is being learned about the world around us every day. The idea of confining my interest to the parameters of a home and family—even if that home be as grand as Pemberley—is a limitation that my mind and heart rebel against!"

Seeing now that the subject was not just a philosophical one for his daughter, Mr. Bennet responded with more empathy. "We are all presented with limitations, Mary my dear, whether we are men or women. There are those who have broken through such barriers that the rest of us have learned to live with, and the world has become a better place for their accomplishments. If you choose to test yourself as one who will do so, it will require bravery and determination, and because you are a woman, it will also require a bit more skill than what is found in general even among men. This, of course, is not fair, I grant you, but when one is seeking to go beyond the bounds of what is commonly accepted, it is what one will be confronted with."

"My resolve to set out on this course will come from the unfairness of women's situation and will, I believe, harden to steadfastness when confronted with the obstacles you have mentioned. As for my skill, I can only hope my talent will rise to the occasion. Be assured, Papa, that I am not seeking to change society; I am only concerned with pursuing my own interests, which at this time have nothing to do with finding a husband and raising a family."

Hearing Mary express herself with such clarity of thought borne from sober contemplation and seeing in her eyes the flame of determination, her father wished to do nothing to dampen her spirit. He therefore said, "As you know, your mother knows no other interest, but let me tell you now, my child, you have my blessing to push ahead in whatever direction your interest inclines you."

"Thank you, Papa," Mary said with sincerity. "And ... may we at the start of this endeavor of mine, by way of a symbolic gesture, now break with tradition between men and women and shake hands upon it?"

For the first time that he could remember, Mr. Bennet looked with pride at Mary. "I will wholeheartedly give you my hand," he answered, and with mutual respect, they reached out to one another. "Do you know what it is you wish to pursue, my dear?"

"Not really. I have been under the guidance of my mother this past year, and initially I was a willing pupil. But inside there was *something* calling to me that finally I could not ignore, like the words of the poet who said, *'The wind through the trees tells of tales faintly heard by my soul, and until now is their calling being made more clear.'* So I have been struggling more with the issue of following those feelings or submitting to Mama's instruction and marching to the same tune as all other women. Now to have your kind blessing for taking my own course in life, I can begin in earnest to find a path that does interest me."

After saying this, she looked out the window of the carriage with a feeling of real freedom and excitement, the sound of the wind's calling being made more clear. Mary Bennet spent the rest of the journey considering just how vast and wonderful the world looked at this moment.

# Chapter Three

Arriving at Pemberley, they were informed that Elizabeth and her husband had just returned home themselves from a brief visit into town. She and Mr. Darcy's younger sister Georgiana had taken to the shops while he was secretly picking up a very special gift he had commissioned to be made for the two of them. Each had been told that she was to keep the other busy for the sake of the surprise, not knowing the full extent of his plan.

Therefore, Mr. Bennet and Mary were shown into the sitting room until Mrs. Darcy could be informed of their arrival. Elizabeth, upon hearing the news, quickly dressed and came directly downstairs. "Papa, Mary, how delightful to see you," she said as she entered the room. A sudden apprehension caused her to add, "We had no idea of your coming ... surely all is well?"

"Yes, my dear," her father answered, "there is no cause for alarm. We have been sent by your mother. In point of fact, I fully expect she will send a letter, despite her dislike of writing, to ensure your getting the proper message. Though learning has never been her strong suit, she has at least learned, on matters such as these, that I am not to be trusted with passing on such delicate information. Not to mention, I am sure there will also be extensive instructions as to what she expects you to do."

Darcy now entered, making the same declaration as Elizabeth had, to which he received a shorter version of Mr. Bennet's reply. As often was the case, Darcy did not comprehend Mr. Bennet's answer, but without pursuing the matter, he graciously suggested, "May we all sit down and call for tea?"

The Darcy's servants were always prepared for guests, and therefore refreshments were quickly brought in. Once they had all been served, Elizabeth asked more specifically, "Papa, for what reason has my mother sent you both here?"

Mary was aware her father could answer Lizzy's question without mentioning what they had talked about in the carriage, although it seemed logical that he would. This prospect was met with mixed emotions, for she was not sure she was ready for the world in general to know of her desire to put off pursuing a match for some as yet unknown interest. Therefore, she turned to listen carefully to what her father would say in answer, looking at him with earnest anticipation.

"Your mother sent us here for Mary to see firsthand the joys of marrying the right sort of man, since in your mother's opinion, your sister has not sufficient interest in the notion. As you know, Mary has never cared much for balls and those sorts of activities which are generally believed to advance such a thing as matrimony." Elizabeth stole a look at her sister to see how she bore this information but could not make out its effect on her, as Mary was still intently turned toward her father.

Georgiana, who had been on the verge of going in, halted so as not to interrupt when she realized Elizabeth's family was there. From her vantage point, she could hear what was being discussed and sighed out of sympathy for Mary, for since Elizabeth's marriage to her brother, Georgiana and Mary had discovered they had much in common and a growing friendship was evolving. "How thankful I am that neither my brother nor Elizabeth are urging me to make a match as Mary's mother does her ... I know I am eighteen now, but the prospect of being singled out by someone in particular for the purpose of courting me is frightening! ... how glad I am my brother understands my fears and is kindly helping me to deal with them. Elizabeth too gives me strength, for she is not afraid of any man ... how diverting it is when she makes me laugh at those men that have come within our circle. But poor Mary must bear her mother's insisting on her own ... but wait—what is it that is being said now?"

Mr. Bennet was continuing, "On our carriage ride here, Mary expressed her desire to set off on a path that did not include luring some eligible young man into matrimony. Your mother can think of nothing else, as you well know, and will be thrown into a panic involving spasms and such things if she hears of it. So it is my determination that she not learn of it any time soon, and that she continue in whatever sort of blissful ignorance can be hers while still having one unmarried daughter." Pausing with a shake of his head, he finished with: "All that about your mother aside, I must say that Mary is not idle, nor is she passing her time in frivolous pursuits as your younger sisters used to do, so I have given her my blessing to follow her aspirations, even though they may be contrary to what is expected for young ladies. And there you are, Elizabeth, at this point I have delivered your mother's message on why we are here as well as telling you my feelings on the subject."

Elizabeth now addressed her sister: "Mary, may I ask what it is you intend to do?"

"Father and I have only just discussed this in the carriage on the way here, and though he has given me his approval, I have had no time to set my course."

Georgiana, still listening unobserved, thought, "How brave of Mary! She wishes to set her own course, like a sailor setting out on a mysterious voyage." She now felt this was an appropriate time to enter the room, and as she did, she received greetings from the visitors. Not wanting anyone to know she had been listening, she said, "Mr. Bennet, Mary, it is always a pleasure to see you here at Pemberley. I hope all is well?"

The conversation then moved on to their trip to town, and suddenly Darcy called everyone's attention by standing and saying, "I believe this is an excellent time to bring out a surprise I brought back from London for *a certain someone.*"

His wife tried to act as if this was an unexpected announcement just as his young sister was making the same attempt, with both saying, "Surprise? For whom? What is this all about?"

Darcy, observing the forced expressions on their faces, was gratified, and continuing his pretense, gave each a knowing smile. "I shall return momentarily," he announced and headed out of the room. The family began to express their wonder at what surprise Darcy could have, with Elizabeth and Georgiana each thinking what a wonderful way he was going about his scheme!

When he returned, he carried a single beautifully wrapped package about half the size of a hat box. Lizzy and Georgiana were sitting together on the divan, and the anticipation each was feeling at being a part of surprising the other could hardly be contained by either of them. Coming to a stop, Darcy proudly set the box down on the table before them, which drew the impulsive response from both wife and sister: "*Surprise!*"

Now the two ladies looked at each other with a puzzled expression as Darcy laughed and said, "Well, I suppose the fun is over. Georgiana, while we were in town I picked this up for you—I hope you like it."

"For me??" Georgiana exclaimed. "You told me the surprise was for Elizabeth!"

"And what better way to surprise my sister than to tell her I intended on surprising my wife? Young ladies being such keen observers as you are, I had to do something so as not to raise your suspicion," he said, very pleased with himself.

Georgiana, taking up the package, opened it with all the pleasure that accompanies being so pleasantly honored. But once the box was opened, she let out a gasp. "*What is this?*" she asked in astonishment. Pulling out two smaller boxes even more elegantly wrapped, she set them on the table as everyone exclaimed how lovely they were. With eagerness, Darcy told her to look at the bottom of the boxes. "One says *Georgiana* and the other says *Elizabeth*," she read aloud and handed one of the packages to Lizzy.

Taking it with a look of totally unexpected delight, Elizabeth cried, "Well, my dear, how clever you have been!"

Laughing at how expertly he had carried this off, Darcy said, "What better way to surprise my *two* favorite girls than to tell each of them I am trying to surprise the other?"

As the gifts were being opened, expressions of satisfaction and awe came from Elizabeth and Georgiana, and with great pleasure they held their gifts up for all to see. Each held identical necklaces, a lovely pear-shaped ruby with a square green emerald from which it was suspended. Darcy explained after the thanks and hugs were over: "Georgiana, you may not remember that our mother had a pair of earrings set with these jewels, which were her favorite because Father had them made especially for her on their first anniversary. She gave them to me with her instructions that I give them to my bride some day, but I thought what better use could I put them to than to have them made into these matching necklaces and give them to the two ladies that mean the most to me?"

This, of course, brought on anew the expressions of love and appreciation from Elizabeth and Georgiana, as Mr. Bennet and Mary also conveyed their own approval and warm commendation. Although more was said on the subject at hand, the party spent the rest of the time enjoying catching one another up on what had been happening since their last correspondence.

* * * * *

After tea, the Bennets wished to change and excused themselves to do so. Mary soon found her way into the library where she came upon Georgiana, who was specifically waiting for her. "Mary, it is so nice to have you here again. There are few people whose company I can enjoy and be relaxed with like I can yours."

"Yes, it is so pleasant that we have the same regard for each other, Georgiana. I'm so glad to see you again as well and am looking forward to spending some time with you while I am here. And I must say, I was very eager to have the Pemberley library at my disposal when Papa informed me of our coming, but if you prefer to be left alone, I can return this evening."

"No, please don't go! To own the truth, I supposed you would want to come to the library and so I came to await you. I wish to talk to you ..." but she was cut short, for at that moment Elizabeth entered the room.

"Mary, I thought you would come directly here," she began, then went on, "Oh, forgive me, am I intruding? I did not know Georgiana was here as well. I don't wish to interrupt you two; perhaps we can talk later."

With that she was turning away, but Georgiana spoke up, "No, don't go, Elizabeth, I am sure what you have to say to your sister is more important. I shall leave the two of you, and we can get together at another time."

Mary was sure Elizabeth had something to say on the subject which had begun earlier. If there was one of her sisters Mary could be considered close to, it would be Lizzy. To be sure, Jane was kind and considerate and one might think this would engender a stronger bond between Mary, the one overlooked, and Jane, the tender-hearted one. But Lizzy's more open and outspoken personality moved her to be the sister that would often stand up for Mary when she saw her being criticized or singled out as sport for those who wished to poke fun at her. Mary respected and admired this about her and truly wanted to hear what Lizzy might have to say on this subject.

Elizabeth, on the other hand, often did not quite understand Mary, as she was very different from the rest of the girls. But upon hearing of her sister's endeavor, which would again likely bring ridicule, she wanted to *'stand up for her'* now, realizing that, in order to do so, she would have to learn more about what Mary was thinking. So she began the subject this way: "Mary, may I speak to you about what Papa informed us of on your arrival? I have no wish to make you feel compelled to discuss this with me, but if you are so inclined, may we discuss it at greater length than what was allowed when the subject was first introduced?"

"By all means, I would appreciate us doing so. However, as I said earlier, I may have very little to add since the matter was only settled between father and myself in the carriage ride here."

"No, I have no wish to talk of specifics, but I do wish to give you my assurance that you need never fear having a home, for Jane and I will gladly have you with either of us. I wish to ease your mind of any compulsion you might have to pursue a course that will provide for your needs in some other way."

"You are very kind, Elizabeth, but I am not driven in this present course to somehow guarantee my being self-sufficient."

"That's a relief to hear you say, but please, do trust the sincerity of your always having a home. However, another concern I have about your idea is for your *happiness*. Do you believe you could be content being alone—that is, without being married?"

"Alone ..." Mary repeated, with a complete comprehension of the word. "Lizzy, *alone* is what I have been for most of my life. Kitty and Lydia have always been paired, just as you and Jane were. I harbor no resentment to any of my sisters for having a ready companion within the family—you must believe me to be sincere in saying so, especially since my talents, if there are any for me to lay claim to, have kept me happily employed in my solitude. After all, happiness is said to come, not from our circumstances, but rather, from our attitude toward them."

Lizzy, struck for the first time how she and her sisters had so completely isolated Mary, cried, "Indeed, Mary, how very selfish we all were to ignore you in this way! Yet you bore it so well, never complaining or despising us for it. Your kind forbearance to us in this matter shows that Jane is not the only one with an angelic aspect to her spirit! I am mortified at this revelation of our .... our *mistreatment*. There is no other word to use than mistreatment!" Moved with compassion, she rushed to her sister and kindly embraced her.

With such emotions being forced to the surface, the sisters wept with each other, saying nothing until Mary was able to speak, "Of all my beautiful sisters to be compared to, I would never have thought it would be Jane!" Their tears now turned to laughter, and they spent above half an hour sharing other thoughts and memories together.

In sincerity, Lizzy ended the conversation with: "My dear sister, I feel that father was quite right in giving you his blessing for you to pursue your desires wherever they might take you. And in honor of your undertaking, I will direct the cook to prepare your favorite dish of roast duck with all the trimmings." Mary thanked her from her heart as Lizzy quitted the room to go speak with Mrs. Prescott.

Looking about the library, Mary considered how many more books must be here than at Longbourn. "I dare say, in a library this large one needs some assistance. It is obvious you can spend as much time looking for what you want as you can reading ... it is a true saying that *'time misused is life misused.'*" She was alone in the library for some time, thinking of all the knowledge contained in these volumes and those yet to be written. Becoming fairly carried away, she was lost to time, until being made aware of just how much time had passed when the door opened again and a servant was calling her to dinner.

At table before they began the meal, Elizabeth requested that her husband allow her to address the group, which of course was granted. Standing and looking at Mary with a smile, she began, "I ordered this roast duck especially for my sister, since she is very fond of the dish. I wanted to do so in honor of her setting out to see what a woman of intelligence and determination might achieve in today's world. I remember once saying to Aunt Gardiner, *'what are men to rocks and mountains?'* Now our dear Mary is forsaking the one to climb what mountains she may find."

Everyone in the family began to give their compliments, all of which Mary took to heart. She now heard Darcy ask, "Do you have some plan on how to proceed with what you might want to do?" Georgiana was glad to hear the subject being introduced by *him,* for she was beginning to believe everyone had been purposely avoiding it while she was present.

"Not as of yet," Mary replied. "However, it is said that any journey must begin with the first step, so it seems I must now determine in which direction that first step will be. And with such warm wishes to start me off, I pray I will not disappoint."

"Well, Mary," said her father, "there is time for all such deliberations. You are still young."

His daughter, who had been looking delighted at all the encouraging and supportive comments, now took on a troubled look at hearing her father's words. She had been feeling like one of the young sunbirds in her book, about to take flight from its nest. But suddenly it seemed she was being pulled back, as if he was saying that now was not the time to spread her wings to the sun.

Georgiana, having observed this alteration and understanding its meaning, felt herself safe to offer this proposal: "Perhaps, Brother, I might take Mary into town. I know Pemberley is wonderful, but as to prospects, town is sure to have much more to offer her."

"That is a splendid suggestion, Georgiana!" Mary responded. "Father, if Mr. Darcy allows it, may I go?"

The excited pleading of Georgiana did not go unnoticed by Mr. Bennet, but it was the earnest look in Mary's eyes that deeply touched him. "Well, Mr. Darcy, it appears my daughter's experiment to break new ground for women is at this early stage dependent upon us two men. What say you to our opening the door wide for your sister-in-law to make her start?" Mr. Bennet did harbor a secret thought that as soon as Mary had run across an obstacle or two she would quickly end the pursuit, but he knew if he were to prevent her from pursuing this venture, she would be certain to have a regret over lost opportunities, and he wished to spare her from this. He likewise believed that if things did not turn out as she hoped, it would not break her spirit, but she could at least be satisfied in the attempt.

Darcy, though, was glad to hear Georgiana speak so eagerly of any endeavor in which she wished to be of use, for he was always concerned about her shyness holding her back from growing more socially mature. Elizabeth had been very helpful in getting her out of her shell, and noticing her look of approval at the scheme, Darcy said, "It seems, Mary, the door has now been thrown open for you to take your first step on your journey."

# Chapter Four

When dinner was over, Georgiana asked Mary if she would join her in a duet on the piano forte. Elizabeth and Darcy braced themselves for Mary to play with the same pretentious manner she had always done in the past. The piece that was chosen was a complicated one entitled *The Swan and the Eagle*, which has some very dramatic changes with its flowing movements, evoking the graceful action of the swan as contrasted with the graceful yet ominous flight of the eagle, and then the highly animated fingering when the swan and the eagle encounter each other. Of course, they were quite prepared to hear Georgiana excel, and as the girls approached the instrument, Elizabeth grew anxious for her sister to be seated with one as accomplished as Georgiana. "Perhaps it would be better for each of you to play your own piece. After all, duets require some practice, do they not? Would you not prefer to play on your own, Mary?"

Not perceiving Lizzy's concern, Mary replied, "No, not at all. A duet with Georgiana sounds lovely, for she plays so well, surely any lack on my part would be overcome by her performance."

Elizabeth was not accustomed to hear Mary talk so modestly of herself, especially with regard to her playing, since she took mastering the piano so seriously. But she felt with that speech, at least any deficiency on Mary's part could be overlooked tolerably, especially considering those who were present. However, as the two played, it was growing ever more apparent that there was no need for apprehension, for since she had last heard her play, Lizzy found that Mary had become every bit as competent as Georgiana! There was a bit of clashing of fingers, with the two laughing along with the rest in the room, but at the conclusion, the little group clapped in earnest at what they had just heard. Indeed, it was evident to Elizabeth and the others that Mary had outgrown what her father had always described as being *silly*, for she had definitely become more proficient in her playing. And though this was just a small gathering of family, it was clear to them that Miss Mary Bennet may very well make a go at whatever she applied herself to.

Later that evening, Elizabeth asked her sister to join her out in the garden. "Mary, it seems you have changed during this past year."

"Changed?" she responded with a surprised tone.

"Well, if not changed, perhaps ... grown ... matured."

"It is said that *wisdom gives one the ability to see what once was not seen*, and I do hope I have acquired at least a measure of wisdom. With all that has happened within the family this past year, I would have had to be an ostrich with its head in the sand not to have ... well as father would say, not to have *'grown in good sense.'*"

"What do you mean, Mary?"

"I took a good look at myself over this past year and came to see my follies, such as when I played and sang badly at the Netherfield ball. I realized I could not make myself be what nature had denied me, so I gave up the notion of enthralling a gathering by singing. But I knew I could improve in other areas, so I applied myself to that. In addition, I looked at my sisters—you and Jane have made a good match for yourselves in your choice of husbands, and are both excellent examples of what a wife should be. Also, I am not ignorant of the imprudence of Lydia's marrying Wickham; she has guaranteed herself a life of misery if he does not substantially alter his character—and I suppose I should justly add, if she does not also. Mother, though, believes any marriage is to be preferred to the alternative. Mama constantly urged and tried to mold me to be pleasing to men in general—you know her mind on the matter: deny your own intelligence; make yourself agreeable no matter the cost to your personal dignity; laugh, be coy; remember your appearance is to be considered above the edification of your mind—in short, she was asking me to deny myself for the sake of marrying, regardless of who that might be!

"All the while, I was devoting myself to my reading and playing, and the more men I was introduced to, the more apparent it became to me: if I were to marry a stupid man, we could not converse with any intelligence on subjects of real worth, yet he would believe himself superior to me just because he was of the male sex.

Seriously, Lizzy, why are men who don't give themselves the trouble to be agreeable to women and who know nothing more than how to hunt, choose a good horse and breed dogs, to be considered acceptable marriage partners? I know I have just rambled on, but if I have changed, these notions have been the catalyst for it."

"Well, you *have* succeeded in improving yourself, and I would add that if any man were to win your heart, he could not do better. And as to men and their ways, I would not disagree with you, Mary, although I would not put *my husband* among that number. But you might just find that falling in love with someone has a way of making any differences between the two of you become far less of an obstacle than they would be when considered from a purely rational point of view."

Darcy was now heard approaching, and as he came upon them, he asked, "Are the two of you ready to join us in a game of whist, or should we leave you to continue your private conversation?"

Elizabeth responded, "I believe we are quite ready, are we not, Mary?"

"Yes, but if you think it proper, Elizabeth, may I ask Mr. Darcy to comment on what we have been discussing?"

Darcy now came closer, gratified to be allowed to be a part of this sisterly *tête-à-tête* which he believed undoubtedly had to do with Mary and Georgiana setting off for town. He was therefore taken aback when Mary asked, "Sir, Lizzy and I were just observing that men are not expected to put forth the same effort as women to make themselves agreeable to one another. What is your own opinion?"

To this, Lizzy appeased her husband with, "We were speaking of men in general, darling, not of men like you."

"Thank you for making an exception for me, my dear, and acknowledging the possibility that there could be more than one," he laughed. "But I would say men experience the same feelings when wishing to please a woman whom they are interested in, and therefore do try to make themselves agreeable to the lady."

"Why, then, do men often have so little to say that is of interest to women? They speak of their sports and other petty matters which are of no concern to women."

Looking at Elizabeth, Darcy saw her anticipation for his answer. "May I be allowed to say that men will talk of what interests them, and what you have mentioned *is* usually the extent of their interest."

Mary countered, "Yes, but that is the point, Mr. Darcy! Why are women expected to show an interest in what men talk of, when those men have not given themselves the trouble to learn anything of interest to women? ... all the work is on our side."

Darcy, now turning from the face of his wife to that of Mary and back again, considering what response he could make to this, finally spoke, "In the face of such facts which cannot be denied, may I observe that no man has gone through more to make himself agreeable in pursuit of a wife than myself. And I would hasten to add, I shall never repent doing so." Squirming somewhat, he continued, "What other men do on the point will be their own loss. Now if I have at least exonerated myself on this subject, may I suggest we go to the game now? For in conducting this exchange in behalf of all men, I fear I am doing my sex no credit."

With that the ladies had mercy on him and did not press the point any further as they all left to enjoy the evening's entertainment.

## Chapter Five

It was determined the young ladies should leave for town within the next day or two. Mr. Bennet was particularly satisfied with the scheme of their going to London during The Season, since it would at least have the appearance that Mary was stationing herself for the pursuit of a husband, which should be sufficient to placate Mrs. Bennet, who as predicted, did write to Lizzy. With an odd mixture of amusement and reluctance, Lizzy opened the letter and read:

"*My dearest daughter,*

*I have sent your father and Mary to you there at Pemberley for a most particular reason, for try as I might, I am unable to bring Mary to understand that in order to be appealing to a potential suitor she must learn to be more pleasing to men and develop those qualities that they find interesting. She prefers her books—I am sure that is the reason she must wear glasses, which most men do not find attractive at all, but nothing can undo what has been done. Her always reading requires she wear her glasses, and as you know, men cannot bear a woman wearing glasses who also is to be found with a book in her hand. The girl wishes to discuss only subjects that she feels have some merit of intelligence, and what man wants a smart wife? Try as I might, I cannot bring her to reason! I have told her men only talk to other men about such things, (excepting your father, who seems to talk to no one, as he is always in his library), and then women talk to women about marriage, and once they are married they talk about their families. That is the way of things—why is that so hard for her to understand?*

*You must have balls and dinner parties where there will be gentlemen who, upon learning that she is your sister, will be drawn to her in consequence of her connection to the Darcy name. Mary simply is not handsome as the rest of you girls are, nor does she have Lydia's lively manner that men always find pleasing, but of course, Lydia and dear Wickham have nothing to recommend her going to them. But surely your sister's connection with you and my dear son-in-law, Mr. Darcy of Pemberley, will be something to give her an appeal to the men in your circle. Of course, you must see to her clothes, for you know she would not recognize true fashion if she were not guided. Can you not take her shopping and buy some things and not leave the choosing to her? Please do your best for your poor sister Mary, and see that she is presented to as many men as you can. Perhaps in numbers there may be someone to see something like charm in her.*

*Your loving mother*

"Poor Mama .... poor Mary!" Elizabeth sighed, as she folded up the letter. "If my mother were to learn of Mary's plans, it would set her nerves on edge! Well, I must give my reply due consideration, as I would not want to start an uproar."

# Chapter Six

The day for the two young ladies to set off was quite different from any other day that had seen two young ladies, one being a modest eighteen years of age and the other almost one and twenty, leave for town. The air had something more akin to the pair sailing off to some foreign port with all its accompanying unknown challenges and mysteries. There had been talk of Mr. Bennet going with them and returning the next day, but he felt "what more appropriate way for Mary to begin this brave journey than to take the first step toward this horizon without a man present? After all, she would be exploring what the world has in store as she is disregarding what men may think and giving regard only to her own preference."

In the carriage, Georgiana showed herself to be the more excited of the two by declaring, "I think you are very brave, Mary, to make your sentiments known about not wanting to start a family any time soon and instead to see what prospects might be found that interest you. I am in great anticipation of seeing how you are going to begin!"

"To own the truth, I feel much more nervous than I do brave."

"But why? You are intelligent and capable."

"I have expressed an ambition which there may be no way to fulfill," she said hesitantly. "And it is made all the more apparent to me in the fact that I know not in what direction I should proceed." Having now begun the journey, Mary was beginning to doubt herself, wondering if she had taken on a scheme that was beyond her grasp.

"Yes, but that is what makes it even more adventurous," Georgiana exclaimed enthusiastically. "And besides, all you have asked for is to be allowed to pursue something other than what lies within the domestic circle. Consider this: say it was your purpose to do as most women and simply find a husband—there is no guarantee that would end in success, as many women can certainly attest to. I would say, Mary, the mere fact that you are going to London to see what there is to be found, whether you find something or not, is not the point. It is my opinion that you have succeeded by making the attempt."

"Indeed, Georgiana, you are quite right!" Mary once again began to feel all the excitement she had when first voicing her idea to her father. "I have said nothing of succeeding in a particular endeavor or accomplishing something specific over which this venture might be considered a success or a failure. As the poet says, *'Dreams you dare not bring to light are dreams not worth remembering.'* Georgiana, you have already proved to be an invaluable companion, and we have only just begun! I am at a loss of words to express how you have unburdened me with your keen insight. Thank you, my dear friend."

Georgiana smiled with delight, even though she proved not to be a convert of the poet, for she had not expressed her own private desire to leave off this most common business of women. Feeling as if she were being put out on display, like some item for men to look at and determine her value as they would a horse, was so unpleasant for her. Do they find her pleasing to look at, does she possess those charms men find most agreeable in a woman, or is she a bore and plain? The idea of this sort of scrutiny was well worth every effort to try and avoid. This was her primary agenda she planned to stick to, in addition to being of some use to her friend. All the gratitude she had heard Mary just direct to her, she was silently expressing back to Mary for being bold enough to take this step and allowing her to have some small part in it. Now instead of suffering separately in their own way over a similar issue, they could join together and not be concerned with such things.

* * * * *

Arriving at the London home, the ladies were glad to be out of the carriage. After a change and tea, they both felt like a walk, subsequently making their way out to the garden. "It has occurred to me, Mary, that tomorrow we might pay a few visits to some of my family's acquaintances and discreetly inquire for some information that could be helpful to you. What do you say to that?"

"I believe that sounds like a very good way to begin. Honestly, I fear if I do not start doing something right away, I will grow more intimidated about this endeavor. So may I say again, you are proving to be the support I need."

"I am growing more and more excited for you, and hope I will continue to be of use to you."

"Georgiana, I don't know if other women feel as I do, but I need to do something other than fit neatly into some space that has been molded out for me and for which, at present, I have no inclination and, I am sure Mama would say, am ill-qualified for." Having had no one to share her feelings with whom she felt would really understand, it was comforting to Mary to hear Georgiana's enthusiasm, but nevertheless she added, "Surely the world need not be alarmed at what I am doing."

"Mary, I don't know how the world in general will react to what you are doing, but as to your feeling intimidated by it, may I say: you are starting on a journey to who knows where? Is there anyone that would not be at least somewhat intimidated? When my father died leaving my brother the responsibility of all that comes from being *the* Mr. Darcy of Pemberley, he likewise was nervous. Though we were both grieving for Father, I heard him and our cousin Colonel Fitzwilliam talking of his fears and, you must understand, my brother had been educated by our father all his life for the task! You are pursuing a goal for which your own talents will naturally lead, and if you are kept from it by society or some other type of obstacle, the fault will lie with those who prevent you, while you will at least have had the courage to try—and if you should be prevented by society, it would be a great loss, for I believe you have much to offer if you are allowed."

"Fear and courage seem to be bouncing around inside of me, both taking their turn at being the most dominant, so there is comfort in what you have just told me about your brother, for he strikes me as one who would be undaunted by any task."

"Yes, I quite agree. But what helped him was to think of why he must not shrink from the challenge that was set before him. You must do the same, Mary ... remind yourself of why you wish to take this course and that will help *you* face the challenges."

"That is excellent advice, Georgiana, and if you could bear to hear it I would very much wish to tell you about one of my motives, though you have heard some of it already."

"Please tell me, Mary, for I find strength for myself when I hear you talk about the way you feel."

"I read books of serious subjects, words that have shaped the lives of men for generations, and ask myself, were these words written just to inspire men, or are they not written for all mankind? Why else do they strike a chord with me? I am no less a woman than any of my sisters, but they have so happily and easily taken to becoming a wife; whereas, I find myself needing to bend my inward inclination to do so, and my spirit will not give way to it."

"I have heard Elizabeth say of your father that he has been described as having a will of iron. It seems you have gotten that from him. In men, such a will is often admired, unless he is a fool, but I would say such a will is not often met with in our sex, at least not outside the home."

"Well then, let us proceed on these visits with eyes wide open. Who knows what we will encounter? I realize I may undertake something only to find I dislike it, but the experience I gain, I believe, will be invaluable. In fact, I might find it is the experience itself that I am craving. And I feel I cannot thank you enough, not only for your help but also for your company."

Georgiana realized from this speech how very different her motives were than Mary's. She wished only to be spared those uncomfortable feelings that originate from her shyness among strangers *(and men in particular)*, whereas she saw in Mary a much more noble cause for her action. Georgiana determined she would not deceive herself into sharing any merit, though she did feel a sense of pride in being in company with someone like Mary. Putting thoughts of herself aside, she said, "Yes, Mary, do not lose heart! You will see your spirits rise once we begin. Before supper, I will send cards around to some acquaintances I feel might give us their help."

# Chapter Seven

The first person they were to go see was Mr. Bartholomew Barrington. He and Darcy had often worked together on various projects, and Georgiana thought this was a good indication that he was an active individual with much to do and would consequently be a source of numerous options for Mary. On being shown into the drawing-room, they were met by Mr. Barrington, who greeted them with: "Ah, Georgiana, how glad I am to see you! And this must be Miss Mary Bennet, is it not?"

Georgiana's astonished look was clearly evident. Mary, of course, only took it to mean that she had informed him of their being in company together, unaware that this was not the case.

"I see you are surprised that I know your friend's name. I assure you I have not become clairvoyant, Miss Darcy," he chortled. "Your brother wrote me a day or two ago informing me of your coming, inquiring if I might not have something for his sister-in-law."

Now, most women who have grown to merely the age of twenty have by this time learned that when men seek to be helpful to women they often only complicate matters, and Georgiana's education along that line was well on its way. "Did he? How very kind of him to alert you in our behalf," she replied demurely.

"Indeed it is," answered the gentleman, "for a situation has just arrived in which Miss Bennet, if she is so inclined, could be of great help to us."

Perhaps that quip about men was said prematurely? Georgiana looked excitedly at Mary and responded, "How kind of you, Mr. Barrington! And how good our timing has proved to be. Pray, what is it you are speaking of?"

"Just three days hence, I took on two nieces—they are five and seven—and I was in the process of looking for a governess for them when Darcy's letter about Miss Bennet arrived," he said. Addressing Mary, he jubilantly offered, "It seems, Miss Bennet, *Providence* is working for both of us! What say you, shall I call the children for you to meet them?"

No, it appears that men have once again lost ground in the area of being of use to women when their help has not been asked for! Upon hearing this news, Georgiana turned to her friend in disbelief and saw the same disappointment in the eyes of Mary, who nevertheless bore it well, with her expression changing but little.

Miss Darcy was about to speak in behalf of her friend, when suddenly she heard Mary's own voice: "You are very kind, Mr. Barrington, and I am sure the children are dear little girls. However, I was not looking for a position as a governess. I hope the delay this misunderstanding has caused you will not prove to be too much of an inconvenience."

"Think nothing of that, my dear young lady!" he replied sincerely. "But, may I ask, what other position might you be considering? After all, what else are women of your station in life capable of doing besides caring for children?"

Mary, restraining herself to continue very much the gentle young lady, declared diplomatically, "At this point, I'm not quite sure, sir, but I intend to find out."

"I mean no slight to you young women, you understand. But does not nature itself teach us that children and the home are the domain of your sex?"

Georgiana now wished she herself had the nerve to reply, even though nothing in particular was coming to mind. She was therefore glad Mary was at no such loss! "If indeed it was nature's intention to keep us within the bounds of the home, why then are we blessed with the capacity to learn and understand far beyond that realm? And I would hasten to add, why endow females with the desire to do more than simply be homemakers?"

"In my experience, women have always desired marriage and children," he replied, somewhat startled at her boldness. "You, of course, are young, and perhaps it is your youthful spirit that chafes at what may only seem at present to be the limitations of a home and family."

"I have not spoken of chafing at the prospect of becoming a wife and mother, Mr. Barrington. I have only spoken of having the desire to do something other than that while I am still young. I would point out to you that nature has obviously given the role of father to the male; however, that has not prevented men from restricting their interest and activities solely to that which revolves around the family. Would you not agree that it would be wrong to limit what men can do only to that part of life? Has not the world benefitted from man's activities that have gone far afield of the home? What, I ask, is the world being deprived of by thus limiting womankind in that way? Would we not be ignoring what makes us human, and not just man and woman?"

Mr. Barrington, now having nothing to say in response to Mary, turned to Georgiana: "Well, my dear Miss Georgiana, I am sorry I have proved to be of no help to your charming friend, but it was ever so lovely to see you again. And Miss Bennet. unfortunately I must bring this little visit to an end, as other matters call for my attention. Please excuse me, my servant will escort you ladies out."

When they were back in the carriage, Georgiana could not help but express her mirth: "Mary, did you see how you left him completely speechless? I was mortified by what I was hearing from him and kept wondering, what possibly could be said in response? Yet each time you showed a keenness of mind and greater astuteness than Mr. Barrington, who is twenty years your senior! Now I cannot keep myself from laughing at the memory of his face in total disbelief at your logic and sense."

"You do not think I was impertinent, do you?" Mary inquired a little self-consciously. "I had no wish to be so."

"Do you mean like he did not intend to insult women with his comments? I dare say if you had been impertinent, you would have compelled him to acknowledge his error."

"Well, that may be true, but is this the way for me to find what I am looking for? It is said, 'one cannot go about making enemies when one is dependent.'"

"My dear Mary, you have not made an enemy of old Mr. Barrington. You have taught him, I hope, to think differently of women, however. There is no doubt, should he ever run across your path again, he certainly will not look at you the same, regardless of his opinion of our sex in general. I can picture him now approaching the first woman he sees to ask her opinion and observations of what he has just heard from you."

With that image in mind, the two amused themselves until they realized they had given no directions to the driver, and quickly had the carriage stop so as to consider where they would go next.

# Chapter Eight

"Now that I know my brother has sought to be of use to you, I really must try to think of who on my list he would least likely have contacted," Georgiana began. "I am sorry his involvement altered our plan of action."

"With reference to our first visit, I consider him as having done us a favor," Mary put in. "Because of your brother's letter, Mr. Barrington came right to the point, which saved us from spending half the morning in small talk in an effort to ascertain some kind of information."

"Were he to know of it, that would bring him pleasure, for he was trying to be of use! But, now more to the point, who should we go see next?" she mused. "I have it, let us go to the home of Mr. and Mrs. Morton! They are a fine couple that are better known to me than to my brother, so it is doubtful he has written them." She then gave directions to the driver and they were off. "Mr. Morton is a gentleman who has a high regard for his wife, and he is a banker, which is why I thought it might be worth our while to see them... although I will admit, they were in my mind to visit as a last resort. Well, never mind that, we shall see what there is in that corner."

"If nothing comes of it, we may at least consider it a practice at being discreet in discovering something useful. Otherwise, we may learn too late that we do it ill."

With that somber thought hanging in the air, the ladies tried to prepare themselves in their own minds for this next encounter. As they exited the carriage and reached the door, they looked at each other with a countenance that declared, "I hope we are ready."

Mr. Morton was home at this hour, for he had left some important papers behind, and when the girls came in, he was only too glad to postpone leaving directly so as to sit and visit. He and his wife dearly loved to have company; therefore, the gentleman was content to put off his work and enjoy this unexpected interruption. Upon meeting

Mr. and Mrs. Morton, Mary found they were younger than she had anticipated. They made a natural pair, for they were both short and plump, he being possessed with a jolly look and she a very kind, gentle appearance.

"My dear Georgiana, how pleasant to see you!" he cried. "I cannot tell you how surprised I was to receive your card yesterday, and look how promptly you have come to see us."

"Yes, sir, it is quite nice to see the two of you as well. Mr. and Mrs. Morton, I would like to introduce you to my sister-in-law, Miss Mary Bennet."

After a few pleasantries, Mr. Morton quipped, "I suppose you young ladies have come for The Season—I can well imagine two men's hearts are soon to be captured! May I suggest you not make your conquest too soon, however, for one never knows who is to come later, is that not right, my dear?"

"My husband is speaking of when we met," Mrs. Morton laughed. "You see, he was delayed in making his appearance by business that had taken him to the north."

"Indeed, I found my lovely Trudy quite monopolized by a certain Wilmer Task. It was only because of my ruthless skills learned as a banker that I was able to make an opening for myself." It was obvious to the friends that Mr. Morton could still vividly recall the incident.

Mrs. Morton, reaching for her husband's hand with a smile, teased: "He prefers that version of our getting together to the truth. I believe it makes him feel as if he had to struggle to succeed against another man to win the fair maiden's heart." The couple looked at one another with love in their eyes as she continued, "The reality is, there was no comparison between the two, you know. Mr. Morton was far and away the superior man, though he was not much of a dancer! But, truth be known, though everyone said I did it ever so well, I cared little for dancing myself."

"Whichever version of the truth you two young ladies prefer to accept, I will leave to you, but the lesson of not settling too soon should never be lost, for the latecomer may be the very one you're searching for," he said proudly.

As the discussion was centering on balls and meeting men, the two girls gave the appearance of listening with great interest, but all the while they were searching for some way of turning the topic. Just how much *"practice at being discreet"* they might need was about to be revealed. Georgiana was the first to attempt it: "Mary and I did not come for The Season, Mr. Morton, we had other matters of interest that brought us here."

"Two young, attractive ladies not come for The Season? That is a novelty," he returned. "What other matters could possibly interest you here in town besides The Season?"

The girls hesitated, looking at each other with uneasiness, when Mrs. Morton intervened, "My dear, London is a place one can have several reasons for coming that may have nothing to do with balls and dinner parties."

This was said with more kindness than conviction, and her husband, still in disbelief, could not help asking impulsively, "But I don't understand—what other occupation could there be for two unattached young ladies?"

"Indeed, my love, whatever that occupation may be, perhaps it is one they prefer to keep to themselves," his wife said, sounding just as baffled, looking at the two girls with an odd, quizzical expression.

"What? Why, you are among friends here, Miss Georgiana, you can speak openly," Mr. Morton insisted.

"Surely, my love, there are any number of reasons they might be here," his wife suggested, " ... although, nothing comes to mind presently..." In the absence of even one of the any number of reasons, an awkward silence ensued.

Seeing Mrs. Morton struggling in behalf of themselves and her husband being overwhelmed by the notion of two girls not being in London for The Season was beginning to make Georgiana and Mary very uncomfortable. Georgiana's impulse was to rise and declare, "Oh dear, excuse me, I have just now noticed the hour! We stopped at Mr. Barrington's earlier and still have some other calls to make ... it was so good to see you again."

"My dear, please don't let our going on so among ourselves be the reason for your leaving, that is just the way it is among husbands and wives, you know."

"Yes, now that my brother is married I have grown to understand just what you say, but indeed, we must be off ... we shall see you again another time," Georgiana replied hurriedly.

"Please make it soon if you can," Mr. and Mrs. Morton called out as they followed the girls to their carriage, wishing them well and waving to them as they parted.

Without a doubt, because this visit definitely was not fruitful even in the smallest measure, the question of how the girls would fare on their next visit was uppermost on their minds.

# Chapter Nine

Once again in the carriage, Mary said thoughtfully, "It seems we will need a great deal of practice if we are to succeed!"

"I'm sorry, Mary, I did not know what to do. I feared they were going to talk on about how they met and what prospects might be here for us. I simply could think of no other way of turning the subject."

"Do not alarm yourself, Georgiana, as you saw, I did no better. How were you to know what his reaction would be? We have at least learned that the direct approach seems to be too startling for people to hear."

"Perhaps we should just go home and think how best to proceed," Georgiana replied dejectedly. "What do you think?"

"No, if it's all the same to you, let us continue," Mary answered. "I believe we should try to anticipate that The London Season is foremost on everyone's mind, so let us introduce some other subject before they have an opportunity to bring that up."

"Yes, that at least has the sound of working!" With that, Georgiana opened the slide and directed the driver, "Gerald, take us to the Randall home." Turning back to Mary, she asked, "What topic do you propose we introduce?"

"How soon shall we arrive there?"

"Ten minutes or less, I'm sure."

"In that case, I think we should stop so as to give us more time to contemplate." Georgiana now gave directions for the carriage to stop, and as they sat, she kept looking at Mary, expecting that at any moment she would suggest an appropriate subject.

Becoming disconcerted, Mary grumbled, "Forgive me, but may I ask that you not keep looking at me? No subject is coming readily to mind and you are making me nervous! Could you perhaps try to think of something also?"

"You are quite right, of course, they do say two heads are better than one," Georgiana apologized, and looking out the window, she realized the situation was already putting pressure on the two of them. Try as she would, however, nothing was coming to her mind that would direct people's thoughts away from The Season.

After passing some minutes in silence, Mary finally declared, "I think the problem is, any subject that does not have to do with these festivities will provoke the same kind of response we received from Mr. Morton."

"What, then, are we to do?"

"I believe if we raise a *hypothetical* situation that does not involve us, we may achieve our goal without sounding like two young ladies out to turn society on its head." Now with something that sounded like a good plan, they were once again on their way to the Randall's. These old family friends were not particularly forward thinking people, but after the last couple of visits, there didn't seem much danger of this visit turning out to be any less productive.

* * * * *

They found Mrs. Randall quite ready to receive them. At her age, young visitors were not frequent, and upon the receipt of Georgiana's card she was eagerly anticipating the call. They could not have found anyone more ready to talk, as she started a topic she believed to be uppermost on their minds: "You girls are exhibiting kindness to an unusual degree in coming to see me when there are so many more entertaining activities to be participating in during The Season! You do your parents proud, Georgiana, remembering me in this way."

"It is a duty that is more of a delight, Mrs. Randall. I could not come to town without seeing you."

"And who is this you have brought with you?"

"This is Miss Mary Bennet. It is her sister Elizabeth who married my brother."

"How fine for you, dear girl, to have gained a sister that can be a companion for you in your brother's happiness."

"You observe correctly, Mrs. Randall. Mary and I are very glad to have each other as sisters."

"But surely the two of you are wasting precious time in coming to see me? There can be no benefit to spending time with a companion such as myself, for I certainly cannot be of use in finding a young man for either of you, I am sorry to say."

Mary now spoke up abruptly, "What would be your opinion, Mrs. Randall, of a young lady who had the inclination of pursuing something other than marriage? Someone that wanted to explore what avenues young ladies do not—or better said, what is considered things that young ladies should not do? ... I am speaking hypothetically, of course," she barely remembered to say.

Surprised at the question, Mrs. Randall looked from one to the other, and walking over to a table which had several miniature portraits on it, she picked one up and returned, taking a seat closer to the girls. Looking at the picture with tenderness, it was clear her mind was occupied with the memory of the person represented, though the girls had not as yet seen the image.

The older woman held out the picture for them to see, which was a portrait of a young lady. "This is ..." she faltered, paused, and looked up. "Excuse me, girls," she said, looking troubled as she carried the photo over to the window.

Mary and Georgiana could only look at her, wondering what could have caused this reaction. Mary whispered, "Who is the person in the picture?" and Georgiana shook her head, quietly replying, "I do not know."

After what seemed like five minutes, Mrs. Randall turned from the window, and walking over to the girls again, handed them the portrait and went back to her usual chair by the fireplace. "The picture you are holding is of a dear friend of mine whose name was Margaret James. I knew her from the time we were children, and I dare say, I cannot imagine any real sisters being closer than the two of us were ... from the time we were young, she disdained the notion of learning how to sew," she stopped, looking amused as she recalled, "I cannot think of one handkerchief she ever finished! She was not content playing cricket with other girls, she wanted to play against the boys. On more than one occasion, she actually donned a pair of men's breeches and went riding, sitting astride like a man!" Then looking about herself as if to verify no one else was present, she leaned forward and said, lowering her voice as she smiled, "Once Margaret even talked *me* into joining her on such a ride! I felt ever so wicked, but Margaret looked like a bird taking to the air, and I just had to try it myself. This, you must understand, I have never told anyone, not even Mr. Randall," she said confidentially.

"As we grew older, she continued to resist what was commonly expected in young women. Her father, who was convinced that it was all just a phase, did little to bring her under control, thinking when she was older, nature would call her to her femininity. I often heard him say to her mother, *'After all, no matter how stubborn she is now, even she will have to surrender to the inevitability of being a lady when she becomes one.'* Sighing, she stopped with: "My own mother and father soon directed that I limit my association with my dear friend."

The two visitors, sitting captivated by what they were hearing, inquired, "Did you lose touch with her?"

"No, thankfully my parents did not insist on my absolutely not seeing her, for they knew how attached to each other we were, and they knew my own inclination. They felt sympathy for Margaret, I know, because we would often talk of her. And they did not want her to be without a friend, realizing her course was not going to induce anyone to befriend her."

Mary asked, "Did she finally conform, as her father believed she would?"

"She did not, Mary. And I'm afraid most people did not take the time to even try to understand her. They believed her problem was envy for her brothers' status in the family and an inordinate desire to embarrass them. But that is not at all what was driving her! She resisted the idea that women are, by nature, weak compared to men. She knew, of course, that men are physically stronger, but when she saw women servants working as many long hours as men, she concluded their stamina was not inferior to the men. Her own experience convinced her of women not being *weaker of mind* than men, for she could understand such things as designs for bridges and layouts for drainage, while her brothers were having difficulty getting the sense of these things. We heard her own father often times reproaching her older brothers, *'Your younger sister understands these things better than you!—do I need to bring her in to explain? If only she could inherit, she would make a proper master of my estate when I am gone!'*

"You know, when she was a mere child, it was a novelty to have a girl taking an interest in subjects and activities that are thought to be for boys only, but as she got older, her interests and abilities did not change as her father had anticipated, for she continued to outshine her brothers. I honestly think he took great pride in having such a daughter, but outside the home, in the world, her talents were not appreciated. And so, being prevented from engaging in what interested her simply because she was a female roused her sense of unfairness."

Mary and Georgiana, looking concerned, asked, "What became of Miss James?"

"Some men made promises to allow her to pursue her interest in land development, only to keep her under their thumb and use her for nothing more than filing papers. When she would protest to them, it was always the same thing: *'In time, be patient.'* After five years or so of this, she went back to her father and related the prejudice she was encountering. He blamed himself for her plight, because he encouraged her at home. So in an effort to assist her, he sent her first to India, where she discovered women have less freedom even than here. Then he sent her to an estate he held in Jamaica and, as a representative for her father, being in a land where the culture was far more relaxed in all its views, she was finally able to have an outlet for her talents. It was not all a bed of roses, mind you," Mrs. Randall halted, as if to caution the girls. "She did have to prove her abilities, and the climate there is altogether different, but she managed."

"Did she ever marry?" Georgiana now wanted to know.

"No, which for me is the saddest part of her history. Having been so frustrated by men, excepting her own father, she often repeated in her letters to me that she would not voluntarily submit herself to the whims of any man."

Mary, feeling perplexed by what she had heard, asked, "If she lived as she wanted, why then do you say you are sad for her?"

"My dear girls, when you have lived as long as I have, you are able to draw certain conclusions. One is," she reasoned, "that such a spirit as Margaret's is rare, and I am saddened in the knowledge that in not getting married and having children, her beautiful spirit has not been passed on. The unhappy truth is, she did not tolerate the tropical climate and was often unwell, but she preferred the illness to the stifling restrictions here. She died when she was only forty years old, and in the last letter she wrote me, she declared she felt no regrets and thanked me for my friendship and for not abandoning her when all her other acquaintances had." Sighing deeply, she quavered, "She told me to thank my parents for not making me break off our friendship. I remember her words well, *'Such loyalty is not often met with in this world, and I will not leave it without expressing gratitude to those who have shown it to me.'*"

At this, Mary and Georgiana saw her gray head turn toward the fireplace as she sat in silence. Waiting for a few moments, Georgiana sympathized, "I am sorry, Mrs. Randall. We certainly did not intend to bring up a painful memory."

Turning back toward them, she reassured her, "Sweet child, Georgiana, you have done no such thing! At my age, I do not often get to talk about my life and memories ... it seems all the young people today are consumed with what lies ahead of them and are not much interested in the past goings-on of an old lady like myself." With a far-off look in her eye, she admitted, "This is something, I know, at your age the two of you will not comprehend, but time rushes past, leaving us with just glimpses of what we have lived. I am grateful to you both for listening while I remembered my dear friend Margaret. I know very well there are more entertaining things for young ladies to do than this."

"Would you mind my asking, Mrs. Randall, what is your own opinion of how your friend Margaret lived her life?" Mary could not hold the question back, as this story of Margaret James was touching the depths of her heart: "Do you believe she was foolish and wasted her life?"

Mrs. Randall, looking thoughtfully at Mary and noting her clear eyes and eager expression, understood she may very well be in the presence of another such spirit as her own dear companion. "Life is too short to live in fear of regrets, Mary. We make decisions every day, the most of which are of little consequence, but there are those moments in which we are confronted with a choice that will have lasting consequences. Margaret understood what she was doing." With a little regret, she shook her head, "Many times I wished she had chosen to marry, then she and I could have continued our friendship as married women having our husbands and children to laugh and cry over. And, yes, she may still be alive today." Suddenly she was standing up tall, with a sparkle in her eye, as she finished, "But then, she would not have been *Margaret,* my best friend and a *person*—I say person, because Margaret would have liked it that way—a *person* who was my best friend ... *the* person I admired most. So no, Mary, I know for a certainty Margaret was no fool, and one thing she never wasted was life!"

"Are you therefore saying that it would be good for a young lady to do as Margaret did?"

"Only if the young lady in question understands what my friend did, that she must be the person she wants to be. Margaret did not try to urge me to do as she was doing, for she understood I did not have the same desires as she did. When I chose to marry, she did not feel I was making a mistake." And reflecting thoughtfully, she added, "I believe the lesson of Margaret's life, for any who would care to know it, is, *'Do not be afraid to live as you choose, yet be prepared to live with what comes from your choice.'*"

Mary Bennet listened carefully to all the words of Mrs. Randall. She had not imagined that this day such rich information, so pertinent to what she was trying to do with her own life, would have been presented to her. "You have been more helpful than any words could express, Mrs. Randall," Mary said sincerely, "and I can assure you that spending this time with you has been so much more than entertaining. I do not believe we could have spent it better anywhere else."

Miss Darcy agreed it was so. Having spent this lovely time together, the ladies all were sorry to see it end, but turning to Mary, Georgiana asked, "Are you ready to go?" Mary nodded that she was, and they left Mrs. Randall, who gave them leave to stop at any time, happy with the memories she had shared and the joy of having been of some use to the youthful expectations of her dear visitors.

# Chapter Ten

Mary and Georgiana now had much to talk over. "What an extraordinary story we have just heard!" Mary exclaimed.

"It must have excited in you a stronger desire to pursue your dream, did it not?" Georgiana was inspired by what she heard Margaret had done also, but for herself, it was the possibility of living without fear that struck her more than anything else. She knew all too well how her own fears had been directing her life and was unsure she could muster the strength needed on her own. For that reason, she was hoping her association with Mary would give her more courage, for at times she seemed to lack the will even to say to *herself* what it is she wanted out of life.

Mary professed, "It has inspired me to rethink what it is I am doing, I must say."

Georgiana, looking at her with confusion, said, "What? Rethink what you are doing?! How could that be? After hearing about the life of Margaret James, who lived as I have heard you say you would like to do, how can you say such a thing?"

"When Mrs. Randall summed up her friend's life and the lesson that is to be taken therefrom, it struck me as particularly insightful. She said—now give me a moment, for I want to say it just as she did—*'Don't be afraid to live as you choose, and be prepared to live with what comes from your choice.'* That is exactly what she said, is it not?"

"Yes it is, but I still don't understand what it is you are saying, Mary." Georgiana was now concerned that her own motivation was in danger if Mary was beginning to waver, for she was hoping for further stimulus from her friend's example.

"Please do not make yourself uneasy for me, Georgiana. All I am saying is, those words helped me to see there is much more to what I am about to embark upon than just what it is I may *want* to do. I realize now I must also give due weight for what will come of my choice. Miss James faced many obstacles in her course and finally had to move to Jamaica to live as she wanted ... I must consider just how far am I willing to go."

"Mary, I can't believe you will have to move to Jamaica or anywhere else quite so far off and exotic to find something that would interest you," Georgiana objected.

"That may very well be, but you are missing the point. I have not really thought out this endeavor."

Georgiana, no longer concerned for herself, was now fully drawn into this exchange. "I feel you are making a very big miscalculation, Mary."

"Really, how so? I am admitting I have not calculated enough."

"Ask yourself: did Margaret know when she began that she might have to move to Jamaica to fulfill her desire? Did she, at the beginning, say to herself, *'I will be willing to move to Jamaica if need be?'* I tell you, she did not! Upon making what efforts she could and being presented with difficulties along the way, she then made her decisions. It was *along the way* she determined how far she was willing to go, not at the beginning. I don't believe you understood what was meant by Mrs. Randall's words to *live with the consequences of the choices we make.*"

Mary, accustomed to looking at things intellectually and not emotionally, was not affronted by Georgiana's assertion that she had misunderstood. She was curious to hear more from her friend. "Please continue," she importuned.

"I did not take her comment about living with what comes from our decisions to be referring to her moving to Jamaica. Rather, I think she was referring to all the decisions she made along the way. Her friend did not regret missing out on what might have been because she had a burning desire for what she was reaching out for—a life doing the things that mattered to her."

Mary interrupted, "But would you not say her living far away from her friends and family were part of the consequences she had to live with?"

"Yes, certainly. But the mistake I think you are making, Mary, is that Margaret did not at the start think she would need to live in some faraway land. She simply began down a path that led her to make first this choice and then some other choice. If you think you have to consider whether you will be willing to move far away in order to fulfill your ambition, you are putting yourself in the position of having to make a choice that is *not right in front of you*. Margaret did not face that hard decision until she came to it. You should ask yourself if you are willing to live with whatever decision there is to make *today*, not one you may never even have to make."

Mary, with her steady bright eyes, looked intently at her friend. Georgiana, who had grown accustomed to Mary's ways, held her gaze likewise, knowing this was the way to give due weight to what she had just spoken and that in a moment Mary would speak. Sure enough, Mary responded, "I said earlier to your old family friend Mrs. Randall that the time we spent with her was well worth it. Now I can honestly say with the same feeling that I am glad it was you who was with me. You are perfectly right, Georgiana, there is no reason to think I must make such a life-altering decision at this point," confessing, "The idea of saying goodbye to all I know was giving me pause. But this much I can say I have decided..."

"And what is that, if you don't mind my asking?"

"If I do end up moving to Jamaica, you will have to come with me."

# Chapter Eleven

The next two weeks proved to be no more productive than their first day's efforts. It seems the world has no other occupation than to see those who are not married end up so, or at least being participants in the minutiae of its workings! During this period, the girls stuck to their resolve of not seeking out those whom Darcy may have contacted by letter in his effort to be of use. Georgiana did receive a letter from her brother, however, which went like so:

> *Georgiana,*
>
> *We are all well here at Pemberley. As you might imagine, a great deal of our conversations are about you and our interest in knowing how matters are working out for my wife's sister. I must confess, I was certain we would have heard from you by now, informing us that your endeavor had been successful and that Mary was now engaged in a pursuit she found satisfying. I would have thought that a favorable outcome had preceded you there ... If I did not know the two of you as well as I do, I might be tempted to think you are now enjoying the festivities of The Season rather than that more serious enterprise which took you thither.*
>
> *It would be of no significance if you were enjoying yourselves instead, and please feel at liberty to do so if that is your inclination. It may prove to be more difficult to be resolute when everyone around you is so differently occupied. But I must say, the picture of you and Mary being caught up in those amusements is a straining of the imagination.*
>
> *I feel I must explain why it is I have expressed my surprise at not hearing that Mary has found something at which she could be employed. Immediately upon your departure, I took it upon myself to send letters ahead of you to some of our acquaintances, explaining her desire. It therefore puzzles me*

*that none from among them have resulted in anything useful. But perhaps as I am sending my correspondence, you have already sent your own, informing us that things have been settled.*

*Let me warn you now, Elizabeth has been trying to make some excuse for going into town to see how her sister is doing. I have dissuaded her thus far, but I am not sure how long I will be able to get her to resist her sisterly impulse to do so. She may not have my flare for handling matters such as this with the needed prudence, but she is very anxious for Mary, that she will be able to succeed in finding something which could give her an outlet for her aspiration.*

*Do understand, we are all wishing you both well, and I especially am filled with pride at your willingness to help Mary with this scheme. I know you believe her to be the brave one here, but acting as a friend and supporting her the way you are is commendable, indeed, and requires its own kind of courage. If there is anything you require in the way of assistance, all you need do is ask.*

*Your admiring brother,*
*Fitzwilliam Darcy*

Certainly, Georgiana was grateful for her brother's encouraging words and there was comfort to be found in hearing of his and Elizabeth's willingness—really, great *enthusiasm*—to help. But at the same time, she recognized that any further assistance in the form of letters from him would work against their interest. For this reason, she composed her own letter in reply with more than the usual care she normally did when writing Darcy.

*My dear brother,*
*How pleasant it was to receive your letter. I laughed at how well you know me, with your reference to Mary and myself trying to be lively participants at the festivities surrounding The Season! Before continuing, however, I feel I must also beg your pardon for making you be the first to write, when I should*

have anticipated Pemberley's eagerness to have some news from us.

We have been busy with visits to some of our friends, particularly finding Mrs. Randall a most interesting companion. She told me expressly to convey her best wishes to you and Elizabeth, by the way. I believe Elizabeth would be most satisfied with the acquaintance, and if I am not much mistaken, Mary is very likely relating the same information to her in her own letter. We have been to see her several times since our arriving in town, and each time we find ourselves longing to return her way again soon. In some ways, our visits there have been most beneficial toward our goal. I know spending our time with someone who goes out but little and does nothing even remotely connected to The Season would make Mary and myself the laughing stock of our peers, but to us nothing could be less of a concern. I can see why Mother and Father cherished her friendship.

But alas, I should not fill the paper with our visits to Mrs. Randall. Our first visit was to Mr. Barrington, who informed us of receiving a letter from you. He was unable to be of service, though he was willing, offering only a position as governess and, as you know, Mary's interests are in a different direction. She was very much gratified by your attention and believed your letter was helpful, nonetheless.

We are of the opinion that approaching our friends without their being aware of Mary's intentions will put us on a better footing to discover discreetly if there is anything to inquire about, however. We are well aware that our being young ladies setting out on such a project predisposes us to making mistakes. But honestly, Brother, the mistakes, if that is what they have been, have proved to be educational—and since I am speaking to you, I will allow, somewhat amusing. If you were to permit Elizabeth to come, I believe the amusement would greatly increase. You know her sense of humor so well ... it certainly would not fail in some of the circumstances we have been in!

On perusing my letter just now, I fear I may be giving you a false impression of our attitude in this pursuit. Truthfully, we are both in earnest about what we are doing here, and if you could have seen how very well Mary has handled herself, I know you would continue to give us your kind support, albeit from a distance. Be assured, if our spirits begin to falter or we find ourselves at our wits' end, we shall ask for you and Elizabeth to come give us the benefit of your wise direction.

For now, we are still doing well and continue to look at each new day with a positive attitude.

Your loving sister,

Georgiana

# Chapter Twelve

A letter was also delivered to Mary from Elizabeth, and upon opening it, she was pleasantly surprised to find one also from her father. His proved to be only a few lines, which is what one might expect from Mr. Bennet, since he is not fond of the business of writing. It was as follows:

> *Mary,*
>
> *I hope things are well with you and your pursuit. It being The Season, there may very well prove to be some young men about the place that, upon being confronted with ladies of serious stamp, are likely to turn on their heels and run. Although, in the whole of my existence, I have come across so very few of the creatures that I would say most men doubt their being any. However, if there be anyone among your sex that can set the record straight, I am convinced it is you.*
>
> *As always,*
> *Your father*

Before reading Elizabeth's letter, Mary felt compelled to answer her father's:

> *Dear Papa,*
>
> *I received your letter today and want here to give it my prompt attention. Mercifully, we have seen but little of the young men you mentioned, although there have been those who have attempted to set their cap at Georgiana's feet. As you pointed out, her being earnest and sober-minded does not have the attraction that her inheritance does. We have, however, developed a most effective way of dealing with these interlopers. I now relate some of these, for I am convinced you will find our scheme diverting.*

*A certain Milton Bean was the first to arrive and inquire after Georgiana. He had met her at his uncle's home last spring and, upon learning she had arrived in town unaccompanied, wasted no time in furthering the acquaintance. She was taken by surprise, even though he had sent around his card, not expecting he would make an appearance so soon afterwards. Georgiana finds him a bore, since his primary topic of conversation is talking of what a splendid coupling his inheritance would be with hers. She asked me, therefore, if I would sit with him and see if I might somehow frighten him away by such means as you have suggested in your letter.*

*After introducing myself and making Georgiana's excuses for not being quite prepared to receive visitors, he began by asking if I were wealthy like Georgiana. I know this is going to sound cruel, Papa, but the impertinence of him asking such a thing! Putting on as regal an air as a Bennet girl from Longbourn can muster, I declared, as I looked steadily into his eyes, "Wealth is a relative thing. One with only thirty thousand pounds may be considered by those that have eighty thousand as quite unfortunate. To which group may I put you in, sir?" He began to fidget and swallow hard as he struggled to say he had "not quite so much."*

*I have had so little practice at putting my nose in the air, but Papa, I do believe I do it ever so well. Even so, he seemed not quite ready to quit the room. For that reason, crossing my arms definitively, I inquired with a superior attitude, "And what sort of business can you presume to have with my friend Georgiana Darcy?" Based on his reticence in informing me just how much his inheritance was, I was sure if I assumed a posture expressing objection and astonishment to his being there for reasons other than common courtesy, I would have worked further at moving him toward the door. He stammered and repeated some inarticulate something or other, till he remembered where he had met Georgiana, and felt he should do his duty and inquire after her. Not wanting to lose ground, I became quite bold and asked condescendingly, "Is it your practice, sir, to ask how much money someone has on beginning an acquaintance? To be preoccupied with money is a sign that one has not enough of it—into how many homes are you allowed to ask such a question? I am sure my good friend might extend some consideration to one in your position, but she is often too kind for her own good." This was sufficient enough to make him most uncomfortable, bringing him to his feet. To drive him the rest of the way out, I told him that 'Miss Darcy will be detained somewhat longer, but if he wished to continue talking with me he could stay.' ... He promptly left! After he had gone, Georgiana told me she had been trying to enter the room, but could not for laughing at what she was hearing.*

*Well, Mr. Bean was followed by a Mr. Langston Wiffle. Georgiana attempted to inform me what it is about him that she found disagreeable, but I pointed out that no excuse or explanation was required, it is enough for me to know she wished not to be bothered with him. I perhaps should have waited for her explanation, for I have never seen anyone so intent on saying* nothing *in my life. I have heard Lizzy's account of Mr. Darcy being silent, but he at least had the good sense to visit with Mr. Bingley, who did carry the conversation. Mr. Wiffle sat silent, as I have described, and for the first few moments I kept expecting him to say some nonsense which I could use against him as I had done with Mr. Bean.*

*Father, had the servants come in to offer tea, I believe the man would have been taken as a piece of furniture! He is of average height with curly hair, which he keeps rather too long to be manageable, and he sat straight as a board, like a soldier at attention. I was at the point of introducing a subject, when the idea of looking at him without my saying a word as well came upon me. I would turn my head from side to side, as if I were trying to make something out about him. This brought on his first movement, as he began to shift about in the chair, after which he would stealthily glance over at me to verify that I was in fact looking at him. His self-consciousness starting to get the better of him, he seemed to desperately want a mirror in order to look at himself. When he could take no more, he stood and quickly ran his hands across his hair, saying he had just remembered a piece of business that he must tend to, asking that I give Miss Darcy his apologies for not being able to stay.*

*There you have it, Papa. Aside from this little bit of fun at the expense of these young men, I have yet to come upon something I find interesting. I suppose I might hire myself out as a person who chases away unwanted suitors, but unless I am much mistaken, that office is generally taken by the fathers of young women.*

*Please be assured I am gratified by your kind note to me and continue gratefully looking forward to this opportunity you are allowing me to have.*

*Your daughter,*
*Mary Bennet*

Now taking hold of Elizabeth's letter with keen anticipation, Mary opened it and began to read:

*My dear Mary,*

*I trust all is well with you and Georgiana; be assured all is well here at my home. I am longing to hear how things are working out for you, even though you have only been gone a little more than a fortnight, but I cannot imagine anything could have come your way in so short a time. My husband insisted on writing to some among his acquaintance to see if they could be of assistance to you ... he is a very dear man, and I hope his involvement has not somehow complicated things for you. He means well, as I am sure you know, but often well-meaning persons make matters worse, and I am confident you have some fine old saying on that point. It is our sincerest desire to be of whatever use we can be to you. This, of course, may be the tenth time I have said that, and by this repetition, I count on you to take it as an honest expression of our readiness to act upon it.*

*Father continues with us, so if you are to send a separate letter to him, send it here, for he is in no hurry to return home—you know his disposition and how he loves Pemberley. And if Jane and Kitty were not abroad with Charles, you are aware of what well wishes would also come from that quarter.*

*It being The Season, I hope you have not found everyone more in the mood for merry-making than for giving you an opportunity to explore what possibilities might be open to you. With town being half crazy with matchmaking, you and Georgiana may have your hands full dodging suitors. I would suggest, to ward them away, your straightforwardly informing them of your not being interested. But it is often the case that when a lady expresses such a sentiment, to some men it has the effect of triggering an internal mechanism which makes them want what has just been denied them all the more! One day you must allow me to tell you of Mr. Collins' proposal ... even if it does not illustrate the point exactly, it is nonetheless an amusing story. I cannot account for this action of some of the male sex, nor can Mr. Darcy, although he does offer, by way of some explanation, that it may have something to do with their fondness for sport. But to be honest, men chase after ladies and ladies chase after men, so it at least has the attraction of being a sport that females are allowed to play as well as males!*

*More seriously, Mary, nothing could make me more proud of you than what you are attempting to do, and I know I am joined in this by father, though he would not express it so openly. You are as familiar with his ways as I am, but I must relate to you that at dinner he does not fail to mention how his daughter is at this moment, or has at some point in the day, been setting society on its ear. I have rarely seen or heard him half so pleased than he shows himself to be at the thought of you confronting men of society with your notions. In both our eyes, you are already proving to be a success. Please do not allow some early difficulties to dissuade you from pursuing this until you are satisfied with your effort. And if you should feel discouraged, only give me the smallest hint and I will be by your side as quickly as Mr. Darcy's carriage can convey me ... although the thought of you, Georgiana, and myself in town with no men about us may be enough to alarm the whole of London.*

*Please give Georgiana my love. I look forward with great pleasure to hearing from you at your earliest opportunity.*

*My love to you ~*

*Elizabeth*

Elizabeth's letter conveyed all the good wishes and words of encouragement that Mary could have hoped for. She recognized in it an eagerness on the part of her sister which demonstrated her determination not to neglect her. So with pen in hand, she began her own letter in response:

*My beloved sister Elizabeth,*

*Thank you for expressing so earnestly your willingness to help me as I proceed in a direction on which I may very well need to avail myself of it. Please understand, I feel all the force of what you expressed in your letter and hold you all the more dear as a result.*

*At this point, I find myself equal to the difficulties that have presented themselves. Actually, in saying this, I am not giving Georgiana her due. Had she not been with me, I am certain this letter would be for the purpose of requesting the support you have offered. She is very intelligent, level-headed, and has proven to be most invaluable, and our friendship has deepened from this little time we have spent together. I am sure she is much like her brother, which accounts for your respecting and loving him as you do. In speaking of your husband's well-meaning intentions on my behalf, you did indeed call to mind an old saying on the subject. For whatever it is worth, it states, "Meaning well does not always mean doing well." Although in our case, the saying has thus far not applied.*

*I find it interesting that your depiction of London during The Season is quite accurate. Sequestered as we have been all our lives in the country and hearing only vague accounts of it, since none from among our society participated in it, I was quite surprised to see all this nonsense. You mentioned half crazy, and that about sums it up so far, but perhaps after a whole month here, we may have to include the other half also.*

*There is some advantage to The Season, one would have to admit. After all, to have a place where those gathered have the same agenda of finding a prospective partner for life, what could be more convenient? For myself, though, this parading about in an attempt to look acceptable, while likewise looking for someone acceptable yourself, reminds me of cook's description of going to market for melons or some such thing—'look at the color, consider the size. Does it look fresh, or has it been on the stand too long?' For those that have found someone to marry, they return next Season to display the success of their first year. Any older couples who come do so either to relive the past or they now have their own son or daughter to put out on display. I believe I may say with some assurance of not being contradicted, Mama and Lydia would be in their natural element here.*

*I do have some experience with the notion of being put on display, however. This past year, as you know, our mother endeavored to have her least fortunate daughter groomed to be pleasing to someone and did everything possible to show her work to as many as she could. So perhaps the country is no insulation from these proceedings. It is the scenery alone that is different.*

*On the subject of home and what my formative years were like for me, my dear Elizabeth, please do not feel you have some penance to make. I sensed in your letter a desire to make up for my sisters finding ready companions within the family, whereas I did not have that luxury. I did not suffer because of it, but the sentiment does you credit. However, it will injure me to think that you are pained by the retrospection. We might as well despise Jane for being so beautiful, or you for being father's favorite. Only the most foolish look at what has passed* with such a strong regret that it affects their present. I have never felt bitterness over my place in the family, and I forbid you to feel it for me. Each of us can choose what affect yesterday will have on today, and I prefer to be grateful to have two older sisters with sense and good judgement whom I can model myself after ... and as for our younger sisters, I have at least a direction in which not to go.

I do believe Georgiana and I would very much like to see you all at least by the end of the month. Until then, I shall be determined to write more often, as I should. I suppose I was waiting for something worth reporting. You may count on hearing from me with more regularity, whether there is news or not.

Your sister,

Mary

## Chapter Thirteen

The two girls decided to spend this day at home, feeling that a break from going out would give them time to take a fresh look at things. They determined to use the first part of the day doing whatever would take their minds off the many things that had been occupying them. Georgiana was in the drawing room, doing—of all things— some drawing. There was a very large vase in the room, the silhouette of which caught her eye as a very interesting shape for the legs of a table she had been sketching, and she set to work incorporating the design into her piece.

Mary could be found in the library, looking to see if it held a work she wanted, believing it to be *The Essays of Sir Francis Bacon*. There was a particular quote of which she wished to have the exact wording. If her memory was sound, it seemed to say something such as: *"A wise man will make more opportunities than he finds."* Even though she was supposed to be using the morning to get her mind off her mission, having once recollected something so directly related to what she was doing, she was determined to find that sage advice in print. While attempting to do so, she was once again struck with how wonderful it would be to have such a quantity of books. And yet, what vanity in not knowing where to find the one for which you search! Before being able to get much further in this contemplation, however, there came a sure indication of someone at the front door. Hearing this, Mary quickly went to find Georgiana to determine if it was yet another young man needing to be dealt with in her own unique way.

The carriage that had arrived bore the crest of Lord Dewey, the Earl of Essex, whom Darcy knew quite well. On more than one occasion in recent years, Darcy needed assistance in working through some intended improvements for Derbyshire, and he wisely turned to the older man for his advice. It seems one man's *improvements* are another man's *worsenings*, but with Lord Dewey's added weight behind each project, the opposition crumbled. Happily, Darcy was able to return the favor, and their friendship developed nicely from this mutual cooperation.

Going straightaway to the drawing room, Mary asked if Georgiana knew who had arrived. "It is a friend of my brother's," she informed her. "It is Lord Dewey ... we are acquainted, but he is my brother's particular friend. They have worked together on some business concerns and most likely he has come merely to speak to him. He is a good man, very gregarious, although a little loud. Anyway, I feel it is likely that when he learns it is only you and I here, he will leave directly."

The servant was told to show Lord Dewey into the drawing room. With her first look at the man, Mary was struck by his size—he evidently loved pork, for he bore a remarkable resemblance to that creature! Georgiana certainly had not exaggerated his being loud either, for he burst into the room with all the rush of the north wind, bringing with him a happy countenance and expressions of sincere gladness. "Miss Darcy, how well you look," Lord Dewey bellowed, "and would you please present me to your friend?"

"Yes sir, and how wonderful to see you," she replied. "This is Mary Bennet, whose sister Elizabeth married my brother, as you know."

"Indeed, I do know, and I have no need to ask after your brother, Miss Darcy, for I have had a letter from him. He told me you young ladies were here and that Miss Bennet was looking for something in which she might put her talents to good use. I have been waiting for you to make a call on me, but when more than a fortnight passed and still no Miss Darcy and Miss Bennet, I came directly to you myself, as you see."

At hearing this, the two girls looked at each other, thinking the same thing! Suddenly, Lord Dewey's demeanor changed as he looked around the room, unable to meet their gaze any longer. Inhaling deeply, he continued in a much less cheerful manner, "Young ladies, there is something very distressing that brings me here."

Georgiana took on a concerned and compassionate tone, saying, "Indeed, Lord Dewey ... but where are my manners, please sit ... should I ring for tea?"

"No, dear lass, for my heart is too heavy with grief." He hung his head and the friends were pulled to the edge of their chairs out of concern. Anxiety as to what could be troubling the great man and what, of all things, either of them could do to be of help shown on their faces.

"Forgive me, girls ... I do not mean to carry on this way, but Mr. Darcy spoke so highly of Miss Bennet, being serious and intelligent and very reliable ... and I know enough of you, Miss Darcy, to say the same." Again he had to pause, for he was overcome with emotion. The girls' anticipation was growing with each passing moment as to what it was he had to relate, and what it was he wanted from them.

"I beg your pardon, I am not usually this emotional," *(as if any Englishman ever had to offer such an observation),* "but my reason in coming could not be of greater concern to me nor so dear to my heart," Lord Dewey groaned. "Miss Darcy, you have heard of my wife, have you not?"

"Yes, I have been told that she is seldom in the country and spends much of her time in her native Italy," Georgiana affirmed.

"I do not know if you are simply being discreet in what you say, but the purpose that has brought me here requires that I not speak in couched phrases or merely make suggestions. I must speak plainly. Now please, I beg of you young ladies, if what I say begins to make you uncomfortable or is too delicate, then tell me at once and I will say no more—be assured my feelings will not be injured. Will you promise to stop me if either of you is so inclined?" he implored.

The two friends could not have had a more sympathetic look. Georgiana readily accepted, "You have my word."

Mary in her turn said, "If what you are to relate is troubling to me, I shall inform you just as Miss Darcy has agreed. But may I be permitted to add with the same strength, if there is anything we can do to bring some relief or comfort to what distresses you, we shall do whatever we can. We are young, as you know, but it has been observed by the poet, *'Youth not idly spent does give him what is highly regarded.'"*

"How glad I am to hear such words from you, Miss Bennet! It is just as Mr. Darcy has written about you, and your kind reassurance does much to soothe my troubled heart." And gathering his composure, the kindly gentleman's story now began to unfold:

"What I have to relate has to do with my daughter Alice, whom you have never had an opportunity to meet, Miss Darcy. She is sixteen and is in need of a true companion. Her mother is not *often* in Italy, as you suggested—she is *always* there. Bella left Alice and me when Alice was but nine years old.

"Let me start at the beginning of our history ... my wife's father arranged with my own for the union. It was a marriage that really served our fathers more than the two of us. I saw her disappointment in me when she first laid eyes on me ... as you can see, I am not quite the picture of the handsome Englishman, and to Bella, physical beauty is everything, for she herself is quite attractive and, sadly, also quite vain. She could not bear to be seen with me in public, and being ashamed as she was, she very often would visit her family in Italy.

"I knew the reason for her going so often, but would tell myself, *'she misses her family.'* I did secretly hold out the hope that my wife would learn to love me. When Bella was gone, I would always make some change about the place, seeking to make our home here be more like what she had where she had grown up. However, for some reason, it only served to make her more disgusted with me. She believed me to be as stupid as I was unattractive."

At this point, both girls' emotions were being deeply touched by Lord Dewey's efforts to win his own wife's heart and the insensitivity of such a woman. They were not overwhelmed with his story, but Georgiana could not hold back a tear. As it started down her cheek, she turned away to hide it from him.

"Miss Darcy, have I said too much? Should I refrain from going on?"

"No, Lord Dewey, my heart goes out to you, that is all. Pray, continue."

"Very well, if you are sure ... things went on like this for a year or so, but on learning she was going to have our child, there seemed to be a change for the better in her. Seeing this as an opportunity to improve matters, I did all in my power to assist her goodwill toward me by giving her full allowance to do whatever she wished to the nursery or any other part of the house and grounds in preparation of welcoming our child. As a consequence, she stayed at home without so much as a hint of going to Italy. I even went so far as to bring her mother and younger sister from there to stay with us and contribute to her feelings of satisfaction. It really seemed that this would be the beginning of her happiness with our marriage.

"In due time, when our dear Alice was born, I could not have been more happy, and Bella seemed to take to mothering as any husband would wish. We named our daughter Adele ... you will soon learn why she is called Alice now. When Bella's father and other relatives came to see the child, I had never seen my wife so happy. Everyone talked of how lovely the baby was, and with each reference to her beauty, my wife would beam. I have since learned to look at this very differently than I did then, but as I have stated, you will come to understand why."

It occurred to this dear man just now that he should explain why he was giving them this history. "I believe, young ladies, I should mention here, I have not come simply to unburden myself upon your kind indulgence. What I have to ask of you will soon be made understandable by what I am unfolding to you."

The two young ladies declared, "Please, Lord Dewey, there is no need for you to feel we are growing weary of your biography. You have wholly captured our attention."

"Your kindness in saying so gives me hope in the purpose for which I have come! Well, let me proceed then ... you girls are aware of all the hustle and bustle that accompanies the birth of a child, which shortly gives way to daily life with an infant. During these early years, Bella continued to give me hope that things had changed for us. Not that her view of *me* altered, but she at least tolerated things better while Alice was a toddler, with all that is adorable naturally attached to that stage of life. But as she began growing into a young child, it became apparent to everyone that, instead of possessing her mother's beauty, she had rather taken after her father." At this recollection, his Lordship turned away from his audience, and when that was not sufficient, he stood and stepped over to the fireplace.

From there, while he kept himself facing the fire, he continued: "It is with shame and extreme emotion I must tell you the rest of this sad story ... Bella would scream at my daughter about her weight ... she would insult her and call her names, trying to shame Alice into losing weight! I tried everything to comfort her, but a child, as you can very well imagine, has not that capacity for understanding such conduct from her mother. No matter what I said to my wife, she would not be reasonable with our daughter."

Then turning toward them, he said, "In short, she had become as ashamed of Alice as she had always been of me. Her visits to Italy now came as regular and often as before. At length, doing the only thing that seemed open to me to protect my little girl from the abuse of her own mother, I directed my wife not to return from Italy, and to leave us in peace. She of course was well compensated for complying with my wishes.

"You may deduce from this why she is called Alice instead of her birth name. Anything that is a reminder of her mother has been changed—everything I could do to return my home to what it was formerly has been completed ... if only the hurt done to my Alice could be removed as easily."

Having unburdened himself of the woe he and his daughter had been through thus far, Lord Dewey now came to the point of his journey to Miss Darcy's home:

"For this reason, I have come to see you two young ladies, and you in particular, Miss Bennet, having been made aware of your desire to put your talents to some good use. I put it to you, can one human do any better than to come to the aid of another? I wish to *employ* you, not as a governess, for she has had many—and yet there is something sorely lacking in my girl. She is sad and discouraged, without friends, for all the young ladies are consumed with looking pretty and having the finest clothes, wishing to parade themselves about to be noticed by eligible men—if you could but teach her how interesting life can be aside from that which is commonly done by young ladies! I know I am asking you to take up a task of great significance. You may feel someone older, motherly, is what is needed, and this is what each governess has attempted to be. I am afraid though, that with all of them having been older, there has failed to be a sense of *relating* that I imagine only someone closer to her own age can have with her. This is the explanation for my visit, and I will not try to work further upon your heart by pleading with you. I can well understand this prospect may not be at all what you were looking for, to say nothing of getting involved with a troubled young girl like Alice, so if you choose not to accept my request, I can understand. And I will not think the worse of you for it," he concluded, with a mixture of sadness and hope in his eyes.

Georgiana looked with great empathy at Mary and was anxiously biting her lower lip, feeling the pressure of the moment. Mary's bright eyes continued upon his Lordship, then turned to consider what her friend might be thinking, noting only deep concern from her. It was while she was looking at Georgiana that Lord Dewey spoke again, "Miss Bennet, I have no wish to hurry you in your deliberations. Let me leave you to consider the matter carefully, for I can easily comprehend there may be others you wish to consult with before giving me your answer."

Mary responded, "Thank you for not pressing for an answer right at this moment, Lord Dewey. I could not but hear Heywood saying, *'Look ere ye leap.'* You have painted a clear picture of how things stand with Alice; however, before I will be able to give a definite answer, I feel I will need to come see her. But I shall not keep you in suspense of my intentions and will let you know of my answer as soon as possible."

Addressing Mary, he said, "I could not hope for anything more, and your taking the time to reflect soberly upon this request of mine only confirms what Mr. Darcy has said about you. Might I add please, Miss Darcy, there is no slight meant to you. It was only Miss Bennet that your brother pointed out as being someone who was looking for employment."

Georgiana, not wanting to say anything either to give hope to the gentleman or to influence Mary, simply bowed in acknowledgement. But as they walked with him to the door, she restated their heartfelt concern for Alice and himself, and his being certain of hearing an answer soon.

# Chapter Fourteen

Over tea, the girls spoke together of what a sad account they had just heard. To believe such selfishness, coupled with so great an ego, was to be found in a mother was difficult for either of them to fathom.

Mary remarked, "Mama has put me in uncomfortable situations, but what we have had recounted to us is far beyond anything I ever experienced. My mother at least was motivated by what she thought was best for me."

Georgiana shared her own feelings: "I have had no mother for most of my life, yet sad to say, that would be preferred to having a mother like poor Alice."

These expressions were followed by a few more that were not too different, along with words of commendation for Lord Dewey standing up for his daughter, even at the expense of his marriage. They both agreed that, though neither of them would be considered expert on the subject, what he had could hardly be described as a marriage.

"But enough of our recounting this horrible story," cried Georgiana. "Do you know what you are going to do? Have you made up your mind, Mary?"

"At this point my mind is fixed on the question, am I *capable* of helping?"

"Are you capable! Mary, what is there to think about? Surely you intend to offer to do whatever you can for poor Alice!" Georgiana's tender heart was wishing to have gone straightaway with Lord Dewey so as to begin trying to be of assistance.

Mary, though, was not going to let her emotions overrule her head. "Dear Georgiana, my heart yearns to help Alice just as yours does. But you must consider how much more hurt we could inflict if we begin to try to help, only to find we have taken up a task beyond our resources to deal with. Would that not be cruel? Regardless of the good intentions, I will not begin without first giving this endeavor its due consideration."

Georgiana, looking as if she had just been pulled back from a precipice, exclaimed, "Indeed, Mary, how wise you are! All I could think of was trying to help. It truly would be devastating to know that in an effort to do so, I had only made things worse for her."

"It is not my wisdom, though, that should be credited. It is a Lord of a different sort who said we should *'sit down and first count the cost to see if we can finish what we set out to do.'*"

"I will grant your being correct about the greater wisdom belonging to the author of those words, but yours is the sort of wisdom that remembers such things, as well as how to apply them."

"Yes, I am glad I have a good memory and have put things worth recalling into my head. Nonetheless, there is still the matter of deciding about going to see Alice. By the way, don't think it has escaped my notice that you keep saying *we* in all of this."

Georgiana smiled, but with a serious look, urged, "If you will allow me, and Lord Dewey does not mind, I simply cannot sit by and not offer my assistance. I will make no more rash statements about charging in, but please, do use me as a sounding board for your deliberations."

"That I will do, but this talk about doing harm to Alice without intending to has made me think of something we should waste no time in doing. Please send a note to Lord Dewey asking him if he has not already informed Alice of coming to see us—I feel it would be better for him to remain silent on this matter. Tell him no decision on our part has been made yet, but it may be for the best if she were not aware of any of this."

As Georgiana went to the desk to write the note, she asked, "Why would it be best for Alice not to know about his plan?"

"There are two reasons for hoping he has not informed Alice, which I believe if we are to take on this responsibility, we must consider," Mary stated. "First, I do not wish for her to get her hopes up when nothing has been decided. As we have been discussing, it certainly would not be beneficial to her if no help thus followed. Second, she may have learnt not to open up, for fear of getting hurt as she has been by her mother, and if she thinks we are coming for her sake, we could be confronted with her closing herself off. On the other hand, if we go under some other pretense, we could very well be in a better position to reach her."

Hearing this, Georgiana began thinking Mary was inclining more to help than not, for why else would she have thought so far ahead? After dispatching the note, she asked, "Considering the fact that so many things about this scheme cannot be known without seeing Alice, what in particular are you thinking will determine if you will even take the first step of seeing her?"

"I think primarily I must answer the question, do I want to get involved in this person's life? When we left Pemberley, you know, I had nothing specific in mind. All I wanted to do was expand my horizons as a person ... well, there is no need to repeat what you already know ... anyway, in some respects what I am thinking sounds terribly selfish, I know, but still—it is *my* life and someone is asking me to take a portion of it to use this way. It would be so easy to say yes and thereby make myself feel useful, because it is completely unrelated to the female scheme of the sort I am avoiding ... I suppose I could in this way say I have accomplished what I have set out to do ..." It was obvious that Mary was struggling to make this decision.

"Does it bother you that accepting this is, in effect, taking the easy way out? As if to say because there were no obstacles to overcome in finding this opportunity that it somehow lessens the honor of what might be done?"

"No, that is not what it is at all. It shames me to think of such a thing when this poor girl is at the crux of my decision, but put simply, I must say—do I want to obligate myself to this?—will it satisfy my inner hunger? I do fear the appearance of callousness if I were to choose not to accept this responsibility, and yet, it is distasteful to me that I should feel compelled to accept this offer simply because it is the moral thing to do! Georgiana, you must know, I could not speak so plainly to anyone but you. Do I sound as unfeeling as the girl's mother?"

Georgiana now came to sit next to her friend. "Mary, if you choose not to take up this responsibility, you will in no way resemble Alice's mother. *She* shirked a responsibility that was hers by the laws of man and the laws of God. I would say, to abandon her child because she felt her daughter was not pretty enough is an act so despicable only the most heinous crimes could be compared to it! *You,* on the other hand, have no real obligation here, and the fact that you are struggling with it as you are shows how far superior you are to her mother. You have every right to pause as you are doing. It is your future that is set before you, and you should be the one that determines what that future will be."

Mary drew a deep breath, and spoke softly, "Thank you, Georgiana. I would now like to walk out into the garden to think by myself." Thereupon, she quietly rose and left the room.

## Chapter Fifteen

Mary was glad for the change of scenery, thankful for the fragrant scent and dazzling display of roses, absent-mindedly contemplating how that is the reason we tolerate the thorns. She considered too the strangeness of being out among such beauty while having to determine so serious a matter. Her thoughts were interrupted by a noise and some movement on the other side of the hedge, and curiosity drew her near to see what it was.

The gardener, a middle-aged man who was rather thin and not very tall, had come to tend to the roses and was carefully examining the last two plants at the end of the row. As she went closer to have a better look at what he was doing, he turned to see her approach, greeting her with: "How do you do, Miss?"

"Hello," she answered. "Would it be a bother for me to watch what you are doing?"

"I work just as well with an audience as without one," he said jovially, adding, "if there is anything you would like to know about these roses, Miss, please ask away. They are my pride and joy."

Stepping closer, Mary could see the condition of the two bushes that had his attention. There were several unopened buds on the ground, and even though the other bushes were alive with blooms in their splendor, these two had no opened flowers. "Why are the flowers on these two bushes not opening?" she wondered.

The gardener, looking thrilled to have someone with whom to talk about his roses, said, "I was afraid this might happen to these two, but you never can tell until it's time for them to start blooming. You see how near the fence is? Well, that alone would not be too much for my babies, but as you can see, the tree has been so impolite as to send its branches far enough over that now our two darlings here don't get enough sun and that makes them stay too moist. They call this *flower balling*, and it happens to flowers like roses or peonies that need plenty of water. But they also need plenty of sun, along with good air movement about them, to keep them from staying damp."

Mary ventured her opinion: "But I thought if plants did not dry out, it was called *root rot.*"

"I see that you know a bit about gardening, but it is a good thing this particular garden is left up to me and not to you, Miss," he chuckled. "Root rot is what happens when the roots do not dry out, but what is happening here is the *top of the plant* is not drying, and that is something altogether different."

Information to Mary was like the sun for these roses, for she loved to learn. Her expression showed her interest. "I see, there can be no question the two conditions are very different despite moisture being the culprit in both problems. Obviously, with the ground retaining too much water, the solution is to rectify the drainage. How will you remedy this moisture problem?"

"Well, since the two plants here were doing just fine next to the fence, we can see that this limb overhead is what has done the mischief," he explained, "and since Miss Darcy prefers the blossoms of these roses to this limb from that tree, and the tree itself won't mind me cutting back this limb, I think that should do the trick. Then these fine roses can feel the warm kiss of the sun, and these blooms can come out and show the world just how pretty they can be."

Mary reached down to pick up one of the unopened buds, saying more to herself than to the gardener, "How sad for these flowers to have come this far, and then lacking the bright rays of sunlight, they should just fall to the ground, never reaching a full bloom."

"You must have a tender heart, Miss. Only a person with such deep feelings would look so at a fallen flower. But don't you mind, as long as I can do something about it, you can count on seeing these two plants being put to rights."

Still holding the bud in her open hand, Mary said, "Thank you, sir, for letting me talk to you." As she turned to leave, she heard the gardener saying to himself, "What a good girl. The world could do with a few more like her."

Mary took a seat on one of the benches out in the garden. She could hear the gardener working nearby, just as he said he would, putting things right for those two rose bushes. She really meant it about feeling sad for the unopened flowers, but acknowledged something else was on her mind as well. "For not having the warmth of the sun, these blooms would not open ... I can well imagine how a child would be affected, being deprived of the warmth of its mother's love and care." Holding gently onto the bud, she closed her hand around it, stood up, and marched with purpose directly into the house to see Miss Darcy.

Calling her name as soon as she entered the house brought Georgiana quickly out from the drawing room. She could tell by the look on Mary's face that she had made up her mind about Alice. Full of suspense, she could scarcely wait for Mary to speak, hoping that look meant they were about do something for Miss Dewey.

"Georgiana, if there is something that can be done for Alice to put her right in some way, we need to try!"

This was exciting news for Georgiana, who affectionately grabbed Mary by the hand, exclaiming, "I am so glad to hear you say so, my heart has been aching for her ever since his Lordship left!"

"Now, mind you," Mary said soberly, "we must only commit to *meeting* her to see how difficult the case might be. We owe it to her and to ourselves to keep our wits about us. We certainly want to help if we can, but we dare not do any more harm than has already been done. As I said earlier, her spirit must be fragile beyond what either of us could ever imagine."

Accepting Mary as the one responsible for the decision in this matter, Georgiana inquired, "Should we write to his Lordship, or would it be best to ask that he return so we can speak with him directly?"

"We should talk to him in person. I would prefer having the freedom of speech with the ability to clarify matters, and I want to see if he does not also feel it would be best to be introduced to her under some other reason than calling for the purpose of trying to befriend her. Once we meet, we can see how best to continue, or ..." Mary stopped herself, for she could tell Georgiana would rather not hear the possibility of their not continuing after this initial visit, but her sensible side could not deny it being a possibility. For her friend's sake, therefore, she finished with, "Well, one step at a time, is that not what we agreed?"

## Chapter Sixteen

"Mary, how is it you seem to know so much about melancholy?"

"I have a book of poems that was collected and published along with insightful observations by a Dr. Burton Roberts. The title of the volume is *Words From the Darkness*, and all the poems are written anonymously by patients who were in the doctor's clinic. One of them was written in verse, divided with a bit of prose; for some reason this one captured my attention. Not for any beauty of form, you understand, but because the thoughts convey clearly how someone suffering in this way can often feel. I memorized it ... I think, in a way, I just wanted to carry its sentiments with me, so I would not forget how painful life can be for some. And I myself do not want to take the gift of happiness for granted."

"Would you recite it for me?" Georgiana asked, curious to hear what it had to say.

"This poem is called *Mara*, and it goes like this:

*The world has come and brought me bitterness*
*The light looks for me and sees my littleness*
*Blackness is all I have come to see*
*Shame is all I have come to be*
*Keep your cheerful words, they are not for me.*

*My worth is the worth of fools*
*I shall bargain no more for any just due*
*For who could love one rightly despised?*

*Leave me as you have found me*
*The blame would not be yours*
*Rather, care for one worth caring for.*
*Bitterness is the color of my sky*
*The taste upon my tongue*

*The caress on my skin*
*My cup is filled with bitterness ...*
*My name is bitterness!"*

"Oh my, it is sad, indeed!" declared Georgiana. "Do you think Alice is feeling the way the poem describes?"

"Based on what Lord Dewey related to us, it would be a wonder if she does not. I can imagine The London Season only intensifies her despair as well, with all its emphasis on making oneself pretty in an attempt to be found attractive to someone."

"Mary, I must confess, I myself find this primping and putting oneself out on exhibition unnerving, to say the least—and if I were to be completely honest—I would say I hate it! Thankfully, I do not have her reason to be thrown into such depression over it, but I do shrink from it. In fact, when I heard you talking about your intentions of pursuing some field of endeavor, I rejoiced at having something with which to be employed that did not involve balls and dinner parties."

Mary looked at her friend with empathy. "Yes, I have come to realize that about you and feel it is one of the things that has drawn us to one another, for I feel quite the same about being *exhibited,* as you say. It seems that there could not be two more perfect persons to try to help Alice."

"But Mary, I must ask, why would a doctor compile a book of poems, of all things, along with his observations?"

"It was compiled for the benefit of the nurses that assisted him at the clinic, for them to read. He wanted each nurse to have a better understanding of the persons they were trying to help."

"How did you come to have a copy?"

"Mr. Manning, the owner of the bookstore in Meryton, had a niece who tried her hand at nursing and was preparing to work at Dr. Robert's clinic when the young man she had been seeing came into a fortune, thus allowing them to marry. Having no use for the book any longer, she sent it to her uncle. Knowing me as he does, he informed me of it right away. The poetry, as you have just heard, is of questionable talent, but when read along with the doctor's observations, it becomes much more fascinating."

"Do you have the book with you?"

"No, I am sorry to say, it is at home, but if we need it, we can arrange to get it somehow. For now, we must set the wheels in motion and send a message to his Lordship." … and it was dispatched within the hour.

\* \* \* \* \*

The request for Lord Dewey to return at his earliest convenience was received, and so anxious was he in hearing what Miss Bennet had to say, that when the girls heard someone at the door, they believed it was a servant of his Lordship, telling them when to expect him, but instead, it was the man himself, having come directly without bothering to even write a reply! He was quick to say he understood Mary's cautious approach to this delicate matter, admired her insight into his daughter's condition, and was heartened to hear of Georgiana's desire to assist as well.

In fact, all that was needed now was the pretense for their coming. The idea of Miss Darcy bringing some correspondence from her brother was offered, but Mary said such would not do, for it would only be reason enough for them to be there that one day. It must be something that would allow them to return frequently, so that Alice would feel comfortable with them.

After several attempts, his Lordship stopped trying to think of something, and as he looked up at the ceiling, a tear rolled down his face, which did not go unnoticed by the girls. "You dear young ladies, giving yourself so much trouble for my poor Alice …" his giving voice to the emotions caused the first tear to be followed by many others. "Your deciding to come see her is the first glimmer of hope I have had for my sweet child in so long a time … now do not worry, Miss Bennet, I have not forgotten this visit does not mean there will definitely be others … I honor your wisdom in this, but if it is all the same to you, I am unable to refrain from hoping." He finished by sobbing quietly into his handkerchief.

Hearing this, Mary resolved right then and there that the situation with Alice would have to be one requiring more expertise than just loving concern before they would turn away from trying. She therefore observed to Lord Dewey, "Shakespeare pointed out to us that *a friend is one that knows you as you are, understands where you have been, accepts what you have become, and still, gently allows you to grow.* Rest assured, sir, the two of us will do our utmost to allow your daughter to gently grow."

A brief moment of silence was concluded when Georgiana thought to ask his Lordship, "What is it that Alice likes to do?"

"She enjoys reading and drawing, I know," he answered. "Let me think ...I am a little sad that she has never taken to the piano ..."

Mary stopped him by asking, "Is your Lordship's library very large?"

"Indeed it is—a person would be hard put to find one better stocked!" he proudly boasted.

"Have you a librarian, sir?"

"Heavens, no, each new book is placed on the shelf in the order in which it comes into the house." The look on her face made him ask, "Have you an idea forming, Miss Bennet?"

"I do. Since Alice enjoys reading, she must be quite involved with books, and I can speculate what a difficult time she must have trying to find any particular volume in a library as large as your own. What if you were to have us come to organize the library? With it being done for her sake, we will unavoidably need her personal input, for you want it to be done over to her liking."

"Capital idea! That should take little doing to arrange," the old gentleman exclaimed. Hence, the three agreed that, with this objective in mind, Georgiana and Mary would arrive at Lord Dewey's sometime after Alice customarily had her breakfast the very next morning.

* * * * *

That evening, Lord Dewey determined to speak to Alice after dinner. "My dear, I have something planned for you that I hope you will take pleasure in."

"What is it, Father? Or is it meant to be a surprise?" she looked up at him innocently.

"Perhaps *surprise* is not the word. I have arranged for two young ladies to come tomorrow ..." he got no further, for Alice interrupted him abruptly with, "Father! Please don't introduce me to anymore young ladies!" There was desperation in her voice. "All they ever do is look at me as if I were a Medusa, while they talk of ... of everything that ..." She could not finish her words, as she began to weep.

Coming quickly over to her, he took his daughter's hand as he put his other arm around her. "No, no, my dear, you did not let me finish. I have invited some young ladies, but the purpose is for them to do over the library, so that it is more to your liking," he persuaded.

"What? What did you say? The library?"

"Yes, indeed, the library," he replied gently. "I know how you cherish your books, and I am hoping to contract them to make over our extensive library to your liking."

Alice stopped her tears, but being still a little suspicious, she faltered, "But ... why two young ladies?"

"Come, come, dear, would any man know what a young lady such as yourself would like?" Remembering how Mary suggested matters should best be related, he continued, "Do not worry yourself, your presence will be required only occasionally, so that your own tastes and preferences will be given proper attention. The rest of the time they are here, you need not concern yourself with them."

"Is that true, Father? You are not expecting me to play the host to them, are you?"

"My darling girl, you know I will not have you made uneasy, for I understand very well your feelings on this point. But am I to do nothing to bring pleasure to my Alice?" With a broad smile, he beamed, "You must allow me this indulgence. When it is all done, I am in high hopes of your being made very happy."

# Chapter Seventeen

There was, in the carriage that was winding its way to Lord Dewey's estate, a pair of nervous young ladies, the like of which could not be found in a single barouche in London that day. Not that nervous girls in carriages was anything new to the fair city, but it could safely be said that rarely have two young ladies been going somewhere with so much at stake. For how could making an appearance at a ball or dinner be compared with trying to help a troubled heart find peace and learn to bask in the light of the sun?

They were unaware that, inside the home of Lord Dewey, there was another equally disquieted young lady. Even though Alice believed her father about the reason these two were making an appearance this morning, her apprehension was growing every moment as the time for their arrival drew near.

With the sound of their knock, Alice moaned to her father, "I cannot meet them—please don't make me meet them, Father, I beg you!"

"It is fine, my dear, go into the other room and observe them from there. If, after you have seen and heard them, you are up to coming in, well and good. If not, you will have at least had a look at them."

She did not have to be asked twice, and found comfort in being thus hidden. When Mary and Georgiana entered the room with his Lordship, Alice took note of the fact that these girls were obviously women of good taste in their dress but not the sort that reveled in a style that proclaimed a self-indulgent attempt at drawing attention to themselves. This was promising, she thought. They spoke well and were at ease with his Lordship, and their being comfortable in her father's presence made her like them all the more. The sound of their voices did not have that sound of emphasized femininity that so grated on her either, which was so much like her mother's way of speaking.

She heard her father's loud voice saying, "It is good to see you young ladies here! My daughter may join us, she is at the moment in another part of the house. I know you are only here to look around, but if there is anything that can be done to make the library better suited for my daughter, I want to assure you that you will have my full backing. You being young ladies that are as fond of reading as my Alice is, I have the highest hope that you will have some sort of recommendations for it. I have been quite anxious about your coming, for I do so want something to be done. Money is to be considered as of no importance—spare no expense, for I will spare nothing in order to make my girl happy, you know."

At the sound of all of this, Alice's heart gave way to a sense of gratitude to her father, and she could not help wondering what ideas they might have for the library. She heard Mary ask, "May we see the library, sir?" and her father led them away.

As the moments slipped by, Alice remained hidden, wanting very much to know what suggestions were being made. It soon got the better of her and she sent a note by way of a servant for her father to come to her. When he appeared, she confessed, "Father, I so much want to know what is being said about the library, but I dared not go in by myself ... please, will you take me in?"

"Yes, indeed I will," he replied, holding back any excitement, for he did not want to do or say anything that would cause her to change her mind. "And if I do say so myself, I think you will find the two young ladies tolerable. They certainly seem to know their business."

"I did have a favorable impression of them from what I saw and heard from my vantage point."

"Good, good. That gives me hope that between the three of you, you will be able to get the library improved just as you would like it." Upon entering that room, Lord Dewey was smiling as proudly as the day his Alice was born. "Young ladies," he said calling their attention, "may I present my daughter, Lady Alice Dewey."

Alice was rather plump, with a round face which was pale as a consequence of not getting out-of-doors. Her hair was black, the one thing she did inherit from her mother, and its darkness made her paleness stand out all the more. Her eyes were green, though Mary and Georgiana received only a glance, as she quickly looked down upon entering the room and would only half look up at them when each was introduced in her turn. Her clothes, although made of fine material, were plain, considering who her father was, but he would not insist upon her dressing in any other way than what was pleasing to her, for her mother had constantly tormented her about her attire, and now any reference to putting on something that would be considered more befitting her station was painful.

"Alice," said her father, "this is Miss Mary Bennet, and here is Miss Georgiana Darcy."

The name *Darcy* caught Alice's attention. "Darcy? Do you not have dealings, Father, with a Mr. Darcy?" This was said in such a low voice she was scarcely heard by the girls.

His Lordship looked up at Mary with a bit of alarm written on his face, as if to ask *'how was he to answer this question?!'* Not wanting some slip of the tongue to sink their effort before they even got started, she spoke up, "Pardon me, Miss Dewey. Did I hear you correctly—did you ask if Miss Darcy has a connection to the Mr. Darcy your father is acquainted with?"

Startled to be addressed by one of the girls instead of her father, she turned her head slightly up. Mary, not wanting Alice to feel any more insecure than she already was, continued, "Miss Georgiana Darcy is Mr. Darcy's sister, and Mr. Darcy is married to my sister. It was Mr. Darcy who informed your father about us and our interest in libraries." Directing attention away from the young lady, she went on, "I must say this is a fine room! After we get the dimensions and draw up the library as it is, we will be able to start sketching out some ideas. Miss Darcy loves to draw and is quite good at it, and I might ask, if you have an interest in drawing and would like to put something on paper, we would be only too happy to see it." Mary busied herself by walking around looking at everything except Alice, so as not to put any pressure on her. "Your father is insistent on this being done to your preference and whatever recommendations you have will be attended to. Perhaps when you are at your leisure you can also write down what colors are your favorites and things such as that, but for now we must get the measurements and allow Miss Darcy to sketch out the room."

Lord Dewey took this as an indication that Mary had determined to continue. Otherwise, he thought, she would have made some excuse for not taking on the commission. He looked at her with such satisfaction as to leave no doubt of his belief in it. This was not lost on Georgiana, and she dearly wanted to know what observations Mary might have made on so short a meeting. Putting her desire aside, however, she pulled out her pad and paper and positioned herself in the middle of this very large room, saying, "I will start with the entrance. How much detail would you like in the drawing, Mary?"

Mary smiled at her friend, showing her approval at her saying this, for she believed the more Alice would hear before quitting the room, the more convinced she would be of this being about the library and not suspect it was about her. She replied, "We will not need great detail. Put in, of course, the design of the door and frame and just a general outline of the woodwork."

Alice immediately whispered, "But Father, I don't want them to change the door ... will it be necessary to change it?"

"All you need do is speak to them, child, your word is law to them," he returned, in as quiet a voice as he could muster. "And since I will not always be at home, you might as well begin now with me by your side."

"Miss ..." Alice said shyly. When both Mary and Georgiana looked towards her, she froze, and appearing half-frightened, she turned to her father with imploring eyes to speak up for her. "Miss Bennet, my daughter is wanting to keep the door as it is, if you please," he said.

Mary kindly responded, "Miss Dewey, this is exactly the sort of thing we need from you, in addition to the other things we have asked you for. And as your father has said, we are to suit *your* taste, not our own. Of course, if you feel more at ease to write down your directions for us, that will do also, but we may still need to consult with you on certain matters."

Alice, still not looking at Mary, bowed in acknowledgement and was turning to leave when Georgiana ventured to say, "Miss Dewey ..." This stopped her, but she only half-turned to listen as Georgiana proceeded, "Your wanting to keep the door shows you have fine taste. It will be a pleasure to hear any other observations you have for us."

Alice smiled, saying loud enough for only her father to hear, "Thank you."

Lord Dewey, wanting to follow his daughter out, said to Mary and Georgiana, "Thank you, Miss Bennet and Miss Darcy, you have my deepest gratitude." Alice, who had not walked away, heard her father's words and was struck by the depth of his expressed gratitude for what little they had done so far. Knowing what a kind man he was, though, she dismissed it with no further thought.

The two girls promptly set about on this prospective work on the library, not wanting to enter into any conversation that could betray their ulterior motive. Neither of them thought there was any danger of Alice coming back into the room, but they wanted to be cautious. With the sketching soon done and the dimensions taken, they were prepared to leave. His Lordship, seeing them to the door, asked, "Should we expect you tomorrow?"

Before they could answer, Alice came rushing in with paper in hand, and taking a position next to—or more accurately stated, *behind*—her father, she anxiously gave the paper to him. "And what is this, my dear?" he asked. Speaking softly, her reply was, "These are my favorite colors ... that Miss Bennet and Miss Darcy asked for."

Georgiana smiled so widely a person would have concluded that she had just received news of soon becoming an aunt! Lord Dewey was likewise overjoyed at his daughter bringing herself forward in this way before the girls had quitted the house, declaring, "There's my girl!" as he patted her hand. Looking proudly at the paper, he passed it on to Mary, which produced a smile from Alice.

"Oh, this is wonderful, thank you very much, Miss Dewey. And yes, your Lordship, we will be back tomorrow, but probably not until after lunch."

Lord Dewey, feeling that things were going so well, proposed something he thought might be helpful by saying, "May I suggest, young ladies, since you will be here for some time to come, that we be permitted to address you by your Christian names, and that you do the same with Alice?" Turning toward his daughter, he added, "Does that suit you, my dear?"

"Yes, Papa, that will be fine."

The two other young ladies accepted the proposal in as friendly a manner as it was presented, and after wishing one another a good evening, they thus parted.

\* \* \* \* \*

Without delay, upon leaving the house and entering the carriage, Georgiana could not contain herself a moment longer, and her words came in a flurry, "Obviously you saw reason to continue, but was she as bad as you thought she would be, or was she better? ... was not it a good sign that she came to give us the information you asked for? ... oh, and are we really going to redesign the library now? That was not just pretending?"

Mary laughed at Georgiana, "And which of the many questions that you asked should I try to answer first?"

Now she was laughing too, "Yes, I know, how unlike me! But being there all that time without having an opportunity to say anything to each other on the subject was making me feel like I was going to pop at any moment! And you, looking as impenetrable as a stone except for when you smiled at his Lordship and then at me—how I wanted to hear something from you! I feared saying anything until you smiled at me ... I hope I did not misread the expression on your face ... really, Mary, *please* tell me your impressions, and I promise to speak no more until hearing them."

Her friend replied optimistically, "It seems we have hit upon the right thing with this library arrangement. And, yes, it appears we *will* have to redo his Lordship's library, unless he tells us not to actually do anything but carry on some pretense. So we should look at your drawings and see what sort of changes we might recommend."

"Yes, yes, forget all that—I know I just promised I would say nothing, but what *are* your impressions of poor Alice?"

"I agree with your view of her. It was a good sign that she came with that list of things, as was her coming into the library earlier. I would say it seems she is not as overtaken by melancholy as those poor souls in the doctor's clinic. The trauma with her mother has definitely left her feeling insecure and with low self-esteem ... she most assuredly is lonely and isolated. I would say the love and tenderness of her father has prevented her from sinking too far into the darkness that overtakes some persons in similar circumstances. But if we continue to take it slow and not try to force her to open up to us, I think we could become her friends on the basis of this mutual enterprise."

Georgiana thought aloud, "She must care a great deal for her books and that library."

Mary agreed, adding with deep feeling, "Those books and that library must be a safe haven from the uncertainty of dealing with people and the potential of getting hurt! ... but seriously, we do have to come up with some ideas for tomorrow. Not knowing how long it will take for Alice to warm up to us, it's a good thing we will be busy with the library. And our not knowing exactly what we're doing may actually work in our favor from that point of view."

"Well, as long as Alice is helped, I doubt if Lord Dewey will much care about the library."

# Chapter Eighteen

After dinner, the girls were surprised to have the servant announce that Miss Dewey's father had arrived and wished to see them. When he came into the room, he was the picture of happiness, eager to have an account from the girls. "I beg your pardon," he greeted them, "but this visit must be attributed to the anxiousness of a father. I gather from your committing to another visit you did not think it a hopeless case with my Alice?"

Mary answered, "I saw much to give us courage, your Lordship. We were talking on the ride home about how the subject of the library is one she is truly fond of, and by this means it seems we will have a very good basis for establishing a friendship with Alice."

Hearing Mary talk of being *friends* with Alice touched the great man to the core, and once again he was instantly overcome with emotion. "You dear young ladies, to hear you express the intent of being friends with Alice ... this is something I have not heard as a part of our vocabulary since she was a child! All her childhood friends have, like her mother, abandoned her." Pausing momentarily to collect himself, he went on, "It does me good to hear the word being used about my sweet child. I should tell you, she was disposed to think well of the two of you, I am certain, for otherwise she would not have spoken as she did when you were leaving. And when you were gone, she showed herself to be very enthusiastic about the library, even admitting that the prospect of dealing with you was *'not too terrifying.'* I know this may not sound like the most promising statement, but if you knew her as I do, you would see reason for much hope in it."

Georgiana, not forgetting what Mary had said about the library, brought up this question: "Sir, about the library—it seems that though we have chosen well under what pretense we are to enter your home for Alice's sake, we had all neglected the fact that we might really have to do something! I feel I must prepare you ..." she hesitated. "You may find that you have chosen poorly on that head."

His hearty laugh rang out, as he commented, "My dear girls, it matters not to me if the library is left in shambles after you are finished! My only concern is Alice. Do what you will with the library, and take as long as is needed to accomplish our main goal." Changing his attitude, he continued, "Now that you have determined to proceed, there is something else that needs to be addressed, and I wish to discuss that forthwith. You are so kind to speak of friendship with Alice and I am convinced of the sincerity of this intention. Equally important, however, we must not forget that this is also a business arrangement that I am engaging you in. Let us not be reserved on this point—have you any idea of a fee?"

Georgiana impulsively exclaimed, "Lord Dewey, I hope you know in this there is no reason for any such consideration for myself! I am only too glad to be of service to Mary, and of course to Alice, but as to any monetary requirements, it need not be a wonder that I am in no need of such compensation."

"Miss Darcy, one does not forgo payment for goods or services simply because one is rich. This is the way of the world!" he pointed out frankly. "I have more of the stuff than even your brother, and believe me, I still find satisfaction in the prospect of being compensated for my services. You and Miss Bennet are taking on a weighty charge, one that includes working on Alice's library, do not forget; so please show no scruples in this regard and let us come to an understanding on the subject."

She made no reply, though the idea of getting paid for trying to be a friend to someone was rubbing her the wrong way. The wise older man detected as much. After years of doing business, he had learned to understand the looks on faces, and even though he had yet come across someone who was insulted for getting paid, the look of not being satisfied with the amount offered was the same as what he saw on this young lady's face. With this in mind, he stated persuasively, "Only think, Miss Darcy, how many make their living by becoming governesses. Are not these persons, in effect, being paid to be a companion to some child or children? The concept, you see, is not as distasteful or rare as you might suspect, as is evident by the number of governesses there are to be found. If though, the idea of being paid is something you feel is beneath you, please consider this: neither your brother nor I, as I have already mentioned, ever take such a position."

He was speaking in as kindly a manner as one can when talking business, yet Mary was looking for a way of settling this matter quickly so that the distastefulness of it might be dismissed. "Lord Dewey, you spoke of the matter involving the library—may we not settle this pecuniary problem by payment for our efforts in that work? Having no experience in such matters, clearly we will be dependent upon you to help us determine how much compensation is generally regarded as fair. Then we can consider our drawing close to Alice as a delightful consequence of that endeavor, and you will have the satisfaction of having done right by us. In this way, we can feel all the serenity of helping Alice for a more noble cause than receiving payment. We will not lose sight of that being our main objective, I assure you. Our hearts have been touched too deeply for that to happen."

This was agreeable to all three. Georgiana now looked relieved, his Lordship was satisfied with the idea, and Mary's pleasure was found in the realization that what she had set out to do as discussed with her father and Lizzy was coming to fruition. She was struck with the roundabout way it took to come across this project to which she could put her talents, but she could not help but feel good about everything at this moment.

\* \* \* \* \*

As soon as Alice's father had gone, Georgiana said with concern, "Mary, I do hope what I said about payment with regard to myself was not somehow insulting or offensive to you. I am afraid it made me appear as if I felt superior to you, and nothing could be further from the truth! I have reason to believe you know just how I was feeling because of the way you cleared things up for all of us."

"Georgiana ..." Mary said reprovingly, yet with all the love of a sister, "what will society come to when the Darcys of Pemberley have to apologize for their station in life? Only consider what things would be like for me if it were not for you and your brother! Instead of staying in such a fine home as this while I searched for something to do, I would be in a horrible flat which I would not even need Caroline Bingley to point out the lowness of. My spirits would then have *those* conditions to contend with, as well as the challenge of trying to find my own way all alone, without a companion such as yourself."

Georgiana tried to object to this description, but Mary would not hear it. "Now, if you please, Miss Darcy—for I will have you know the truth of how surpassingly fortunate I know I am to have this connection with you—how could anyone like myself have ever imagined being noticed by Lord Dewey, the Earl of Essex? I will tell you how: it is by having, as my own dear sister, *Miss Georgiana Darcy*. And so, even if the thought of being paid had insulted you, as if you were simply *Mary Bennet*, it could not—it would not—make me wonder in the least. I am fully aware, though, that this is not what was troubling you about all the talk of money, and it only makes me love and respect you all the more."

With the air cleared of that issue, they could now enjoy the things they had accomplished thus far. Mary felt her satisfaction over the way events were progressing was such that it was time to pen a letter to her father and Elizabeth with the happy news of their commission to work on this excellent library. Discussing the idea together first, however, the two agreed they should say nothing about being asked to help Alice, and with that, Georgiana likewise proceeded to compose her own letter to her brother.

# Chapter Nineteen

It was now time for the girls to take a look at Georgiana's drawings. "I must say, I do agree with Alice about the door to the library, for the carvings are magnificent. I very much dislike when library doors are painted to look like a shelf of books—allow some man to go in with a decanter of spirits and very likely he will not be able to find his way out!"

"In a room as large as theirs, one could very well find it difficult to locate the door, spirits or no," Mary replied. "And I do agree, the door is wonderful. Did I see you draw it out in detail?" Georgiana shyly pulled out the sketch she had done with the door prominently displayed, and Mary was pleased at how well she had captured it. "This is worthy of a frame," she praised.

"If it does not make me sound frightfully conceited, I was thinking the same thing."

"No, not conceited at all, just one who recognizes a drawing that is well done, even when it has been done by your own hand. Now enough admiring of your skill as an artist, however. Do you see something we could suggest doing tomorrow?"

"These two half-pillars on either side of the door ... what colors did Alice say she liked?"

Mary read the list: yellow, violet, and gray were listed first, with secondary colors being pink, blue, and orange. Georgiana commented, "She has chosen some wonderful colors, even somewhat surprising ones! I would suggest we recommend the painting of these pillars in light shades of one of these colors. All the mahogany in the room is fine for men; they seem to be drawn to those dark earth tones, or maybe they just prefer a darker room. Perhaps it gives them the sense of being isolated in their own cave."

Putting their heads together, the two discussed several options, some of which were immediately discarded as not very practical. Being inexperienced and youthful did not discourage them, for despite Mary's disadvantage of not having been much in society, her extensive reading had included publications on home decor. Georgiana had the benefit of her private schooling in the arts as well as having been in several prominent homes during her short lifetime. At length, it was Mary who offered a suggestion: "Georgiana, surely you have seen when something is painted to simply *resemble* marble?"

"Yes, of course! That is a splendid idea, Mary! That would keep the sense of richness and elegance and at the same time lighten up the room. How delightful ... I am enthralled with this plan!"

This was sufficient to enable them to relax for the rest of the evening. It had truly been a long day, and they had been made weary with nervousness. Though the two of them were calm by nature, venturing out on an errand of this magnitude in behalf of a man as dignified as Lord Dewey, the Earl of Essex, would be enough to tax even much more experienced persons than these young ladies. And yet, at this early stage they had reason to be happy with themselves, for who at such a tender age could boast of having negotiated as effectively as Mary had in this case?

It was therefore agreed that to have determined recommending the painting of two columns, even if that was *all* that was decided upon, seemed reason enough to relax and think and talk of something altogether less serious.

# Chapter Twenty

The girls woke bright and early the following morning, happy they had arranged to return after lunch instead of before. They were grateful for having the extra time to collect themselves and their thoughts before starting on their way to see Alice. It occurred to them that the proposed idea of faux marble columns had the advantage of being something that would require her opinion, and they hoped some additional ideas might come to them as well once they were in the library. Several other things occupied their morning until it was time to head out.

As she looked out the window, Georgiana thought aloud, "How splendid it would be if his Lordship was away from home so Alice would have to speak with us directly and not feel she could communicate through him." As soon as they arrived and entered the manor, they were informed by the servant that the master indeed was not present and would not return until late that evening. They were thus shown directly to the library.

"Well," asked Mary, "now that we are actually before the said columns, do you think it is still a worthy recommendation to make? I will, of course, defer to you as the final word since you are the artist, and I dare say, much more accustomed to decorating than I am." Feeling somewhat tense, she added, "Especially for one of the finest homes in town."

"Why, yes, I do indeed," Georgiana replied confidently. "In fact, being here makes me more excited at how lovely it will look. If only we could speak to Alice and get her reaction to the idea! Shall we not have the servant ask her to join us?"

"By all means, let us do so." The servant was thus dispatched, but shortly returned without Alice, and instead with the question, *'Is it absolutely necessary that she come?'* Requesting that the servant wait outside the room, Mary and Georgiana conferred with one another over how to respond to this brief reply from Alice.

Georgiana spoke first, "Do we say yes and see what she will do?"

Mary remained silent, mulling over the question, pacing first one way and then another. A few moments passed, with Georgiana in anticipation of what her conclusion would be, unsure herself what they should do next. Meanwhile, Mary had been turning over in her mind first one plan and then another, dismissing them all, when suddenly she turned to Georgiana and said, "No, we don't ask her to come. Quickly—write a note relating what it is we are thinking of, asking whether she could inform us one way or another if the idea suits. If it meets with her approval, what colors from those she gave us would she prefer? ... I am hoping, you see, that her attachment to this room will motivate her to come hither. If not right away, perhaps later, but either way we will not have given her undue cause for anxiety so early in our efforts. Conversely, if she does not come at all, we will at least have gotten a decision on the columns."

Presently, a note did come back, informing them that she thought the yellow, lavender and gray would make an excellent marble column. Now that they had that information, what were they to do? They looked around the room, searching for something, *anything* that might strike them as being a worthy second recommendation. Georgiana, noticing the furnishings were adapted more for a man's taste, wondered if they should not look at replacing them with something more feminine? Mary acknowledged this as a very helpful suggestion, and entering into the spirit, remarked on how much could be done with the furnishings in the room. Leave some things as they were, of course, for it could not be assumed that men would not be allowed into the place, but she felt if Georgiana would set her mind to what other alterations along that line could be made, they might just earn their pay.

After spending some time taking and making notes, Georgiana declared, "We will need to have Alice accompany us into the shops to look at fabrics for reupholstering some of these chairs and divans. And it will be necessary for her to join us in order to locate some additional chairs and the desk, of course, for this is something that cannot be done through notes."

"You're right, perhaps we should ask to meet with her again to discuss these things. I must admit, I am beginning to think that our not asking to see her the first time may not have been a good idea. The sooner she faces us on her own, the better it will be for her."

Another note was sent requesting that she please join them, relating that there were other matters needing to be reviewed together. As the moments passed, they began to wonder if not receiving an answer right away was a positive or negative sign. At last, a note came from Alice declaring her apology: she simply could not come down to see them today.

Mary patiently accepted, "Well, let us pray that tomorrow her courage will rise. Since you have what we need for the recommendations on the furnishings, we should reply once more stating our wish that tomorrow may be a better day for her to meet with us." This having been done, the girls prepared to depart, not quite as satisfied as the day before, but not losing any determination nevertheless, realizing they had only just begun.

As they were walking toward the carriage, Georgiana asked, "What will we do if we run out of ideas to suggest and she still refuses to see us on her own?

Mary, taking on a thoughtful appearance, replied, "If that happens, we will just have to ask her father to be with her during these first few discussions till she feels more at ease."

"Should we inform his Lordship of this now, or do we wait?"

"I would rather wait," Mary answered. "If we go to him so soon after starting, it might seem we lack the patience to succeed in this endeavor." They said nothing more about this for remainder of the ride home, but both were wondering if they *did*, if fact, have the patience to see this through should Alice not allow them to see her sometime in the near future.

\* \* \* \* \*

When the two friends arrived at the Dewey home the next morning, they sent a note up to Alice straightaway, thinking the sooner she knew of their presence, the more time she would have to let go of enough of her fear that she could present herself. To that end, the note expressed their real need to confer with her, assuring her they were at her pleasure and that it would not be an inconvenience to wait as long as she felt necessary.

Meanwhile, Mary gave voice to an idea she had been meaning to mention: "You know, Georgiana, having been in these much larger libraries than what we have at Longbourn has set me to thinking. How does anyone find a particular book among all these hundreds— or perhaps as this library seems to have—thousands of books?"

Georgiana replied that as for herself, she kept her favorite books within ready reach and had never much needed to search about, although for someone as scholarly as Mary, she could readily acknowledge why such a thought would occur to her. In answer to that, Mary continued, "I have for some time been thinking of the necessity of cataloging the books in these larger libraries and having a written list to which a person could consult, thereby verifying whether the book is even in the library at all ..."

She was interrupted by Alice who, unknown to the girls, had realized that for her father's sake she should at least try to make an appearance and had summoned the courage to answer their request. Hearing the two girls talking, Alice had stopped nervously at the door, but was drawn the rest of the way in as she listened to what Mary had to say. "Yes," she suddenly broke in, "otherwise, you spend all your time looking for the book, which is something I have done on many occasions. And so often I cannot find it, even with the help of the servants."

"Miss Dewey, how wonderful to see you! Thank you for coming to us," Georgiana said with surprise as she rose from her seat. This caused Alice to stop her advancement, but wanting very much to hear what Mary was saying, she could not help asking that she continue.

Mary now felt the weight of the moment, wanting to hold Miss Dewey's attention long enough to help her feel at ease so she would remain with them. To this end, she continued speaking as naturally as she could, "I have not worked out a system as of yet, but it seems that the first step would be to have a listing of all the books and arrange them in categories."

"Why categories? Why not just list them alphabetically?" Alice inquired. Her timid manner was obvious, but the subject was too intriguing to remain silent.

"Well, as I have been contemplating the idea, it occurred to me that an alphabetical arrangement will only give you a list of all the books, and in a library such as this, all that would have been accomplished is moving the ponderous search from the shelves to an extensive list of names on a page, which would prove quite tedious if you were unsure of the book's title. But categorizing the books by subject or genre will direct your search into a more limited scope."

Alice excitedly broke in, "And that would require the books be arranged on the library shelves under these same guidelines! Such a change would make things *much* easier!" As she spoke, she moved closer to the girls, having forgotten herself for being caught up in a topic that interested her exceedingly.

Thinking how nice it would be to extend their conversation, Georgiana suggested, "Should we not sit down? We have some other things we would love to have your opinion on, Miss Dewey." Her self-awareness beginning to return, Alice did sit, but the animation of the moment had passed, for she was uncomfortable at the notion of being consulted.

The two friends, seeing this alteration in her, now sought a return to her excitement. "Perhaps," said Mary to her, "you and I could make notes on this scheme of rearranging books into categories and then compare them. I am sure, between us, we will discover a workable prospect." This did not succeed in bringing her back to a more lively state, but she did acknowledge her willingness to jot down some ideas.

Georgiana thought this was a good time to outline a number of the other changes involving the desk and ideas of new fabric for some of the furniture, with possibly a new piece or two. Her own kind heart being moved toward encouraging the young lady, she gently added, "This will require that we go out into the shops, and we would be ever so grateful for your company and, of course, your views and decisions."

Instead of having the reaction she hoped for, Alice became obviously shaken, looking nervous and not knowing what to do with her hands, as she stammered, "I … I … don't know. My shopping is all done … I mean, I do not go into the shops. Um… is …or … can there be some other way?"

Mary, not wanting for this first visit with Alice to end in such discomfort for her, offered this suggestion: "Perhaps Georgiana can go into the shops tomorrow to see what there is to be found and can bring any samples of fabric for you to examine here. And as for the desk, her doing a search in advance will allow your venturing out to be as short as possible. While she is doing that, if you are of a mind, you and I can continue discussing our ideas for the books in the library."

As she was talking, a certain amount of calm returned to the girl. Picking up on this, Georgiana turned the conversation toward the columns, wanting to give Alice as much praise as she could also. Giving a vivid description of their plan, she concluded, "How magnificent it will look, do you not think so, Alice? The colors you have chosen will create a splendid appearance."

Miss Dewey smiled and said she believed it would. Mary exclaimed, "I would say it will add an atmosphere of grandeur, as if one was studying in one of the great halls of learning." The two friends saw Alice's eyes light up with delight at hearing their warm approval. This was something she never heard except from her father, and coming from him, it simply did not carry the same gratification as it did just now.

Georgiana's sympathy for Alice was growing the more time they spent with her, and her mind was searching for additional ways to extend this visit with her. Considering that one way to do that would be for all of them to have refreshments together, and certain Alice was not likely to attend to it, she asked, "Miss Dewey, shall I summon the servant for tea?" This, again, did not have its intended effect, for it did not go well at all. Certainly it was not because Alice was averse to having tea, but it reminded her that she had been remiss in her office as host. Creating a panic in her, a most uncomfortable feeling that she was somehow being looked down upon by Mary and

Georgiana arose in the poor girl. She immediately stood in an agitation, muttering to herself: *'how abominable it was of me ... how sorry I am to have been so negligent.'* She would not even turn to look at either of the girls, though they each were trying to say something to alleviate her distress and have her stay. But she was gone from the room in a moment's time, still bemoaning her failure to give proper attention to their comfort as she hurried away.

Mary and Georgiana remained looking at each other in astonishment, feeling so disappointed at this outcome. They each felt they should depart as soon as Georgiana had noted what pieces of furniture to recommend for reupholstering. Definitely the pressure of trying to help Alice, coupled with the responsibility of doing something with the library and having no experience for doing either one, was causing greater internal tension for both girls than they knew. This strain was about to seek a release, and without a doubt, it was not going to be pleasant.

# Chapter Twenty-one

Inside the carriage, Georgiana remarked, "I am sorry I mentioned tea! Things were going so well until then."

Thinking of just how well things were going made Mary annoyed at Georgiana for ruining the moment. Out of frustration, she complained, "Was it *that* important to you to have tea at that very instant? You could not have forgone the pleasure just once?"

Instead of reiterating her apology, Georgiana was compelled to defend her actions. "Do you not think much good could have come from enjoying tea together? There could hardly be a less provocative suggestion, I dare say!"

"What we have just witnessed does not verify that statement—this undoubtedly was yet another area of her life that her mother tormented her with, and your bringing it up made those feelings come flooding back! You never should have said such a thing without considering her frail emotions."

"Well, pardon me for not having read your precious book of depressive poems!" cried Georgiana, feeling truly insulted by Mary's words.

"Maybe if you would read more than the same five books you have next to your bed, you might have learned something more useful," came Mary's sharp reply.

"If you would bother to do more than just put your nose in a book, you might learn how tea is an excellent way of getting to know someone," Georgiana pouted.

Mary was tempted to retaliate and Georgiana felt like saying more, but they at least had the good sense to stop there, and rode on in silence. Arriving at home, Georgiana sprung from the carriage quickly, not waiting for the door to be opened for her, whereas Mary took the opposite action and permitted Georgiana to go in to the house while she lagged behind. Addressing her maid servant immediately, Georgiana directed that her dinner be brought to her room, for she wanted to be alone. Mary, feeling likewise, gave the same directions.

If only the girls had been privy to what was happening at the Dewey estate that same evening, their feelings would most certainly have been less inclined toward irritation. "Father," Alice said as soon as he arrived, "I have behaved so badly today toward Miss Mary and Miss Georgiana!"

Feeling distressed to hear such news, her father nonetheless said sympathetically, "My dear, I am sure you did not. Tell me, what happened?"

"We were having a very pleasant time talking about the library and some of the changes to be made, when Georgiana suggested tea. You remember, Father, how Mother would browbeat me and ... and belittle me on the subject," Alice bemoaned, biting her lip. "Well, I just could not help myself ... I began to shake and stammer, and I escaped the room in such a state, I am sure they think me a freak!"

"My sweet child, I am certain they are not thinking anything of the sort; they are good girls and have been brought up not to think meanly of anyone. Surely you can see that in them; do not trouble your heart with such thoughts. Now please, tell me what you talked of that was so pleasant, and let us get your mind off this other matter."

She needed a little more assurance that the incident was not as bad as all that for her mood to change before she could go on to relate Mary's idea of categorizing the books. This, of course, was the most exciting thing to her, and with great joy she explained what a wonderful idea she thought it was. On the other hand, when she began to recount Georgiana's plans of shopping for a new desk and fabric and how they wanted her to accompany them, her father could see that her apprehension about this trip to town was returning. "I am not averse to the idea, especially if I can demonstrate that I am no lunatic who is not allowed out of the house, but Papa, I do feel very nervous about it," she admitted despondently.

Gently, Lord Dewey suggested that she write the girls, informing them that she had changed her mind about going with them and would meet them at the shops at ten, even offering to go with her if she would like. To her father's delight, she accepted the plan, for she was truly eager to make up for what had happened today.

Having agreed upon the subject, father and daughter bid one another good night, both feeling contented with their arrangements for the following morning.

\* \* \* \* \*

Unfortunately, the two young ladies at the Darcy residence did not see each other the whole of that night, both fretting about what had taken place. In consequence, neither slept well. This is as one might expect, for it was the first time they had ever had such a disagreement. As a result of remaining in their rooms all evening, neither of them got the note Alice sent about wishing to join them at the shops!

By ten the next morning, neither Mary nor Georgiana had stirred from their beds, having finally drifted off to sleep in the wee morning hours. When Georgiana roused herself, she did not even look at the time, but could not allow another minute to pass without making up with Mary. Determining to find her friend immediately, she hurriedly rose and headed out the room. Mary, having the same idea, was just exiting her own apartment when she heard Georgiana say her name. "Mary, I am so sorry for having snapped at you yesterday! I had a *dreadful* night because of it—please tell me all is forgotten."

"Don't be silly, it is I who should apologize. You may have snapped at me, but I scolded you as if I were your mother! And, for all things, asking for tea! You were absolutely *right*, for having tea was an excellent idea to promote the friendly feeling we were trying to create with Alice. Who could possibly have known ..." At this, Georgiana raised her hand, gesturing for silence, and gave her friend a warm embrace.

As the two were just making up, the maid servant, having heard their voices, came upstairs with the note from Alice. "This came for you last night, Miss."

"Thank you, Rosie," Georgiana said. "Oh look, Mary, it is from Alice."

"What does she say?"

Looking up with alarm, Georgiana exclaimed, "Dear me, we have not a moment to lose, Mary! The note says Alice wants to meet both of us at the shops." Reading on to find out the time, she said, "We will never make it! I fear they have already arrived in town by now!"

Mary insisted, "We must attempt to join them. Perhaps we should first try their home." They considered it, but the fear of Alice already being at the shops was too strong an image to take them toward the manor first. As quickly as they could prepare themselves, which was made obvious by the looks of their hair, they were in the carriage heading for the shops!

While the girls had been coming to terms, Alice and her father, who had been waiting in front of the mercantile establishment for some time now, were in their own conversation. Alice said dejectedly, "I know what they must think of me, Father ... is it not clear they have no intention of continuing a project that involves dealing with *me?* Can we not go home, please?"

"Alice, you are overreacting," he responded. "These are not the sort of girls that would walk out on such a ... a ... a ..." His Lordship could not find the right word to describe what the girls were doing without inadvertently saying the wrong thing. This, of course, only made it worse for Alice.

"You see? You believe they have no interest in seeing me again after yesterday either."

"No, my dear, I was simply at a loss for words, there was nothing more to it than that. Let us go to their home instead and see what has become of them. You need not step out of the carriage, I will get down alone. After that, I shall take you home if you feel you cannot continue." Alice only barely consented to this as they got into the carriage and started out for the Darcy home.

# Chapter Twenty-two

Just as his Lordship and his daughter left the shops, the girls proceeded that direction and were soon in the town square, heading straight for the nearest place they might locate Alice. When not finding her at the first place they stopped and uncertain exactly where to go next, they began going into one store after another, their anxiety only made worse on being informed by Mr. Russell, the fabric merchant, that Lord Dewey and his daughter had indeed been in his shop earlier that morning.

In the meantime, arriving at the Darcy residence, an inquiry from Lord Dewey after the girls brought the answer that they had left in quite a rush and were overheard saying something about the shops. "Did I not tell you, my dear?" the Earl beamed. "Just as I suspected, they were detained over some business or other, and having become aware of their being late to our appointment, they have rushed off to find us. Now, do not fret any longer. If we hurry back, we will likely catch up with them." And once again, his Lordship's carriage was winding its way through the streets.

Still searching for the Deweys, Mary and Georgiana were so concerned over how Alice might be taking their failure to keep the appointment that they failed to notice their own reflections in the shop windows, revealing how their rushing around had further disarrayed their hair! However, wasting no time, they re-entered the carriage, for both of them determined they must now go to his Lordship's home and explain, and thither they headed.

Well, it is no surprise that at the same time the carriage bearing Alice and her father was heading toward the square, the one carrying the girls was moving along another street in the opposite direction. What a curious circumstance, both parties completely unaware of what was happening!

Alighting once again at the mercantile's, Lord Dewey consulted Mr. Russell about whether Miss Darcy had been there yet and was told of the hustle and bustle with which the two young ladies had entered and exited his shop. Being in no doubt of their intent, he nevertheless felt they had spent enough time chasing the wind. It was now time to take Alice home and begin attending to his own business of the day. Returning to the carriage, he informed her of all he had learnt, saying it was best for them to meet up with the girls later in the afternoon. With this development, the two carriages were now heading in the same direction, albeit one was far ahead of the other!

We find the girls now arriving at Lord Dewey's, hurrying to the door to inquire if Alice was within and learning that she was not. Turning away dejectedly, their pace to the carriage was more befitting that of a lady now, though their appearance would still not answer for it. Back inside the carriage, they also decided it was best to try to meet with Alice later in the day and were thus on their way home. Looking at her friend for the first time that allowed her image to register since they left that morning, Mary suddenly declared, "Georgiana! You should see your hair ... it is a fright!"

"If it in any way resembles yours, I am sure of it!" They began to laugh heartily, relieving some of the tension that had been growing throughout their search. Unexpectedly, Georgiana caught sight of something through the window which made her put her head outside it.

"Georgiana, I don't think that will improve your hair. Whatever are you doing?"

"No, Mary, I think that was his Lordship's carriage that has just passed us! They must be on their way home—we need to go back!" Without delay, they once again headed in the other direction.

Alice and her father had barely entered the foyer when the bell rang. Lord Dewey was heard saying, "Beaman, who is that arriving? ... Perhaps it is our young friends, Alice."

When the door was fully opened, it revealed Mary and Georgiana, looking quite the worse for wear. Heedless of that, they came in, marching directly to Alice and imploring her to forgive their not meeting her at the requested time. Expressing their great concern for her feelings on this apparent neglect on their part, both the girls apologized, saying they wished only to be allowed to try again, for nothing would please them half so much as to go into the shops with her.

Alice, who had been accustomed to only one person in the world expressing so much concern and care for her, with their appearance not being lost on her, felt her heart swelling with such warmth for Mary and Georgiana. She thought, *"Only persons who are genuinely good and kind would care so little about their appearance while expressing such concern for my feelings!"* She looked at her father, saying, "You are absolutely correct about them." Turning to the girls, she took them by the hand and said, "Surely you will want some tea. Please come in and let us have some, I will send the servant immediately ... Father, do you not have a meeting you were leaving for?"

Looking at his daughter with pride and a great sense of calm, the Earl left straightaway, satisfied that his Alice had been introduced to two excellent young ladies with whom a strong friendship would be forged. He blessed the day he had heard the name Mary Bennet and his decision to go see her and Miss Darcy. At this point he was not sure what was going to become of his library, but right then and there, he decided if this new library should turn out well, it should have their names inscribed prominently and permanently for all to see.

## Chapter Twenty-three

Alice had not enjoyed tea with company so much since she was a little girl. They had their refreshments in the library so they could discuss plans. Obviously the trip to the shops would be rescheduled, but within the confines of that room, they looked about themselves and let ideas come to mind. Before long, they were all excitedly giving voice to various schemes.

Georgiana was the first to observe, "Having the columns painted will do something to brighten the room, but I fear it will not do nearly enough."

"Is it possible to make that window larger?" Mary asked.

"Oh yes!" declared Georgiana. "There is a house in the lakeside district that has a fabulous window that juts out, and when you stand there, it is almost like being outside. I had always thought it simply wanted a window seat."

"That of all things would be splendid!" cried Alice, fully absorbed in the discussion, completely at ease now. "Nothing is quite as nice as a window seat, reading with the rain falling all about you, or having the sun shine warmly on your skin. I remember sitting at such a place when I was a child. A larger window with a comfortable seat is a must." She added, "I do wish something could be done about reaching those books on the higher shelves. The rolling ladder is fine for someone more nimble than I, but I am always having to ask one of the servants for help. And of course, not knowing exactly where the book I am looking for is—just as you and I were speaking of the other day, Mary—so much time is spent with the servant rolling the ladder from place to place and still the book I am looking for is not found. Ladders being used for such a purpose is not practical. It would seem a more enlightened approach could be found."

Mary, looking about the room as if she was making calculations, finally said, "What I am about to propose may sound ridiculous at first, but before discounting it outright, please try to imagine my idea." The two girls sat up to pay close attention as Mary rose and walked to the window. "Picture, not just a larger window, but really, most of that entire *wall* being made into a window. Think of what a fine large window seat that would make!"

Georgiana was beginning to say something, but Mary continued in earnest, "No, no, hear me out, please ... to make up for the loss of shelf space that will be replaced by window, we make shelves up higher on the other walls of the room. Then around the rest of the room, we could have a balcony built with stairs leading up to it. This would make the books be readily at hand with no need of a ladder, perhaps only a step stool at most. I'm thinking with the window reaching all the way up the wall and past the balcony, we could incorporate another section of seats on the second floor so you can find your book up there and begin reading without having to come down to the first floor." She turned inquisitively to see the reaction of her friends.

"It sounds magnificent!" declared Alice. "Can all that be done?"

"Yes, that is a grand scheme," chimed in Georgiana. "But I wonder as well, can it be done?"

"I have no idea," said Mary, "but it was exciting to have the picture come to mind. How are we to find out if such alterations can be made?"

The three felt if they were going to make changes on such a scale, they would have to talk to someone with more experience. Alice spoke up, "My father has had much work done to the house; he will very likely have persons we could consult."

It was then settled that Lord Dewey should be conferred with. For that purpose, Mary suggested that the other two draw up some sketches first so that these could be used in talking to him. "Let us put off going shopping so the two of you can use the time for your drawings," Mary directed.

"But I'm sure Georgiana draws much better than I do," Alice said sheepishly. "Perhaps it would be better if she drew the ideas."

"Don't worry about that, Alice. We are not looking for something to hang on the wall, just a rough sketch so your father will have a better idea of what we are planning. Besides, it would be good to compare the different ideas you both come up with."

"In that case, why don't you draw something also, Mary?" asked Alice.

Georgiana began to laugh before Mary could reply, "As you can tell by *someone's* laughing, anything I might draw will not convey a jot of information to your father, except that I should have left the drawing to you two."

\* \* \* \* \*

When they got together again to look at the drawings, there were some obvious similarities, but the differences were interesting: Georgiana had incorporated a circular staircase on one end of the room to take up less space while having the main staircase in the center, whereas Alice had positioned two staircases on either end of the balcony. As for the window seat, Georgiana had drawn a continuous divan spanning the entire length. Alice, though, broke up the space into smaller sections so that armrests were available along with space for lighting in what might be considered more private sections. For the curtains, they both had the same idea of lightweight material that gave an airy feel to the room.

"I believe it will be hard to choose from your designs, they are all lovely," Mary said.

"Not really," returned Georgiana. "This is Alice's library, so whichever suits her is what we should go with."

"Oh, please don't make me decide all on my own," Alice pleaded. "I value your opinions and would dearly love to hear them."

After a moment's contemplation, Mary spoke first, "I like the staircase in the middle. However, I would suggest we make it twice as wide and not have a second one, which would permit us to enlarge the two ends of the balcony and possibly to place a chair or two there."

"Yes, I agree," responded Alice. "The staircase being placed in the middle gives a sense of symmetry that is very appealing to the eye, and having a place to sit at each end is a wonderful touch. What do you say to that, Georgiana?"

"The widening of the balcony at the two ends will be a pleasant addition and having the staircase a bit larger will give the room that look of grandeur that will be most becoming for such a library!" she replied excitedly. Turning to Alice, she added, "And I much prefer your design for window seating—it is more suited for comfortable reading and has that feel of coziness that comes to mind when one hears of a window seat."

"Well then," Mary said pleasantly, "it was not as difficult to decide as I had imagined. When I saw both of your fine drawings, I liked them so much I would not have known how to begin selecting what to keep and what to leave out. You know I had said to you, Alice, that you should not be too concerned with your sketches since they would not be hung on the wall, but I honestly think we should have these sketches framed as an exhibit for all that enter here to catch a glimpse of the beginnings of what, I am sure, will be the finest library to be found in a private home in all of London!"

The two artists were in raptures with the idea and even began choosing where they might be placed, when another less happy thought occurred to Georgiana: "We are getting a little ahead of ourselves, are we not? We have yet to find out if such changes are even possible."

"That is true," Alice said, warmly adding: "but I will have the sketches framed all the same. Even if it cannot be done, the ideas are certainly worth remembering." The memories that were being created today for this lonely young lady were not just the ones having to do with making over the library, and already Alice wanted some way to preserve them before they should vanish.

Satisfied with all they had accomplished, it was agreed that his Lordship should be shown their concepts for the library at his earliest convenience. Privately, each one of the girls was nervous about presenting their concepts to the Earl, and yet Mary especially was elated at how things were progressing. Her hope of doing something different with her life other than being a wife was beginning to take shape, and she determined that evening to pick up her pen and paper and write her feelings about it all to her new friend, Mrs. Randall.

# Chapter Twenty-four

When Lord Dewey was applied to by his daughter, accompanied by Mary and Georgiana, to take a look at their plans, he could see how excited the three of them were. Fully prepared to pretend an interest in what they had done, but truly expecting to find silly plans that he would have to significantly alter, he sat down at his desk, put his spectacles on, and began looking at the sketches they brought. Already in his mind, three things were moving him to approve their plans. To begin with, he had never seen Alice so happy as she was this day—actually, she was more than happy ... she was genuinely involved, speaking of Mary and Georgiana just as he had hoped. That alone would have been sufficient motivation, but he also recalled his own words to the girls, *'If you can help Alice, it matters not to me if the library were left in shambles, give no attention to expense!'* And last of all, he could not minimize his own pride in having one of the finest personal libraries in London; if Mary could improve on it in some way, that would be pleasing to him, for what man does not favor some sort of distinction above his neighbors, even if that man is the Earl of Essex?

Though he had not expected such dramatic changes, the Earl found their sketches quite promising, and with their added enthusiastic explanations, he gave his heartfelt approval. As one might expect where there is enough money, nothing in the way of building is out of the realm of possibilities, and Lord Dewey immediately joined the girls with his own enthusiasm for the project. He explained that there were some modifications needed with the window concept, for columns would need to be added at intervals for support. This would mean that instead of one very large window, the wall would have to be broken up with the addition of more columns, which worked well with the design the girls had chosen for the window seats. The same column design would be used to support the balcony, bringing the look of the room together, since all of them would then be done in the same faux marble look.

Having not only Lord Dewey's approval but also his added input made the girls anxious to get started right away. The books would all have to be removed, and the two rooms nearest the library were chosen as the best location to make a place for them. Therefore, several servants were called to take the furniture away to storage, and Alice even began directing others to take all the books from the shelves to the other rooms to be inventoried. She and Mary had the task of coming up with some system of categorizing them all and were very excited with this challenge of organizing the library.

Georgiana was glad to help, but such work did not suit her and she really did not know what to do with herself. Trying to make her feel more comfortable, Mary suggested, "Georgiana, why do you not return to Pemberley for the next few weeks? The work of remodeling will take longer than that, and Alice and I have these books to tend to. Surely you have things to occupy yourself with there for this brief amount of time, then you could join us again."

"Would that not be abandoning you two? I know there is so much to be done with the books."

"Yes, and we can tell how much you relish the idea of spending all day sitting among them making notes," Alice laughed, for the look on Georgiana's face was quite comical.

"Well, perhaps I can leave town, as you say, *for a while*, but will you promise to send for me if matters progress faster than expected?" Georgiana really didn't want to miss any of this adventure with them and therefore was only going to agree to go if Mary would make sure to keep her informed, which she readily assured her she would.

It all seemed to be a very good plan to Mary and Alice, who knew there would probably be many late nights ahead of them, talking over ideas of organizing and categorizing this extensive number of books. Alice suggested that Mary stay at Dewey manor that very evening so they could get started. At that, Georgiana, now feeling all the more as if she was just in the way, reluctantly agreed. "Very well then, I shall stop by this afternoon to take my leave on my way out of town."

* * * * *

As she left the library, Georgiana heard music coming from the other side of the house and was instinctively drawn to it. She had never heard this particular melody before, and obviously the performer was someone of real ability. She therefore found herself doubly drawn, wanting to know more about the piece that was being played and who could be playing it. Upon reaching the smaller music room and finding the door ajar, she slowly opened it just enough to peer in. There was a young man sitting at the grand instrument, quite absorbed in his playing. Georgiana quietly slipped into the room and comfortably positioned herself to listen.

Becoming absorbed in the beautiful composition, her admiration for both the performer and the piece of music was growing, when he abruptly halted. Not noticing he had stopped to write, she impulsively began to clap and rose to beg that he continue. The young man turned while at the same time attempting to stand, which caused the bench under him to fall. Reaching to prevent it from tumbling had the unfortunate effect of making *him* go tumbling!

Naturally, Georgiana came rushing across the room, circumventing furniture along the way. "Are you alright!?" she cried, now by his side with an awkward attempt of assisting him.

He had bounced to his feet as only a young man trying to make an embarrassing moment be as momentary as possible is able, replying, "I am quite alright, I assure you. I hope the same can be said for my uncle's piano bench, however." He then started to reach for that very bench when he stopped and said sheepishly, "Oh, forgive me for being more concerned for the bench before introducing myself ... I am Lord Dewey's nephew, Van Owen Dewey Thornburg."

Being introduced under such circumstances caused Georgiana to disregard the fact that she was meeting a handsome young man, so without her own usual embarrassment, she replied, "I am glad to meet you. My name is Georgiana Darcy, and I'm here helping your cousin Alice with the library."

Trying to think of something witty to say after his strange exhibition, Mr. Thornburg grinned, "Well, Miss Darcy, after such a demonstration of my uncommon gracefulness, you should do all in your power to prevent me from pouring tea."

"Forewarned is forearmed, they say," she returned with a smile.

He was about to say something in return as he put his hand in his pocket, only to find his pants had ripped during the fall! This created a whole different kind of awkwardness. Now he truly wished for some clever remark to make; however, the rip in his trousers may just as well have been a gag in his mouth! Looking first one way and then another, hoping to compose himself from the shock of his discovery, all at once he remembered the bench. Reaching down to pick it up, in an effort to conceal his feeling of clumsiness *and* the said rip, Mr. Thornburg pretended to inspect it, and glancing at Georgiana out of the corner of his eye to see if she had noticed anything, he turned to place it under the piano. Finally he was able to speak again: "It appears I have not done any damage to the bench," he said, adding under his breath, *"if only that could be said of everything."* He reluctantly turned to face her again, not knowing how to proceed with no other piece of furniture to straighten.

Sensing his feelings, Georgiana wanted very much to alleviate his discomposure. "There is no need for you to be embarrassed, sir. I should apologize for startling you as I did and causing what could have been a very bad fall."

"You are too kind," he said, looking down to try and assess just how bad the rip was without actually calling attention to it.

His turning away made Georgiana feel even greater empathy for him, believing him to be acting as she had herself done many times before, for she remained unaware of what was causing his red face and inability to converse. Her compassion moved her to be less concerned for her own usual apprehension and see if she could perhaps get Van to open up and move past what she assumed was his own shyness. This was quite a different role for her to play, since every time she had been in the position of meeting young men, *she* was always the one needing encouragement to converse. This prompted her to say, "The beautiful music you were playing is my excuse for coming in ... I had never heard it before, and you play so masterfully."

This had the intended effect, for it pulled his attention away from the rip, and he looked up at her with a beautiful sparkle in his eye. "Did you really like it?"

"Yes, indeed! Surely I have not been the first to say so—your modesty does you credit. I must add, I would love to have the sheet music, though I could never hope to play it as well as you."

Van smiled, and the whole room seemed to light up for Miss Darcy. She had been in company with fine looking men who were very much aware of how to put on a charming countenance that was intended to make a young lady go weak at the knees, but Georgiana had believed herself immune to such pretensions since that whole incident with George Wickham years ago. The sincerity of Van's eyes coupled with the genuineness of his expression, however, captured her and held her transfixed, and she began thinking how lovely their chance meeting had been.

Van, on the other hand, remembered his trousers and looked down again, trying to think of some reason for excusing himself other than the real reason that was making him seek an exit. With nothing coming to mind, he abruptly said, "Will you please excuse me, Miss Darcy?" and at that, left the room, keeping the untorn side of his trousers facing Georgiana. This only caused him to walk in a strange manner, bumping into furniture and almost tripping over the rug, which served to accentuate the look of nervous shyness that she believed was driving him out of the room.

Finding herself alone, Georgiana stood looking toward the door Van had just left through. "I have never met a young man so shy who was also quite so good-looking! I know I have, in effect, run away with Mary to avoid being presented to eligible young men, but I do not recall ever running from a room as I have just seen him do!" she thought. Laughing, she turned away from the door, inquisitive to see the sheet music that was still on the piano and was surprised to find that he was, in fact, in the process of *writing* the music she had heard. She now began to think less of his shyness as her admiration for him grew. Reflecting on how handsome he was and how radiant his face was when he smiled at her brought a smile to her own face. Sitting down before the instrument to look more closely at the ledger line, Georgiana could not help but try her hand at this exquisite composition. It was difficult, however, for the score looked more like a child's page with all the mark-throughs, and the notations he had made looked more like they had been done by someone who could barely write rather than a piano genius, so she found herself having to pause often in order to discern the notes.

Before long, unknown to her, Van had changed and returned, but now it was his turn to be at the door listening. At that very moment, Georgiana was having particular trouble; Van thought her stumbling through was an indication of her being just a beginner, not even considering that it could be an indication of his poor penmanship. As she stopped completely to take up the paper and study it before attempting again, he broke into applause, causing her to turn and say, "Oh, you have returned! I hope you don't mind my looking at your music—you are the one writing this, are you not?"

As he came across the room he affirmed that he was. "It is to be a four movement suite."

"How many movements have you done?"

"I'm still working on the first."

"It is *beautiful.* Do you have a name for it?"

Smiling self-consciously, hoping the title would not sound foolish, he replied, "I call it..." hesitating a moment, "... *The Sun.* That is, I am calling it that right *now.* If a better name comes to mind, I'll change it later."

She was expecting some very expressive, perhaps poetic title, but instead his prospective idea struck Georgiana as a bit uninteresting considering how lovely the music sounded. She attempted to hide being unimpressed, yet trying to look as impressed as one can when you are, in fact, *not*, she innocently asked, "Why did you choose to call it that?" However, she had been too well-practiced in the art of open honesty and therefore did not conceal her impression as well as she had hoped.

"Perhaps when one first hears the title, there is something wanting in it, but the music is inspired by the sun's shifting motion through the sky as the year goes by. The first movement is the beginning of a summer's day as the sun starts to shows itself, building in intensity as it reaches its zenith, dominating the sky. From there, I am hoping to capture the sensation of the sun giving way to the passing of summer as it no longer rises to its apex. The third movement is when the sun is at its lowest point and it seems it will never again hold dominance in the sky. As you might guess, the last movement is the sun making its way back. So it seemed fitting to call it *The Sun*," he concluded, somewhat bashfully.

"Well, if the rest of the suite turns out to be as impressive as what you have written so far, it will be wonderful," she replied, trying harder to keep her feelings to herself.

She succeeded in doing so, as this praise was enough for him. "Thank you, it is very encouraging to hear someone say so." Without realizing what he was about to do, Van now showed *he* was not impressed with her piano skills! "I heard you attempting to play it, Miss Darcy. I assure you, it is too difficult for a beginner, but then I was not attempting to write a piece for someone to practice at playing the piano."

Georgiana took pride in her ability, so this comment vexed her, but she simply bowed in acquiescence to his ill-founded opinion of her competency while holding back from making a much deserved remark upon the pitiful condition of the sheet music and his poor handwriting. Thinking it best to move past this, she graciously inquired, "Have you written other pieces of music?"

This was a topic he was eager to be asked about. "Yes, but nothing as long as what I am attempting now. Would you like to hear something else that I have written?" Receiving a *"yes, of course,"* he suggested ringing for tea and playing for her while they waited. Feeling the need to redeem himself with regard to the title of his *Sun* suite, he chose another piece whose title he was sure would sound better. "This melody I call *The Flowers Dance.*"

As he played, Georgiana thought, "His handwriting is terrible, but his music composing and execution is brilliant! He is handsome, to be sure, and on top of all this, he truly does not seem to be conceited." Tea arrived as he had just finished playing, and the servant immediately began arranging the table. Disregarding that, Georgian was moved to say ardently, "That was one of the loveliest pieces of music I have ever heard! I could honestly see the flowers being moved about by the wind—and then you even included what sounded to me like rain falling gently upon the flowers, is that not so?"

Hearing her remarks, he turned from his position on the bench and, even from this distance, his smile was like the full moon on a dark cloudless night. His eyes still holding her captive, she perceived him saying, "You have an excellent ear, Miss Darcy," and then continuing humbly, "Well, I don't mean with reference to your praise of my music, but I mean your comprehending the portrayal of the wind and the rain. I have played that for some and at the end they would ask why I had named it as I did."

He spoke with real modesty about his music, though his playing was of the caliber one hears only in concert halls. Georgiana was quite enthralled and had never felt so at ease talking to any young man as she was now doing. While they sat together for tea, they talked about the music they both loved and other such matters. It seems they both agreed that harp and harpsichord duets are too much of the same thing, being only different enough to prove annoying. And yet, they could not agree on who they preferred, Mozart or Bach! To Georgiana, it appeared they could talk on endlessly.

Pleasant as everything was going, unfortunately the time came for Van to say, "I regret I need beg your pardon once more, Miss Darcy, but I must set about putting the finishing touches to the first movement of the *Sun* suite. My uncle is to have a dinner party tonight for me and I am to play it for him and his guests. I would be ever so grateful if you would come and give me your impression of the finished piece, although in truth, the idea of playing it for you in this way is much more appealing ... but please, do say you will come."

How could she refuse his asking more than once! Suddenly, she thought of her proposed going away to Pemberley, and her hesitation in giving an answer made him address her again: "My uncle will not mind my asking someone of my choosing, if that is what is making you doubt whether you should accept."

Unable to resist the idea of hearing the whole first movement, she accepted. Well, at least she could attribute her acceptance to her wish of hearing his music—instead of the desire to see his face, those eyes, that smile again! Bidding him a good day and her assurance that she would see him again in the evening, she left Lord Dewey's estate, not even thinking of returning to inform Mary and Alice that she would not be going away after all.

Georgiana's thoughts soon ran to the fact that being nervous at receiving a dinner invitation for her usually meant wishing she could find some excuse for avoiding it, or how she might make herself fade into the background and be noticed as little as possible. But now, for the first time, she was joining those legions of young ladies who were nervous with anticipation about the night, hoping, indeed, to *be noticed* by that certain someone.

# Chapter Twenty-five

Mary and Alice, of course, were ignorant of what was happening on the other side of the house, for the work of recording all those books had begun in earnest and it required a great deal of attention to direct all those that had been employed in the business. It was decided between them that Mary take charge of the books in one room while Alice did those in the other.

Consequently, it was not until much later that they had an opportunity of conferring with one another, at which time they remembered that Georgiana had not stopped to say goodbye on her way to Pemberley. Mary suggested she must have found that there was more to do than she had first thought and simply decided to make an early start in the morning. While they were talking over these things, Alice's maid servant called her attention to the dinner party in honor of her cousin, suggesting that it was time to begin getting ready. Startled by the reminder, Alice threw her arms up and looked at Mary, quite disappointed with herself. "I'm sorry, Mary, but I was so consumed with our work that I had completely forgotten about the dinner for my cousin tonight."

"Who is your cousin?" Mary inquired.

"Oh, my cousin Van is a composer, and Father has invited some of the more prominent patrons of the London symphony to hear a composition he has been working on. He plays very well and writes beautiful music—your fondness for music will surely make this evening a very pleasant occasion, and I dare say after all the work that we have been doing, it will be a welcome diversion."

Mary was about to agree on how refreshing such an evening would be after spending all day literally among the books, when she recalled with a bit of a shock, "But I haven't any of my evening gowns here ... I should go home to prepare for the evening."

"There will be no need for that, Mary. We'll send one of the servants to fetch your gowns; that way you may use this time relaxing here instead of rushing about in a carriage."

"Thank you, Alice, that sounds so much better, for I am tired and would dearly love to soak for a bit before getting dressed."

Alice asked, "Should we not send around a note asking Georgiana to join us, since it seems she has not yet gone to Pemberley?"

"If I know her, she will not be inclined to come, but we may as well leave it to her to decide." As things sometimes happen, Mary believed that Alice intended to write the note and Alice thought Mary would do so, and as a result, no note was sent at all!

Later that evening as the guests were arriving, Alice pointed out to Mary who was who as they arrived. How impressive to have the conductor of the London symphony, as well as the first and second violinist, the cellist and the violist all attending this affair! "Are they here because they intend to have a string quartet play, as well as your cousin?" Mary asked.

"Yes, Papa always does so when he has Conductor Wooddale to dinner."

For several minutes, the two girls talked about how Alice expected the evening would go, with her introducing Mary to the few people who came up to say hello to her. There were more guests to come, as many were still arriving outside in their carriages. As Georgiana stepped out of hers, she was unsure what was making her more restless, seeing Van again or having to explain to Mary and Alice what she was doing at this dinner party when she was supposed to have been on her way to Pemberley. Suddenly the girls saw her enter the room, and rushing to her side, they could not help but show how happy they were to see her. She, of course, was all smiles to be greeted by their familiar faces, and if they did notice any touch of uneasiness, they attributed it to being at such a gathering as this.

"I am so glad you came, Georgiana; I was not sure you would. It's a good thing Alice thought of sending around the note inviting you," Mary said.

Alice protested, "I didn't send the note—I thought you did."

"No, I didn't send the note."

Before anyone of them could say another word on the subject, Van appeared by their side to greet his cousin. "Hello, Alice, I'm very glad to see you tonight." Then noticing Georgiana beside her, he turned toward her with, "Miss Darcy, how delighted I am that you're here. I see you have found my cousin .... and Alice, I don't believe I have had the honor of meeting your other friend."

"This is Miss Mary Bennet ... Miss Bennet, this is my cousin Van Owen Dewey Thornburg," and continuing to Van, Alice finished, "She and Miss Darcy are making over the library for Father ... well, I should say, for me, that is."

"Miss Darcy, you have a keen understanding of music and you also make over libraries. How diverse your talents are!" he replied with a grin. Georgiana smiled, and Mary and Alice also smiled and shared curious glances with each other. Before the conversation with Van could go any further, however, he was called away by his Lordship, who wanted to introduce him to others.

Mary immediately asked, "How is it, dear friend, if you did not receive a note from either Alice or myself, that we find you here? Have you received an invitation from some other person?" She and Alice laughed as they saw Georgiana blushing.

Alice now said with a sense of deep gratitude, "My cousin Van is a very fine young man, and aside from my father, he is the only person who has ever been kind to me that has not been paid to do so." At this, Mary and Georgiana exchanged concerned looks, as Alice added, "That is until the two of you have come to us." Just at that moment, Alice was also called away by her father, who wished to speak with her privately to find out if she was being overwhelmed by the crowd.

"How devastating do you believe it would be if Alice were to find out we *have* been hired by her father for that very purpose?!" Georgiana declared with alarm.

"Georgiana, surely you must remember how the matter was resolved by us with Lord Dewey on the point of money," Mary tried to reassure her. "Or have you forgotten how much work still lies ahead of us on the library?"

"No, I have not forgotten … it's just that, hearing those words coming from her was disconcerting, that is all."

"Well, ease your mind on the matter, we are doing a fine work in both areas." Changing her tone, Mary began, "Now seriously, Georgiana, I want to know—how did you and Alice's cousin meet so that he was able to invite you tonight? For he obviously did invite you, am I right?"

Bashfully, Georgiana began, "When I left the two of you earlier, I heard music from the other side of the house and followed it with great curiosity. Finding the room where it originated, I discovered Mr. Thornburg working on the very material he is to play tonight. It is really very good, though I only heard a small portion. I am sure you and I will be delighted with the performance, for he plays uncommonly well."

"Does he play as well as you?" Mary asked.

With more enthusiasm, she answered, "I mean no discredit to your playing, Mary, for I consider you my equal at the instrument. But I must say, if we took *both* our abilities and combined them, we would still not play half so well as he does! However, I must tell you what happened …" With an introduction such as this and with Georgiana lowering her voice, Mary naturally drew closer with all the look of anticipation one has at the prospect of hearing some intriguing bit of news coming from a friend. "Mr. Thornburg left the room unexpectedly—I must say, I found him to be more nervous in my presence than any other young man I have ever met—but anyway, when I saw the sheet music he had been writing the score on, I attempted to play it. But his writing is so abominable and the page was such a mess of markouts that reading it was impossible! When he returned in the midst of my effort to play the piece, which was quite *bad* because of not being able to read the score, in an effort not to say anything unkind about my playing, he said he had not written the piece for *beginners* to practice on! Despite his motive of trying to spare my feelings, that was nonetheless a bit irritating … I mean, we all have our vanities and mine is my playing. But now he thinks I play no better than a child," Georgiana cried petulantly.

As Mary was commiserating with her over such a slight, Alice rejoined them, asking that they come meet the conductor and the members of the quartet before they were called to dinner. Conductor Wooddale was a very gracious and kind man, asking whether the girls were musically inclined. Georgiana was quick to say she is nothing in comparison to Mr. Thornburg, but that she and Mary both loved to play as well as listen. At his suggestion that either of them might honor the group with a tune after dinner, they both objected strenuously, for they dared not presume to approach the instrument with such experts at hand. He then asked about their work on the library and if, upon its completion, he might be given leave to call upon them for their attention to his own library. Georgiana smiled; Mary, though, felt that this might be an indication that she had started down the path that could answer for what she was searching to find. The experience she was gaining was filling her with confidence, and she was thrilled at the prospect of bringing to fruition a workable way of cataloging and arranging the volumes in a large library. She had found in Alice someone who was just as keen to develop such a system, and their two minds thought along so similar lines in this regard that Mary looked forward to once again being at work among the books with Alice. To now have another person interested in doing something with their library who would request her assistance made it seem that a bright day was ahead for Mary Bennet.

# Chapter Twenty-six

The dinner that had been prepared for this grand occasion was, of course, wonderful as far as the food went. There was one thing that would have suited Georgiana more, though. It was arranged that she sit with Mary and Alice, which was better than being placed between two strangers, but if she had her preference, to be perfectly honest, she would not have minded sitting next to Van! However, this night was specifically planned for the talented young man to be introduced to those who could prove to be of some advantage to his music. With quiet resignation, Miss Darcy took her place at table, certain that she would not suffer too much from this deprivation, for the acquaintance was too new—but there was a delightful novelty in her feeling this way.

Mary interrupted her thoughts by asking, "What did he name his suite?"

"He calls it *The Sun*, but that is only his working title. It's very likely he will come upon something much more interesting." She did not understand why she felt compelled to explain the title as she had heard him do earlier, but the words seem to come automatically.

Georgiana's explanation of the concept behind the suite led Mary to ask, "Is the music inspired by the sun?" and then declare frankly, "Because if it is about the sun and its movement, I could not imagine a more fitting title."

Struck with the simple truth of this observation, Georgiana felt a tinge of self-reproach for having thought so little of the title when she had first heard it. This feeling, coupled with Mary's straightforward comment on the matter, made her want to tell him so and to wish him success for the night's performance. To that end, when dinner was over and the assembled guests moved into the concert hall, the quartet began setting up to play, and Georgiana took this opportunity to move toward Van so as to speak with him.

But before she could reach him, Lord Dewey stepped to his side, commanding his attention with: "Now, Van, is it still your wish that I introduce you? Conductor Wooddale said he would consider it a privilege to do so, and I think it might carry more weight for him to do it. The prestige of having someone of his stature introduce you to this gathering of music lovers cannot be lost on you, I am sure." Lord Dewey was very proud of Van and anxious that everything proceed to his advantage.

"You are very kind, uncle, but it would mean more to me if you would do the introduction." Georgiana was close enough to hear that, for she was hoping to speak with him as soon as Lord Dewey had finished. She was moved by the sentiments expressed in Van's choice of preferring his uncle's introducing him to the crowd rather than the conductor ... it had a certain charm to it.

"Very well, lad, as you wish. And what is the name of the suite?"

"Well, as to that, I fear my choice of title leaves something to be desired," he said hesitantly. "Instead of risking disenchanting anyone by the title, you best say nothing of it." Sorely did Georgiana wish to break into the conversation at that very moment, now knowing he intended to play the piece without informing the group of the name of the suite! This she felt certain would be a mistake, and especially knowing it was all due to her own reaction earlier in the day. But of course, she patiently waited for his uncle to finish with his compliments to his nephew.

Now as Lord Dewey stepped away, Mr. and Mrs. Chadwick, an older couple who were known to be very influential patrons, came forward to speak with Van. It seems those involved with the symphony cared for nothing more than to be introduced to a rising protégé, for what credit it gives one to be able to say they were acquainted with a person of the music world before they were famous! And to be able to declare you were at the very dinner that was responsible for launching them into a well-known position was a credit no one among them dared miss.

Having done their duty, the Chadwicks left to speak to Conductor Wooddale, and once again Georgiana stepped forward to get Van's attention. But with frustration did she hear the Tennysons call to him, and turning their direction, he did not even notice her at all. Assuming a nonchalant posture, Georgiana now looked around the room as if she was quite at ease, waiting for her own opportunity to speak with the man. When the Tennysons were drawing their conversation to an end, she wasted no time as they turned to walk away, and with determination said, *"Mr. Thornburg."*

Turning and seeing who it was, he smiled, saying cheerfully, "Miss Darcy, are you enjoying yourself? The music portion of the evening is about to start, and I'm sure someone with your ear will be delighted."

"Yes, but about the music ...."

She got no further, for they were joined by the O'Learys, who burst in with: "Mr. Thornburg, you must pardon us for coming up so abruptly, but I wanted to speak with you before the music started. This is a great pleasure, you know, to be permitted to listen to new music. The old masters are fine, but there is nothing like the spirit and life of you newcomers."

Mr. O'Leary was briskly interrupted by a beautiful young lady beside him, who had the most brilliant red hair. "Uncle, you have forgotten to introduce *me* to Mr. Thornburg."

"No, not at all, dear. Mr. Thornburg, may I present my niece, Miss Penelope Pinch."

"How do you do, Miss Pinch?"

"I am very well, thank you. And I must say I am *ever* so fond of musicians. You are all *so* musical."

Georgiana felt the need to give way to Mr. O'Leary and once again stepped aside. Now in addition to wanting to speak to Van about the title of the suite, she was feeling a *pinch* of jealousy to see him talking to this beautiful young lady instead of herself, for she was quite beautiful despite her pouring on the charm!

Van replied to Miss Pinch, "Indeed, I have yet to meet a musician that was not also musical. May I ask, do you play?"

"Oh, heavens no! *I* have yet to find a music teacher that could be tolerated. But if *you* give lessons, I am quite sure I would tolerate it *very well,"* she said ever so sweetly.

Georgiana thought, "If Mr. Thornburg finds any interest in such a girl as this, I will regret any good thing I have said of him! Why are men turned upside down by a pretty face? Can anything be more shallow than her feigning an interest in music? He cannot be taken in by this pretense, especially after all the grief he gave me about my playing ... she is a numbskull if ever I've seen one!"

Mr. O'Leary begged his niece's pardon, "My dear, if you would but allow your aunt and I to speak to Mr. Thornburg as well, for there is much we want to ask his opinion about. Sir, do you prefer the style of Beethoven or that of Mozart?" Without waiting for his answer, he continued, "I assure you, Mr. Thornburg, we are ready to have you to our own home for such an occasion as this, for there are so many among our acquaintance who are like-minded lovers of the arts."

"Yes, *please*, uncle, settle with Mr. Thornburg *now* to agree to a date for coming," Penelope begged captivatingly. Georgiana wanted very much to hear what reply Van would make to this but found it necessary to step aside, for still others from among the party had come to gather around Van and hear what the O'Learys were saying. With the appearance of Miss Pinch, Georgiana had become conscious that her own standing near Van for so long a time was making it appear she was merely another young lady trying to be noticed by Mr. Thornburg. Her shy nature could not endure it, so she determined to move away. At that very moment, the group was called to take their seats, for the evening's entertainment was about to begin with the quartet starting the affair off. Being the person of honor, Van was placed at the front seats along with his uncle and Conductor Wooddale.

* * * * *

The quartet was wonderful and the acoustics of this fine concert hall were exceptional, but Georgiana could not enjoy it, thinking all the while how much would be missed in Van's performance if those gathered did not have the benefit of the theme of his music. Having Miss Pinch seated just in front of her was not conducive to undistracted listening either, as she was *oohing* and *ahhing* about everything! Calling Georgiana's attention back to the performance,

Mary's comments about everything they were hearing were insightful, making Georgiana realize that she herself sounded rather dimwitted about it all because of her distracted mind.

There being a brief intermission before Van's introduction, Georgiana began looking for him and saw him standing alone. A recommendation by the conductor, which Van was sure to tend to, had caused him to step off to the side so as to make an entrance from there instead of coming from his seat, for this was deemed a more distinguished entry. Telling Mary and Alice she wanted to wish him well, Georgiana now hurriedly went over and called out, "Mr. Thornburg, excuse me for disrupting your attention moments before you are to play, but there is something I must say."

Van could not have been more happy to speak with her at this time, for there was something about her that calmed him. The sound of her voice gave him confidence, and with genuine warmth, he replied, "Nothing could be more agreeable to me than to hear something from you at this moment."

Again, Miss Darcy was momentarily struck silent by the joy of his countenance upon seeing her at such an important moment as this was for him. Recollecting herself, she presented him with, "I have been thinking over the title of your suite, *The Sun*. I overheard you say to your uncle that you preferred not to mention the title, but it seems to me that since it is, after all, music that was inspired by the sun, nothing could be more appropriate than to call it *The Sun*."

"Do you think so indeed? I told my uncle not to mention the title because of the reaction I received from you earlier today," he gently disclosed.

Fervently did she reply, "Yes, I gathered as much, which is why I have been trying desperately to speak with you about it. I must undo what I believe would be a mistake!" Although it was Mary who had convinced her of it, she felt it was her own responsibility to set matters right.

"I could not be more delighted to hear that you have changed your mind on my choice! But I fear little can be done now—I will simply play the piece and see if the music will stand on its own."

"No! Surely something can be done!" she cried, impulsively reaching for his hand. She held it for but a moment till she realized her blunder and, though blushing, she did manage to say, "It is by knowing the basis for the music that your true genius is manifest ... especially with a group of musicians such as we have collected here ... they of all persons will be able to see your wonderful ability for capturing in melody what is seen and felt in nature just as I did with *The Flowers Dance!*"

"For someone who plays as poorly as you do, you certainly have a wonderful sense of music. That is truly rare," he replied gratefully, and hearing her call him a genius made him look fondly at her. Rolling her eyes at his representing her mastery of piano playing in this way yet again, she held herself back from doing what she would have preferred to do—something such as stepping on his foot or spilling a drink on him! Instead, she returned to her seat so he could take his place at the instrument upon being introduced.

Lord Dewey had been prepared to call the party to settle in for the performance when he observed Georgiana speaking to his nephew, which made him prolong that for a little while, for he recognized with what pleasure he received her attentions. Seeing her now walk away, without further ado he called Van to take his place at the piano, but no mention of a title was given for the piece they were to hear. There was polite applause as Mr. Thornburg walked across the room, and as he took his seat, a silence settled in. Georgiana was grieved about the title but tried to comfort herself in the knowledge that she did at least say something on the subject before it was too late.

When he did not begin to play immediately, whispers were beginning to be heard, and Georgiana felt she had made a mistake by speaking to him just as he was to take to the instrument. "I have distracted him rather than helped him. Oh, how many times this day am I to wreck his chances at impressing the conductor and all the patrons gathered here! I should have trusted that the music would stand on its own," she thought, feeling quite wretched.

All at once, the sound of the bench was heard moving back, and Van stood up. Walking to the front of the piano, he addressed the audience: "Please, ladies and gentlemen, I do indeed have every intention of playing for you, but there is something that I would like to say first. Of course, I join my uncle in thanking you for coming this evening and allowing me this opportunity to play for you. I especially thank Lord Dewey for his kindness on my behalf in making it possible that I spend this evening with all of you, including Conductor Wooddale, whose presence gives me great honor and is not taken lightly, I assure you."

At that point, Mr. Thornburg looked around the room, and standing a little taller, went on: "I want to say a few words on the subject of inspiration. The piece of music you are about to hear is the first movement of a four part suite entitled *The Sun*, for it was inspired by the movement of the sun. And when it is completed, it will take us on a musical tour as the sun goes from its zenith during summer to its lowest point during the days of winter. We begin, then, with a typical summer day, from the first glimpses of light that can be seen in the morning to the sun taking its position high during midday." Pausing for but a moment, he continued, "In addition to that, however, there is another kind of inspiration that moves me to play at what I hope is my best." Here he stole a glance in the direction of Georgiana—or was it Miss Pinch? Miss Darcy could not tell, but the happiness on his face was contagious. "I can only hope that my playing will give credit to that source of my inspiration ... and to the patience of all of you, and the honor which you do me in listening." With that he returned to the bench.

Georgiana could not have been more pleased with his speech and was now fully prepared to enjoy his performance. As she listened, the music touched her heart, and when she closed her eyes she could imagine just the two of them as they were earlier that day. Though she was certain the rest of the audience could not feel the same, it was clear that the gathering of music lovers knew how special the music and the performer were. When he concluded, the audience applauded with great enthusiasm and Van modestly bowed, thanking them once again for their praise. Afterward, the playing was declared brilliant and the word *genius* was heard on the lips of many.

# Chapter Twenty-seven

Alone in their own corner of the room, the three friends were expressing their thoughts about the concert. Mary affirmed to Georgiana, "You are quite right about Mr. Thornburg's playing; neither of us could hope to match that level of excellence. And to think he composed those beautiful notes to create such an image of a bright summer's day—he is a master, a genius ... of that there can be no doubt." And turning to Alice, she asked, "What was he alluding to about some other inspiration for his playing? Do you have any idea?"

She answered, "At the time he was speaking, I had none, but observing how close Miss Pinch is to him now, I would guess that he may very well have been talking of being inspired by her, even though he just met her. There isn't a young man that can come into the same room with her that is not soon falling over himself to get her notice. You did see him look her direction, did you not?"

Thinking his notice was directed toward someone else did not have the same effect on Georgiana as it had earlier! She did hazard a hope that he could have been looking at her during his speech and not Miss Pinch, though, and was therefore moved to object, "No ... I believe you are mistaken ... it was not at her that he looked."

"At who then? For he clearly looked her direction, and it seemed quite deliberate," Alice returned.

"Oh ... he was simply looking about the audience," Georgiana offered.

Mary disagreed, "I think Alice is right, for he not only looked at her, but he also smiled." Neither of the girls comprehended that they were adding to Georgiana's distress, and to own the truth, such feelings in this manner about a young man was strange to the young lady. But thankfully for her, their discussion moved on.

"Miss Pinch is a horrid person, though I know I should not say such things. She was one of the girls Papa would arrange for me to associate with not so long ago, and there was no end to her couched taunts of my appearance which she assumed my father would not grasp. He soon discreetly put an end to her visits. Van is far above her in manners and kindness; it would disappoint me terribly if he were to pursue a relationship with her," said his cousin.

Van was, in fact, being congratulated and approached by everyone in attendance. Mr. O'Leary, addressing his niece in the presence of Van, prodded her with: "Tell us, my dear, what did you think of Mr. Thornburg's performance?"

"I loved it dearly, uncle! Sometimes you played remarkably fast, Mr. Thornburg! How*ever* do you manage to hit the right keys when doing so? I mean, I presume you did, since everyone says you played ever so well," she carried on once again, her words sounding as if she had poured honey on each syllable.

This brought an amused smile to his face as he tried to make a sensible reply to such an ignorant question. Politely he asked her, "Aside from the fast playing, was there nothing else that struck you about the piece?"

Delighted to be addressed by him, she simpered, thinking herself sounding quite astute, "I liked it when you played slow too."

Mr. O'Leary, becoming somewhat embarrassed at his niece, believed she had put her musical acumen on display long enough. "We must allow the others to have their share of Mr. Thornburg," he said to her impatiently, and with that he turned away, but Miss Pinch would not follow her uncle's lead, instead staying close by Van. And as long as Penelope Pinch was keeping herself as attached to him as she was able, Georgiana's timidity prevented her from trying to address him, though she very much wanted to express her praise of his music. But, she thought, with persons so closely connected to the London music scene telling him how wonderful it was, surely one who *plays so badly* would hardly be worth hearing from!

"I think I will go home now," Georgiana said to her two friends. "I am quite tired."

"Do you still intend to stop here on your way to Pemberley tomorrow? ... or do you take your leave of us now?" asked Mary.

Georgiana had all but forgotten about her plans to leave, for she was forming hopes of seeing Van on the morrow, supposing she would come to help with the work on the library. Not knowing what else to say at that moment, however, she replied, "Yes, I shall stop, but I shan't come too early, for there's no telling at what hour the guests will be leaving this evening."

"You can come early if you wish, Georgiana, for I am sure we will be retiring soon also, don't you think, Mary?" Alice said. Miss Bennet agreed, for she was anxious to get an early start on the books.

To that end, the girls began hunting for Lord Dewey to bid him goodnight and tell him of Georgiana's going back to Pemberley for a time. "It was good of you to come, Miss Darcy," said he, sounding genuinely sorry to hear that she would be leaving. With pride, however, he asked her, "I am not afraid of being contradicted that my nephew is a rare talent, and would that not be your opinion as well?"

"To be sure, he is," returned Georgiana. "Would you be so kind as to give him my best wishes, Sir?"

"That I will, but why not go and tell him yourself? I saw that you had no problem speaking to him earlier."

"With all those important persons about him, I dare not interrupt what may be a significant discussion," she replied sheepishly.

"As you wish, lass. Although judging from his reaction to your interrupting him before he was about to play this evening, I don't think he would mind! But you will be the best judge of that."

She bowed and began to walk away with quick steps, coloring at his Lordship's words, as Mary and Alice had turned to look at her quizzically. They immediately followed, calling after her, "Georgiana, wait! Why are you running from us? What was he talking about?" Determined to get a response, Mary prodded, "If you don't face us now, we will only make you tell us tomorrow!"

That brought her to a stop. "Can we not go to another room? Or come, let us go outside to wait for my carriage." She was hoping the cool evening air and the darkness would do a better job of concealing her glow of embarrassment than she was capable of at the moment! Making their way outside, the girls resisted the urge of trying to get Georgiana to begin an explanation. Her pace was quite brisk walking ahead of them, and they found themselves out of breath. Having ordered her carriage, thereupon she turned to face their questions, but instead blurted out this explanation, "I told you I was going to talk to Mr. Thornburg to wish him well before he played ... Lord Dewey undoubtedly made more of what he saw than there really was ... that is all!"

Mary, looking suspicious, said in return, "That is all, is it? And such a simple explanation as this required we find another room or come outside?"

*"Hang Mary's quick wit and observations!"* Georgiana said to herself, and then looking as if she had heard the carriage approaching, which was not the case, she hit upon something to say in return: "Did I not say I was tired and wished to go home?"

Alice, feeling for Georgiana and not wanting her to continue in obvious uneasiness, suggested, "My father is prone to make more of things than he should. He may have only been in jest with Miss Darcy, Mary. It is strange, I know, but I believe it has something to do with your being close in age to myself ... it was perhaps a liberty he should not have taken with you."

Georgiana was sorry to hear such an explanation, for she would have preferred the uncomfortable pleasure of thinking Lord Dewey's better knowledge of his nephew made him see something more than she could see in his behavior. Reluctantly she commented, "There, you see, Mary, it was all a joke—nothing more."

The carriage was now near. Mary knew there was something else about all of this, but the girlish teasing had lost its charm. Knowing such a discussion may best be had between just herself and Georgiana, she said, "Well then, what a pleasant way to end the evening, with a bit of a laugh. Sleep well, dear Georgiana, and we shall see you in the morning. Remember to come as early as it pleases you."

# Chapter Twenty-eight

When Georgiana arrived the next morning, Mary inquired, "Are you traveling to Pemberley dressed like that?"

"Oh well, as to that, I've been thinking it over," Georgina replied innocently. "It would be very rude of me to leave at such a time as this. There may need to be some decisions made about the balcony or the windows, or some such things as that, and with the two of you so very busy, it would be remiss of me not to be here to be consulted. Besides, what a terrible companion I would be to think of leaving with the two of you in the middle of your book sorting. I can at least be of some company to you."

Alice was greatly pleased. "Nothing could be better, Georgiana, though I can safely say neither of us would fault you for going."

Mary agreed: "That is very true, Georgiana. I believe the prospect of having your company as we wade through all these books would be most enjoyable. At the same time, we need someone to pass our ideas by that we are forming for cataloging and arranging the books so as to make sure everything will be understandable to someone other than ourselves."

"Well then, is there something you need me to tend to now?" she asked.

"We are still writing down the names of the books in their respective categories, and as you can see, our list is on the verge of becoming as unwieldy as all these books." At that moment Mary had this idea: "Girls, we need to begin moving the books that belong in the same categories together in their own piles. That will slow the list making, I know, but it will make things much easier later on. Otherwise, having these lists will be no more advantageous than having the books scattered as they are."

Alice understood immediately and set off to inform the servants whom she had working in the other room to discontinue the making of lists and wait for them to organize matters. When she returned, she asked, "This undoubtedly will be the first step in establishing our system of cataloging, so how do we begin the separation of the books that we have already listed?"

It was determined that the first major divisions should be by language—French, German, etc. It was hoped this step would proceed with some speed since those books should be easy to identify. Thankfully, there were not that many foreign language books and this task was completed before noon. Taking a step back, they eyed the separated books with satisfaction. Smiling, Georgiana quipped, "You realize there are not more than forty or fifty books in these three stacks!"

Alice verified, "There are *fifty-three* to be exact. But that is not going to detract from my indulging in a feeling of achievement."

Seeing it was time for lunch, Mary said, "I'm going to eat right here so I can look at these three stacks of books, for I believe it will make my food taste better! I'm not sure, but I think Socrates said, *'Food that is eaten from labor, savors longer upon the tongue'* ... there is another part to it ... let me see ... oh yes, it finishes with: *'than food that is brought to you by he who labors.'* Although, now that I have expressed the entire thought, it does sound as if implying that to have complete enjoyment of food, one must prepare it oneself ... in such a case, I think I will dine at the table instead."

Georgiana laughed, "Next time, you must only remember the first part of what he said—until you quoted the whole thing, I was about to join you in eating as we admired our work!"

Alice, who was beginning to feel so much more at ease with her friends, cried, "Hang Socrates! We hit on what will be the best way to continue our work of sorting through all these books! Let us take our meal in the sight of our accomplishment, even if it is a small one."

With that, they began happily eating their lunch, with each one agreeing that the food did indeed taste better. The three friends enjoyed this time together, chatting about things that would only be interesting to females of that age. Soon Mary and Alice began discussing what categories to begin separating the books into, with their excitement growing at the prospect of potentially having the books divided off into workable sections before long.

Georgiana, though, had been expecting Van to come in as they were looking through the books or perhaps during lunch, but he did not. She had resisted asking about him all this time, but now she simply could not hold herself back any longer. Trying to sound only mildly interested, she asked: "Alice, is your cousin not going to take lunch?"

"I dare say he is, but not here. Maestro Wooddale requested that Van go home with him last night. He said there was much he wanted to talk over and it would be best if he stayed with him so they would have time to thoroughly discuss things," she answered without looking up from her plate.

Mary's keen eye, however, caught Georgiana's disappointment flash across her face. She knew Georgiana would not ask another question about him after the teasing that took place last night, but now things were becoming much more clear to her with that look, along with the fact that Miss Darcy was not going to Pemberley. Therefore, with an eye on Georgiana, she asked Miss Dewey, "Was it determined how long his stay would be with the Woodales?" Georgiana's reaction to this question confirmed her suspicions, as she looked up quickly to hear the answer.

"As far as I know, it was not settled how long he would stay, but they do not live far away. It is very possible we could see him at any time. You can only imagine how they must be engrossed in talking once they begin! It's no wonder to me that he stays the night, especially with all the noise of the construction going on here."

"I would hazard to say the two of them are not unlike you and me, Alice, when we start talking about our library system," Mary returned, effectively putting an end to the topic of Van.

The girls now began to discuss how best to organize the books once they had been divided into the major groupings. Alice suggested, "Surely within those major categories we should arrange the books alphabetically. That seems sound to me." The others agreed that it was the most logical way, but the question was propounded as to how the designation of these categories would be made once the books were on the shelves.

Georgiana offered: "I feel that having labels saying things such as *history, poetry*, and so on would look a bit institutional for such a personal library as we are creating. Am I alone in thinking so?"

Mary said thoughtfully, "I suppose you're right ... what is your opinion, Alice?"

"We have only just now come this far in working things out and I have formed no idea of labeling the various sections. I guess we should do that in some fashion, however. What if they were written in an elegant style?" Mary reminded her that this endeavor was to be done to suit her taste, to which she replied, "In lieu of having an alternative, how am I to know?"

Alice and Mary turned to Georgiana, who declared, "Had I known when expressing my opinion that I would also have to have an alternative, I probably would have held my tongue!" But looking first at the books before her and then surveying the others about the room, something altogether different occurred to her, and she remarked, "Believe me when I say, I am not trying to change the subject, but why are book covers such drab colors? They have so little variety in the way of color. It is no wonder libraries have such a dreary atmosphere, with the walls covered by such dark wood and there being nothing in the books themselves to brighten things up."

Mary proclaimed, "Georgiana, that's it! The books do lack color, they are very drab!" and she began picking up several which proved the point.

"Thank you, Mary, for repeating what I said in such a way as to make me sound as if I have just revealed some secret that has baffled great minds, but I have only stated the obvious," her friend laughed.

"No, no, don't you see? You have found the answer to two problems!" Neither Georgiana nor Alice had any idea what Mary was talking about, but Mary jumped to her feet and after stepping a few short paces turned back to them. "Think about this—we are trying to brighten up the library by greatly enlarging the window and adding color to the columns, but when all that is done and the shelves are made, we were just going to proceed to place all these leather bound books on those shelves, and in the process, would be effectively darkening the room again." Alice was about to say something, but

Mary continued, "And we are also looking for some alternative to posting signs about the room stating what books are where. The solution to both of these problems is *color*. Let us just make sure the shelf design allows ample room for painting each section a different color, which will indicate what books have been placed there."

Georgiana and Alice kept looking at Mary, though both were in fact trying to picture such an array of color splashed around one room and were not making much headway. Their confused looks prompted Mary to call for their attention again: "You must remember that these very same drably colored books will still make up a great deal of the color of the room once they are placed upon the shelves. What I am suggesting is that the shelf colors will change that."

Alice questioned, "How do we determine which color will be used for each category?"

To this Mary replied, "Well, let's not get bogged down on such details until we have determined that the concept will do for our system of organizing the library." And thinking aloud, she asked "Or do you think the profusion of colors would give the appearance of someone having run riot with whatever color of paint there was to be found at hand?"

Georgiana was just about to suggest that she and Alice work on drawing a picture of the idea so that the reality of it could be seen when the servant came in and informed Alice that Miss Pinch had come and was asking to see her. "What could *she* possibly want? She is, I dare say, calling on me as a pretense to see Van, mark my word! Just wait till I inform her of his not being here and you will see her retreat as quickly as she came," Alice said, much disturbed at this interruption.

Georgiana offered, "Would you like us to come with you?" Alice said that she would, and the three girls left their stack of books and the question of a multicolored library to speak with Penelope Pinch.

# Chapter Twenty-nine

"Hello Miss Pinch," Alice said with as much civility as her feelings toward Penelope and her own shy nature—which was bolstered by her friends being with her—could muster.

Miss Pinch turned when she heard her name mentioned, obviously feeling superior to Alice. But when she saw that Georgiana Darcy had walked in also, she announced with an air of exultation, "Van has asked me to stop for the sheet music he has been working on. He believes he left it on the piano."

Alice was prepared to watch Penelope be disappointed when she told her that Van was not at the Dewey home, but now in the face of this she stood dumbfounded. Georgiana was also taken back by hearing that Miss Pinch was in company with Van since her musical talents didn't even reach the point of being a *listener* with any degree of comprehension! And besides, he was supposed to be working on his music. In addition to this, there was  that irritating attitude of triumph and superiority that Penelope had assumed once she saw Georgiana, which left Miss Darcy speechless.

Mary, though, had no such reaction. "You must forgive us, Miss Pinch, we were in the middle of a most important decision needing to be made with reference to the library. You say the music is on the piano?" She confirmed that it was. It was obvious she was relishing the moment as she repeated that *Van had asked her to come for it.*

Now Mary Bennet may not have met many Penelope Pinches in her life, but she was Elizabeth Bennet's sister, and that gave her the edge she needed to deal with this. Out of regard for Alice and Georgiana, she determined to knock Miss Pinch off her perch by saying, "Miss Dewey, didn't you and I come upon Miss Darcy and your cousin in the music room yesterday? And is that not where you and he were talking over the music he was preparing for last night's concert, Miss Darcy? He seemed ever so pleased to have you as an audience. Since he was talking the music over with you, perhaps you can take Miss Pinch and see if the music is there, while Alice and I return to our project and await you."

Miss Pinch's assumed air did undergo an adjustment, for now she looked at Georgiana with a sniff, wondering what Van could possibly see in her. Comparing her own beauty to Georgiana's, she felt well aware that her looks and charms were vastly superior. She also knew how to use these assets with men, whereas she saw nothing to threaten her in Georgiana Darcy.

Before agreeing to this and leading the way to the music room, Georgiana stole a quick glance at Mary with a perplexed expression of, *"What did you say that for?"* She wanted nothing to do with Miss Pinch, and Penelope was now directing a superior attitude toward her. Leaving the room with her, Georgiana knew there would be no enjoyment in spending any time alone with Penelope Pinch; however, being the genteel young woman that she was, she searched her mind to find something to say as they headed down the hall. It came upon her to ask, "Is your uncle to give a dinner for Mr. Thornburg? I heard it being talked of last night."

Penelope, delighted to have another opportunity to triumph over Georgiana, declared with smugness, "Yes, he is. But I am sure my uncle will not invite those who were here last night. He wishes to introduce Mr. Thornburg to others in the music world that will be of benefit to him! Mr. O'Leary is very influential here and in Ireland; there has been talk that we will take Mr. Thornburg there."

Thankfully, by this time they had reached the music room where the sheet music was said to be. Hiding her feelings toward that remark as she walked to the instrument, Georgiana said politely, "Here we are."

Looking at the pages of music, Miss Pinch declared childishly, "How am I to know which page he is looking for? I am sure that it was but a single page he requested."

"Perhaps I can locate it for you," Georgiana offered. Taking up the sheets that Miss Pinch merely glanced at, she located a hand written page that was surely what Van was asking for. "Here, this is what he wants."

"And how am I to be certain that it is the correct sheet? After all, you are simply one of the young ladies working on his Lordship's library—what can you know of music? I certainly do not wish to have to return here again!"

Being insulted by someone like Van about her musical prowess was one thing, but being affronted by someone as ignorant and lazy as Miss Penelope Pinch was something else! But Georgiana was a lady in every respect and simply said, "You are quite right. Perhaps to be safe you should take all the pages and he will then find what he is looking for."

"Yes, that is what I shall do so that I don't disappoint Mr. Thornburg." With that, Penelope took all the pages out of her hand, and without waiting for her, turned and walked swiftly away.

Georgiana, filled with surprise and dismay at such manners, watched as she still stood by the piano. She was accustomed to feeling shy and even embarrassed in the company of strangers, but being a *Darcy* she had never been treated as little more than a servant to be ignored as she had just experienced. With Miss Pinch's footsteps clearly indicating she had no intention of waiting for Georgiana to take her to the door, she started slowly back to rejoin Mary and Alice, glad that Penelope's rudeness had at least spared her any further discourtesy while in her company.

Entering the room, she found the two of them engaged in conversation about the visitor. Before either of them had an opportunity to ask what happened, Georgiana, with a look of chagrin, declared, "Alice, you were perfectly correct in describing Miss Pinch as a horrid person, if that was what you said! And if not, I have a few choice words you can feel free to use—such as arrogant, conceited, caustic, abrasive, unfeeling, self-centered, ... well, I could go on but I believe those will do for now ... you catch my meaning, I'm sure!" she finished, her face now taking on a heightened color.

Mary and Alice asked in unison, "What happened?"

"What happened!" she replied scornfully, as the treatment she had just received from that pretentious girl had fully made its mark. "Did I not just say?"

"No, you described her person, quite accurately, I must say. However, you have said nothing of what happened," Mary observed.

"Well, take those words that describe her person and fill in the blanks, and you will know what happened!" Georgiana spoke with zeal.

Alice offered this by way of an explanation: "It is her way, Mary. Miss Pinch just has a way of being offensive by doing and saying the smallest things. She has an air of contempt for anyone she deems beneath her, either by rank or beauty or anything. She believes herself better than others and is determined to have everyone know it. I must say, it is irritating on the deepest level, to say nothing of how she leaves you feeling demeaned. For someone such as Georgiana, you can only imagine how insulting it would be to be subjected to that kind of treatment."

Georgiana, hearing an exact accounting from Alice of what she had just experienced, lost some of the irritation for herself and thought of what it must have been like for her new friend. "Poor Alice," she cried, "how devastating it must have been for you to look to someone who was offered as a friend and companion only to have her be so hurtful to you!" She reached her hand out to her in solace, only to find Alice beginning to cry softly from such kind empathy.

Alice said through her tears, "At least now I have you two ... I cannot relate how lonely and outcast I have felt these many years." Mary came closer and the three girls hugged one another. Alice, with this sensation of sisterly love being demonstrated which she had sorely missed all her life, began to unfold the story of how her mother treated her and the anguish that still resides in her heart. "I feel it is because of *me* that my father now has no wife. If I had not been born and been such a disappointment to my mother, she would now be here with Father. But I did not ask to be born ... I did not ask to be as I am ... how could heaven be so cruel to my father?" she sobbed.

"Alice, you mustn't blame yourself for your mother not being with your father," Georgiana said tenderly.

"Why then is she not here with him, if it were not because of me?"

Georgiana turned to Mary, her eyes brimming with tears, imploring her to say something to soothe Alice's pain. Mary spoke calmly and kindly, but raising her voice a little to command Alice's attention: "Alice, your father explained to us the situation with your mother, and he made it clear that she had spent most of her time in Italy away from him from the very beginning of their marriage. I should add, those feelings she directed toward you were first directed toward your father. So you must understand, your being born was not what drove your mother away."

Alice now stopped crying, for her curiosity was piqued. "Why would Papa relate such information of a personal nature to you if you were to just do work on the library?"

Mary, with complete self-composure, in contrast to Georgiana's look of alarm at the question, replied, "Alice, as you know, your father wanted you to be involved with this project as much as possible. To that end, he informed us of things he felt we would need to know so that we could understand any reluctance we might encounter in working with you. As he outlined matters, I have no doubt of his hoping that in our company you would see that not everyone will find fault with you." Now with great tenderness in her voice she said further, "It is our strongest wish that your father's hopes have been realized."

Stepping to Mary's side, Georgiana added, "Alice, I can honestly say we feel we have found a wonderful friend in you, and not just an acquaintance. We believe your mother has treated both you and your father badly—and you most of all, considering your tender age when her coldness toward you started. I am sure Miss Pinch's character bears a remarkable resemblance to your mother's, although I hope not even Miss Pinch would abandon her family as your mother did you. The loss is all on your mother's side now, since she is missing out on having a relationship with such a fine young woman as you have become, simply out of vanity."

Alice was eyeing Mary and Georgiana contemplatively and the two were unsure as to what impression this information would have on her. Mary and Georgiana stood in silence, waiting in anxious anticipation, their hearts going out to her, but not wanting to say anything more so as to allow Alice to respond in whatever way she felt. The kind, loving concern etched upon their faces coupled with the explanation she had just heard moved Alice to hold out her arms to embrace them again. As she cried she spoke of how grateful she was that it was Mary and Georgiana that her father had consulted. "You two are the first real friends I have ever had." Now all three were crying as the room that had been filled with enmity towards Miss Pinch gave way to the outpouring of sisterly love and friendship.

Alice felt unburdened by having shared her deepest emotions and thoughts. Mary and Georgiana were glad to have been able to finally inform her of her father's intention that having the two of them working on this project would in the process bring them together as friends. Opening up like this permitted the girls to draw closer together in the way that honesty and openness can have on a relationship. Alice now declared, as she cleared the tears from her eyes, "Well, if we had not become friends from working together on the library, I'm sure we would have as a consequence of having Miss Pinch as a common antagonist." Several minutes were now spent in finding humor at the idea of Miss Pinch treating Georgiana Darcy as a servant! Alice pretended to be Penelope as Mary took on the role of Georgiana, and Miss Darcy was almost unable to control her mirth. The three friends laughed heartily at this representation, which was a most pleasant way for this moment that was filled with such strong emotion to culminate.

But the time had come to turn their attention back to the library. It was decided that Georgiana's idea of a drawing depicting the concept of a multicolored library should be implemented. After she traced out a rough sketch of more or less what the library would look like, the girls began to discuss what part of the shelves was to be painted. Mary directed that the headboard and sideboards be drawn wider so that these could be painted, and where two different sections shared a sideboard there would be enough room to paint one half one color and the other half another color. With those directions in hand, Georgiana went off to a quiet part of the house to make the needed changes in the drawing and add the color. With the sketch now fully finished, she stepped back to make an examination of it and gasped, "I hope they're prepared for *this!* Honestly, I don't know if I like it or dislike it." And with some apprehension, she went to join the others to get their impression.

The drawing was laid before them and not a word was said. Their heads could be seen turning one way then another, until taking the drawing up, Mary said, "Perhaps we should set it up on a wall to get a more accurate perspective rather than looking down on it." Subsequently the drawing was placed on the wall, accompanied by the same silence and the same turning of heads.

Georgiana was the first to speak. "It is not as gaudy as I first imagined it would be, but perhaps I have drawn it in too much haste."

"Your depiction of the library is just fine," Mary said with a touch of frustration in her voice.

Alice added, "We mustn't forget there will be a big difference in the actual room being done up this way than just seeing it on paper. Seeing things to scale is quite difficult." The others agreed with this observation.

Finally, though, Mary declared with even more frustration, "It seems plain that the idea has some merit, but in practice falls short of what we are trying to accomplish. We should look for some other option."

For some reason, Georgiana remembered Van's informing her of the name of his suite and her initial reaction. She therefore suggested, "No, let us not discard the idea so fast. There is too much variation yet to consider ... the colors can be changed, the hues altered, the amount of area to be painted minimized. I suggest we leave off any further work on the library and go out for some fresh air and exercise. Indeed, with all that has transpired, I say we not think about the library again until tomorrow! And let us all stay at my home tonight and get a fresh look at this in the morning."

The idea of getting away from the house was greeted with hearty acceptance, and they decided that before preparing to leave for Georgiana's, they would venture to a nearby park. Gathering their bonnets, the three happily set out for a walk, chattering as they roamed the path near the flowering trees. Before long, however, they saw something that they would have preferred not to see—Van and Penelope were themselves taking a stroll. At the sight of them, the three friends gawked, declaring each in their turn:

"I can't stand the sight!"

"I dare not say what I would like!"

"I'm glad that I cannot hear what is being said between them … *'Oh Miss Pinch, what a picture of perfection you are.'* … *'Why Mr. Thornburg, your eyesight is as good as your piano playing!'*" Georgiana cried.

They had an inclination to continue amusing themselves in this manner, but really preferred not to see the object of their ridicule, so they quickly turned to walk away. As they did, Penelope spied them and said, "Mr. Thornburg, is that not your cousin and the two girls that are working on the library?"

"Indeed it is … it appears they have forgotten something judging by their quick pace."

"I dare say they have," she replied, and continuing condescendingly, "I don't think I mentioned to you that when I stopped to pick up the music sheets from his Lordship's, one of them—I believe it was the one that is called *Miss Darcy*—presumed to suggest she knew which of the papers you would want. I, of course, brought *all* the papers so no mistake would be made." A new snobbish remark entered her mind, and she said aloud, "It is a wonder …" then catching herself, she stopped.

Van turned to her, "What is a wonder, Miss Pinch?"

She was on the verge of remarking, *"It is a wonder that Alice could manage to walk at such a pace, being so heavy,"* but not knowing how Mr. Thornburg would take such a statement about his cousin, she thought better of it and said instead, "It is a wonder your uncle would employ such incompetent young persons for this important project as he has."

Thankfully, the three friends were too far away to hear their conversation. They were caught up in their own thoughts, after all. Georgiana, muttering more to herself than for the others to hear, said, *"Of all the ridiculous things!* Why did I suggest a walk here! Is there not a park just as well-suited for walking within easy distance of my residence?" Her comments went unheard by her friends, as did the upset look on her face.

"The only good thing I can think of coming from this is that if Van starts out on the music circuit, we will not have to see the two of them together," Alice grumbled, adding, "Although, even from a distance it will pain me to know he is with Miss Pinch."

Mary alone was calm, except for her feelings for her two friends. She walked on in silence, not wanting to attempt any utterance of comfort at the pace they were making. But upon entering the house, Georgiana and Alice started over again giving vent to seeing Van with Penelope.

"How can he be duped by a pretty face?"

"If he thinks *my* playing is bad ... oh my, she would not even know on what side of the bench to sit!"

Having listened to this long enough, Mary at last said, "Let me remind you girls of what James Austen wrote many years ago: *'What appears to the eyes is not always what it appears to be.'*"

"You are quite right," responded Georgiana sarcastically. "Seeing a young handsome man with the likes of Miss Pinch, what appears to be is *exactly* what one sees!"

"Yes," returned Alice, "the age-old story of a man being taken in by a pretty face, regardless of how hard her heart is applies here. Why are men such fools in that way?"

Seeing the hopelessness of saying anything further on the subject, Mary allowed them to hold whatever opinion they chose about what they saw, although what *she* saw and heard from Georgiana told her a great deal.

Georgiana and Alice were now in a hurry to remove themselves from being in such close proximity to the scene that so annoyed them and to be at the Darcy home, so they left as soon as Alice had informed her father of her plans.

Lord Dewey was glad to see his daughter getting on with Mary and Georgiana and was extremely happy that she felt comfortable enough to want to spend the night away from home with them. After their departure, he happened upon the multicolored drawing of the library, and scratching his head, the kindly old gentleman thought, "Well, at least the important part of this endeavor is prospering."

# Chapter Thirty

The girls had settled in and were discussing what to order for dinner when there was a bustle at the entrance and the sound of familiar voices was heard coming toward them. Surprise was written all over two of their faces, for Mary and Georgiana had quite forgotten that the plan for Elizabeth and Darcy to come had been arranged for the end of this month, and here they were!

Mr. and Mrs. Darcy entered the sitting room where the ladies were gathered, this being the place the three friends had deemed an appropriate location to talk over what kind of dinner to order that would be a suitable insult to Van and Miss Pinch, despite the fact that they would not be there for it. A game of sorts had ensued, with someone mentioning *roast pork*, which sounded better when it was referred to as *roasted pig*. *Duck* was suggested as an allusion to Van being plucked by Miss Pinch and what he really ought to do about it. Mary recommended *'eel*, even though no one in England would eat such a thing even if there was any to be had. In consequence of this exchange of comic ideas for food, there was a great deal of laughter and merry-making in the room, but the sisters hurriedly rose to welcome Darcy and Elizabeth with joy. Introduction to Alice followed and the whole party soon settled down to enjoy one another's company.

Looking around the room, Elizabeth remarked, "It sounded as if we interrupted a party—the laughter could be heard all the way to the front door! I hope our arriving has not put a damper on things."

"No, not at all," said Georgiana. "We were only talking over what we would like Cook to make us for dinner."

In his usual dry manner, Darcy observed, "If food can illicit such a reaction, I can only imagine what the three of you would be like when you are really seeking to amuse yourselves."

Georgiana smirked, "Well, *pig* and *duck* never meant so much as it has today."

The girls again began to laugh and Mary chimed in, "And don't forget *'eel*, if there is any to be had."

"Yes," Alice joined in, "and we do know where it can be found!"

They laughed all the more at this remark, and even though Darcy would not laugh, Elizabeth couldn't help but be infected by the girls' silliness. Mr. Darcy knew it was time to leave the room, declaring, "If it is all the same to you females, I believe you should leave ordering dinner to me, and to be safe, I will go straightaway to give orders to Mrs. Merryweather."

"Please do, dear," cried Elizabeth through the laughter. As soon as he quitted the room, however, she stopped laughing and said, "Alright, who is the young man?"

This question put a stop to the three friends laughing as they each looked at her in amazement. Alice whispered to Georgiana, "How did she know?" and she, looking sheepish, tried to say innocently, "Whatever do you mean, Elizabeth?"

"Well, let's see," Elizabeth began. "You are laughing about *pig, duck*, and of all things, *'eel*. When those words are laughingly said by young ladies, it must of necessity be a reference either to a particular man or men in general. I have known my share of men I would like to see roasted, I must say!"

Alice declared, "Mary, your sister is as clever as you are."

Not knowing how much Georgiana, whom she had not even had an opportunity to discuss matters with, might want to say about Van, Mary said simply, "Alice has a cousin, Mr. Thornburg, and he has insulted Georgiana's performance at the piano. Mind you, unlike other men, he at least has some basis for finding fault with another's playing, for he is a master performer and composer ..."

Georgiana interrupted, "He didn't really hear me play, though. I was attempting some music he had handwritten, but it was so badly put down amongst his notes and marks it was a struggle to read. Regardless of that, as Mary has said, his performance is far beyond what is found in the common way." Feeling somewhat redeemed after throwing that piece of information out, she said no more and turned to Mary for her to continue.

"Yes, he really has not heard Georgiana play at any length, but because of his poor scribbling he thinks she is only a beginner and has made more than one comment on that point. But adding to his insulting Georgiana in this manner, he has been seen in company with someone who has been very cruel to Alice, a certain Miss Penelope Pinch."

Georgiana quickly added, "So that is all, Elizabeth, we were simply having a little fun at Mr. Thornburg's expense."

Elizabeth felt sure there was more to this than what she just heard. One of these girl's feelings must be mixed up with this composer, and she eyed them all carefully. Noting Mary's calmness she could rule her out, but being unfamiliar with Alice, she was not sure whether it was she or Georgiana. "Well, let us be glad that men can offer us some diversion even when they are not present," she smiled as Darcy was walking back into the room.

"Please tell me that remark was not directed toward me. But if my absence is needed for your further amusement, it can be easily granted," he said, joining them.

"No, my dear, we were not talking of you. You are safe from any critical observations, among this room of ladies at least."

\* \* \* \* \*

The visitors were eager to hear about the work being done on the library. Much was said on the major remodeling, which drew surprised expressions from Darcy and Elizabeth. "The scale of the changes are far beyond anything I would have imagined. New curtains and upholstery I could easily see, but this adding a balcony and enlarging the window sounds impressive. You have taken on this project wholeheartedly and proceeded in real earnest," Darcy acknowledged.

Georgiana eagerly replied, "That is only part of the major work being done to the library—Mary and Alice are taking on the gigantic task of finding a workable and simple system of cataloging the books! In many ways, that will prove to be the most impressive change." Elizabeth and Darcy glowed with pride at this account and expressed their desire of being allowed to see the progress if it was permissible. The girls were only too pleased at the prospect, even though it was pointed out that there was more disarray to be seen at present than anything else. Even so, everything was arranged for the whole party to return to the manor the following day.

When Lord Dewey was informed of Darcy being in town, he was thrilled to be able to say in person what he had expressed in letter, thanking him for recommending Mary. Accordingly, he was also there the next day when the girls brought the Darcys over, and after a view of the library being torn apart to make way for its grand makeover, they were shown the drawings that had set the whole thing in motion. The multicolored drawing was curiously not to be found, for Mary had given instructions that it be taken to Alice's room for safekeeping, the girls believing the world was not quite ready to be exposed to such a concept, especially when they were so unsure of it themselves.

After the initial tour was over, Darcy and Lord Dewey began to part from the ladies, while the girls gathered together to talk of the challenges of taking on such a project with no experience, as well as the pleasure of spending money for all those new things that will be needed. His Lordship, hearing the reference to money, boomed from his location halfway on the other side of the room: "Yes, ladies, spending money is a great pleasure, and I can well imagine it is increased when the money is not your own!" He laughed boisterously and in the same loud voice said to his companion, "Come, Darcy, let us leave the ladies to talk without our interrupting." Of course, no one in the room could imagine Darcy bellowing from across the room, but he was nevertheless included by Lord Dewey in any future interrupting that might occur.

When the men were in his Lordship's study, he turned to Darcy with a reflective look, though the joy of his countenance could still be seen in his eyes. "You may never know, my friend, just how profoundly good these two young ladies have been to our household."

"I dare say, sir, such words of praise seem extraordinary even for the grand changes being done to your home."

"I speak not of the changes being done to my dwelling, Darcy, but of the changes to my *household*. Your sisters have helped my Alice so significantly that I count receiving the letter telling me about Mary as blessed as the day my daughter was born. Because of their acquaintance, Alice has become more active and as a result she has even lost weight ... their taking the air together has given more color to her cheeks ... but most of all, she is *happy* and has found fine friends at last! All of this I owe in large measure to you, and if you will permit me, I wish to have a dinner in your honor." Pausing briefly at the look of satisfaction on Darcy's face, he continued, "I have already made preparations for it, informing a few of the guests, but not the girls as of yet. My nephew Van Thornburg will be here to play for us. He is exceptional, even if I say so myself. He has been spending most of his time recently with the conductor of the London symphony, and from what I understand, with the O'Learys, but it is time he put in an appearance here. Please, let us go directly in and inform the ladies—you know how dinner parties are so appealing to the ladies."

The subject, of course, was very interesting to the ladies to say the least, but was also a little disturbing when the girls were informed that not only would Van be there, but of all people, so would the O'Learys—meaning, certainly, Penelope Pinch! The dinner was set to take place two days later, but obviously, very little work was done on the library in those two days as far as what the girls were doing. Oh, they attempted to busy themselves with it, but the subject of Van and Penelope would soon be brought up and all work would cease. The job of cataloging books, it seems, takes a back seat to complaining about men, or rather, a *certain* man! Nevertheless, the servants were making steady progress on separating the books into major categories, but as for any decisions about the system of categorizing, Mary and Alice simply could not keep their minds on it, for that work was hampered by the most distracting prospect of seeing just how close Van was becoming to Miss Pinch.

Alice would say, "Is there not a category of books that describes how stupid men can be? Or how a woman batting her eyes at a man makes all rational thought disintegrate?" And with reference to any books on music, Georgiana would declare, as she imitated Penelope, "Oh *Mr. Thornburg*, musicians are *so* musical! How wonderful ... oh my, you play *ever* so fast, how *do* you manage to hit the right keys ... that is, if you *are* hitting the right keys?" and then reaching for Mary's hand, "*Mr. Thornburg*, you are so *very* clever, for your hands are just the *right* size for playing the piano!"

During this time, Mr. and Mrs. Darcy were appreciative of the bustling about that was being done in their behalf and, for the most part, did their best to stay out of the way. Now and then Elizabeth would join the girls, and during the time she did so, they were capable of restraint on the subject of Van and Penelope. On the day for the dinner, however, Lizzy noticed Georgiana taking greater care in preparing herself than usual, which was confirmation enough for her which young lady for whom Mr. Thornburg was an attraction. Determined to discover more about this, she began searching for her sister, and finding Mary in her room, Elizabeth put the question to her: "Does this Mr. Thornburg really think that Georgiana can't play the piano?"

Taken by surprise at the abrupt question, Mary nevertheless answered, "Yes, and the worst part about it is that he has mentioned it on more than one occasion. Adding insult to injury, the girl he is seeing, according to Georgiana, is so ignorant about the piano she would have trouble even pointing it out in the room!"

"You are referring to Miss Pinch? I understand she is a very attractive young lady."

Matter-of-factly, Mary responded, "Some might say she rivals our Jane, but as you have undoubtedly gathered, she is nothing like dear Jane." With a little hint of concern in her voice, she continued, "We understand that her uncle, Mr. O'Leary, is very well connected in the music world and has taken an active interest in him."

Elizabeth could see that this might be a real blow to Georgiana and asked, "Is the uncle primarily interested in advancing his music career, or does he have designs on him for his niece?"

"I haven't a clue on that head, but from what I have seen, Miss *Pinch* can manage a man on her own. But I follow your meaning, that if he is offering his assistance while also seeking a partner for his niece, the inducement would be strong. Although, with Conductor Wooddale also helping Mr. Thornburg, perhaps he may not feel so restricted about his options."

"Yes, all that is well and good, but what about Georgiana? Just how strong are her feelings for him?"

"They have only just met, so I am sure they cannot be so very strong toward him. To be honest, I think his insulting her playing may have more to do with her feelings toward him than whatever attraction she may have for him."

"It is strange for her not to be glad about his giving his attention elsewhere since she is rather uncomfortable around young men. What makes Mr. Thornburg so different?"

"I know very little of him except that Alice speaks highly of him, and *that*, if you knew her, is quite a recommendation. But as to Georgiana, you are quite right, she definitely does not have the same reaction to him as she does to other young men. And I might tell you another thing that makes it strange for her to react this way to him— he is *very* handsome."

Lizzy, looking wide-eyed and surprised at this bit of information in view of Georgiana's previous shy nature around handsome young men, exclaimed, "And have you no explanation for all this?"

"None whatsoever, except as I mentioned, according to Alice he is quite different from other young men. I can readily believe that. For him to play with such superior skill and write music as he does, he must have spent his time in a very different manner than others of his sex." Elizabeth hid a smile at Mary's opinion of young men. "You should have heard his brief speech that he made before playing; it exhibited all the signs of a modest and humble person. And as I said, for anyone with his abilities to have those qualities is extraordinary."

"Well, Mary, if this girl is to be there tonight, we may be able to observe whether an attachment is being formed between them. We want to prevent any heartache happening to Georgiana." With this in mind, the two sisters agreed to keep an open eye for any signs of particular partiality that might exist between Van and Penelope.

# Chapter Thirty-one

The girls were reacting to tonight's affair very differently than their usual nervous shyness, having developed a bit of courage by virtue of their mutual bond and personal growth, and were now able to experience the joy of contemplating such an occasion as this party for the Darcys, actually having a sense of pleasurable anticipation, and for good reason. Lord Dewey invited only those to whom he was especially close and who had an acquaintance with Darcy which, of course, meant that many of them also knew Georgiana. This gathering of family and friends meant a more intimate atmosphere, which would be such a contrast to Van's introduction into the London music society. *That* was a grand affair with quite a number of guests, whereas this evening of close company would be much more to their liking. And as the evening would later unfold, this would prove to be a great advantage for Georgiana.

The time arrived for the affair to begin, and the guests of honor along with the three girls headed over from the Darcy home in his town coach. Expectation was in the air as several means of transportation were pulling up at the same time. As they were nearing the steps of the Dewey mansion, the four women saw Van likewise arrive and step out alone from the conductor's carriage. Conductor Wooddale was not coming; duties with the symphony would keep him away. Georgiana, who was ignorant of the plan Mary and Lizzy had of looking out for her interests this evening, was beginning to be more excited and nervous about seeing Van again. There was an additional anxiousness associated with what her brother's impressions of him might be.

Their high spirits that were raised at the sight of Van arriving alone were deflated somewhat when they saw Penelope Pinch get out of her carriage and immediately go to his side, extending her arm for him to escort her in. Mary and Lizzy saw Georgiana shaking her head at the sight, so Mary went to *her* side quickly and said, "It seems we will be having *roast pig* and *'eel* at the same table." That was enough to bring a laugh from her friend as Mary had intended, for she did not want her to enter looking downcast, but wanted Van to see her smiling and happy.

Inside, they removed their cloaks and took a look around at how lovely everything was arranged. Right away they also saw that Van had disengaged himself from Miss Pinch and was talking to his uncle, who could be seen nodding his head affirmatively in between saying greetings to his guests. When Darcy and his party approached, however, rather than simply saying *"welcome!"* and turning his attention back toward his nephew, Lord Dewey cried, "Here we are! Mr. Darcy, let me introduce you to my nephew *Van Dewey Thornburg.* And Van, this is the person and his family for whom our little dinner party is being given ... Mr. Darcy and his wife Mrs. Darcy ... the girls you know, but I believe I should mention that Mary is Mrs. Darcy's sister and Georgiana is Mr. Darcy's sister."

Stepping forward first to address Darcy and Elizabeth, Van was all smiles and pleasantness. Lizzy recalled Mary's description of him and believed only this sister of hers could describe such a handsome young man with so little enthusiasm! "I understand, Mr. Darcy," began Van, "we are in your debt for recommending the excellent services of Miss Mary Bennet; my uncle has only the highest praise of all she is doing for him. And we have been doubly blessed in her bringing your sister, who has as fine an ear for music as a person would ever come across in one who is not also proficient at the instrument."

At hearing this Darcy, with a bit of bewilderment, replied, "I'm sorry, what is that you just said?" Standing by his side, Lizzy heard Van's comment as well and turned to Mary and Georgiana with a wry smile that expressed, *"He said that again!"* However, before Van could respond, his Lordship interrupted in order to present the Darcys to some of the other friends who were there. With that, Van excused himself to move toward the other side of the room.

In due time, Lord Dewey began directing everyone to move toward the dining area. Once the group had all assembled at table, he began calling for their attention, which for him was very easily done.

"Welcome again to my home, I am so pleased you could all make it tonight ..." This was followed by a bit of Lord Dewey's chatter, for the old gentleman did indeed love to talk. Finally coming more to the point, he said, "Everyone here knows my dear child, Alice, but you may not be aware that she has a great fondness for books, and I have indulged that by gathering an extensive library." He stopped to smile at her, and even though she was a bit embarrassed, she no longer felt the need to run out of a room when all eyes turned her way. Her father continued, "I could therefore think of nothing more appropriate than to remodel our library into something more befitting my daughter." This, of course, is not exactly the way things had come about, but after all, he is not only her father, but also the Earl, so he is to be excused!

"With this object in mind, a question that needed answering was, *just who was I to entrust with such a project?* My good friend, Mr. Darcy, whom you see sitting beside me, recommended his most excellent sister-in-law, Miss Mary Bennet, as a person whom I should consult. Although being quite young, she is remarkable, I will tell you, and I have met plenty of people in the world for that to mean something!" he boasted, while Mary looked a little uncomfortable with all eyes now turning toward her. Not slowing down, Lord Dewey went on: "But the heavens were smiling on us indeed because Miss Mary came with Miss Georgiana Darcy. I assure you that all that is good in the Darcy family has come to rest in full measure on this one!"

For a moment it looked as if the Earl might become emotional, but he took a deep breath and carried on: "It seems that these two have now taken up with my Alice and the three of them have envisioned something magnificent for the library here at Dewey House! Examine, if you will, these drawings as they are passed to you ... they were done by Alice and Georgiana and are the basis for what will become a library truly suited for Lady Alice Dewey and for this stately manor." With a deep breath, he concluded, "This dinner is to thank my good friend for his recommendation and to express my strongest trust in Miss Bennet and Miss Darcy, as well as to manifest the greatest pride in my dear sweet daughter, Alice." As the applause and the *"hear, hear!"* started, his Lordship boomed, "And when it is finished, we shall gather again to celebrate its completion!"

All three girls were blushing indeed at such praise, but because they also knew the deeper meaning of what was being said, they each held back their tears. Mary was looking at the face of her sister Elizabeth, and both felt their bond growing even stronger with that one look. Georgiana felt her heart swell as she saw the look Darcy gave her, and Alice was sure she had never seen her father beam with such happiness. None of them noticed that it was Van who took to his feet and clapped the loudest, and it mattered very little at this moment that Miss Pinch had procured the seat next to him.

Sometime during the meal, Darcy leaned over to ask Elizabeth if he had correctly heard Mr. Thornburg saying that Georgiana was not proficient in her playing. She informed him that he had. "I don't care how well he plays, only a truly ignorant, pompous fellow would describe her performance at the piano in such a way," Darcy said disdainfully, highly offended that anyone could think such a thing!

His wife could see the need to calm his pride and quickly replied, "The truth is, dear, he has not *really* heard her play. He formed his impression on her attempting to play a piece he had written out by hand, but it was scribbled so poorly she was having trouble making out the notes which, I understand, accounts for her playing very badly."

That worked just as she expected. "I suppose if any man should have empathy for another's having a mistaken first impression it should be me," he admitted, drawing a deep breath and looking up reflectively. Turning his gaze back toward his wife, he flatly stated, "His opinion of her playing, I am sure, matters very little to her anyway, so I need not concern myself with it." Elizabeth smiled sincerely at him, knowing he had come a long way since they first met, but she sighed inwardly at his not comprehending just how much Van's opinion really *did* matter to Georgiana!

# Chapter Thirty-two

Dinner and the customary separation of the gentlemen from the ladies having drawn to a close, everyone rejoined to move into the smaller music room, which was deemed an appropriate location for this small crowd. Lord Dewey notified the guests that Van would not be playing, but he was happy to inform them that the evening would not pass without some musical entertainment. "No, indeed, for I have coaxed Miss Darcy to favor us with a melody. Please, my dear, we are all yours, if you would favor us now."

As she started to rise, Georgiana stole a look at Van to see his reaction, which was one of surprise that turned into embarrassment. Her indignation from what he had said on previous occasions and then again tonight moved her with determination. Here is where her familiarity with the assembled guests worked to her advantage, for her courage would not fail her among friends. So with shoulders back and head held high, she walked across the room. Van was struck with her stately figure, but prepared himself to endure what would likely be a torment, for he anticipated hearing some lovely piece of music turned into a shallow, hideous likeness of its true self! She said nothing, but went directly to the instrument, for she was no speech maker. As she looked carefully through the music that was before her, deliberately creating a suspense, his Lordship reassuringly declared, "If you are not happy with the choices before you, there is a greater selection behind you."

Georgiana smiled and nodded, indicating she had found something to play. Positioning herself and the sheets before her, she laid her hands upon the keys and began playing. She had specifically chosen a piece by a little known composer called *Life of the Unknown Man*. This beautiful piece tells the story of an obscure life, and the slow beginning, which was something she wanted in order to combat the bit of initial nervousness she felt in debuting before Van, expresses how no one expects anything from the man at his birth. It goes through sweeping changes as he grows and begins to dream of greatness then climaxes with the tragedy of an unfulfilled life leading finally to death. The weaving of this beautiful tapestry is quite impressive and far beyond what a beginner could ever hope to play.

Therefore Van, immediately recognizing the piece he had played for his mother many times, began to think she would only attempt the beginning of this difficult composition, but as she continued it became obvious that Georgiana was quite adept at the instrument, performing more than adequately! Van began to sit more attentively, which did not go unnoticed by Miss Pinch. This of course, bothered her immensely. Trying to draw his attention away from Georgiana, she whispered, "When you teach *me* to play, I will be able to entertain at a *much* larger gathering than this little group." He smiled but made no reply and upon her attempting to say something else, he politely shook his head to indicate he had much rather listen.

Sitting quietly while being ignored was something Penelope Pinch was unaccustomed to, and observing Van becoming more engrossed in Georgiana's performance, she took a step that usually had every young man whom she was showing interest in abandon whatever he was attending to and melt under her charm. "I must get some air," she said as she rose quietly and started walking away. Glancing behind and seeing that Van was not coming after her, she pretentiously threw her head back and leered in the direction of the piano, declaring under her breath, *"We shall see,* Miss Darcy, which Mr. Thornburg prefers—*your* playing an instrument tolerably or *my* true feminine beauty! No plain-looking, piano-playing girl will get the better of *me* where a man is concerned!" More perturbed than she had ever been, Penelope Pinch found herself taking a position by the window alone as Georgiana Darcy continued to enthrall the guests.

In due time, Georgiana finished her superb performance and the applause was generous, which served to irritate Miss Pinch all the more. Darcy's eyes shone with great pleasure and pride at the attention his young sister was receiving from her audience. Conversely, Penelope's consternation had something more to endure as Lord Dewey stood to boast about what a sheer delight they had just had and begged that she favor the party with another. Georgiana, however, suggested that if Miss Bennet was so inclined, she would have her come forward to play for them and promised the gathering would not regret it. Mary declared she would be happy to only if Miss Darcy would join her for a duet. Everyone began urging the two of them to accept the challenge, but what touched their hearts the most was the joyful cry of excitement that came from Alice.

Without further ado, Mary joined her friend at the instrument, and even though there was not heard that superior playing of *Mr. Van Dewey Thornburg,* there was entertainment enough for such an evening. The two girls became lost in their music, and once again Elizabeth was touched by how much these two shy sisters of hers had grown in the short time they had been spending together. And as far as Mr. Van Dewey Thornburg was concerned, he found himself torn, wishing to speak to Georgiana as soon as he could, but enjoying listening to their excellent playing and wishing that it not end.

When the brief concert concluded and refreshments were brought in, Van wasted no time in going directly over to Georgiana, Alice and Mary and began, "Miss Bennet, how fine you played, I enjoyed it immensely! And if I may be permitted to say, I owe your friend Miss Darcy an apology."

Georgiana stepped forward with: "For what, pray tell?"

"Should I not explain to them first?" he replied humbly.

"Believe me, they have had an account of it!" Georgiana smiled.

Mary added, "Yes, and we happened to witness it this very evening as we were welcomed by your uncle and you addressed her brother."

Alice agreed, teasing, "Indeed, cousin, you did not hold back your opinion of Miss Darcy's musical ineptitude." All four of them were now laughing at his mistake.

"Oh yes, that quite slipped my mind," Van said sheepishly. "I must appear to be the most high-minded fool, but in my defense, you did play the piece I had written very badly."

"That is no defense at all, Mr. Thornburg!" Georgiana felt she was somewhat justified in saying this, even though the indignation she had been feeling since he first referred to her as a *'beginner'* was fading rapidly with his heartfelt apology.

"It seemed a fairly good one to me. How does it fail with you?" he countered mildly.

"If you would but consider the scribble that only you could make out for notes, you will have your answer," she replied, wanting to hear what he might say to that.

Miss Pinch, observing that Van had entered into an extended conversation with Georgiana, determined to approach the group just then, thinking what better way would there be to show him how terribly lacking Georgiana is in beauty than to give him a side by side comparison? Van was thereby not allowed to respond to what Georgiana had just remarked, for Miss Pinch addressed her instead with: "How fine you played, Miss Darcy." Now turning so that they were both facing Van, she smiled her smile that had made many a young man see nothing but herself and cocked her head in that way that usually rendered men helpless and said, "Is that not so, Mr. Thornburg?"

Not wanting to wait for Penelope's darts to start flying, Georgiana exclaimed, "You are too kind, Miss Pinch, but you must excuse me and my friends. We are wanted by my brother." And bowing to Van, they left to seek out Darcy and Elizabeth.

Miss Pinch congratulated herself in making Georgiana scurry off, thinking, "She is no match for me!" Those near Van could now hear her talking of her uncle's desire to *'take Van to Ireland when next they go'* and *'how pleased she was that her uncle had chosen such a fine young man to promote.'*

As the girls made their way across the room, Alice commended Georgiana, "It was good that you chose to leave when you did. One thing is certain, Penelope speaks well of no one—especially another young lady—without following it with rather vicious barbs couched in polite words and said in as pleasant a tone as has ever been heard."

Mary offered, "Although, perhaps it would have been better if we had stayed so your cousin could have seen what she is really like."

"You're probably right, Mary," agreed Georgiana, "but my first reaction was to avoid her remarks that I was certain were coming."

Alice said, "Well then, if you wish, let us go back and brace ourselves for whatever she might say and know we are doing it to expose her for Van's sake."

Just as they were turning to do so, they were prevented by Elizabeth coming up to them. "Excuse me for interrupting, I'm glad you are all together. Your brother wishes to leave since so many of the other guests have done so. He is presently thanking Lord Dewey—shall we not all go and do the same?" With a feeling of disappointment in not being able to follow through on their plan, the girls replied, "Certainly."

When they had joined the two men, his Lordship exclaimed to Elizabeth, "Ah, what a grand evening this was! I am ever so grateful for Darcy coming and putting me in mind of having this dinner for all of you." Addressing Mary and Georgiana, he continued, "And to think, not only are you intriguing us with this library, but your playing was splendid!" Van now also came to his uncle's side, guessing that the Darcys were leaving. "What do you say to that, Van?" his uncle burst out. "Certainly even you must admit that Miss Darcy and Miss Bennet were a delight to hear!"

"You are quite right, uncle, I would much rather have heard *them* playing than doing so myself. I was quite enraptured and enchanted by the performance." Needless to say, he was referring to both Mary and Georgiana, but his eyes were only on Miss Darcy.

Not noticing that, Lord Dewey, happy at hearing Van express himself in such a fine manner, said, "There! How is that for praise for you two young ladies? I dare say, only if those words were spoken by Conductor Wooddale would they mean more."

As a few final words were being exchanged, Mr. O'Leary and Penelope came forward to join them. She again took a position close by Van while her uncle expressed his thanks for having been asked to be a part of such a warm and intimate evening. Ever on the watch for an opportunity to get the better of Georgiana, Miss Pinch turned to Mr. O'Leary with, "My dear uncle, don't forget your intention of introducing Mr. Thornburg to Ireland's lovers of great music." And without giving him a moment to speak, she continued, "Mr. Thornburg you will be *ever* so welcomed and praised as you so *richly* deserve! Certainly just being *seen* with us there will be much in your favor. *What a sight you would make* on some of the great houses of music in the Emerald Isle! *Oh my*, does not the very expression *'Emerald Isle'* fill you with inspiration? What *beautiful* music would come from your lovely hands there!"

Her uncle, seeking to bring an end to his niece's effusions said, "Indeed, Mr. Thornburg, it would be my pleasure and honor to have you come with us, but we shall talk of this another day." No further comments were made by anyone, and with that the group disassembled and proceeded to their carriages.

## Chapter Thirty-three

Shortly after arriving home, Elizabeth took Mary aside to inquire what she might have observed about Mr. Thornburg's regard for Miss Pinch. Unaware of what had been said, Georgiana came upon them, preventing Mary from answering. However, the subject did not change much, for Georgiana began straightaway, "What do you think of that? I have gone from barely being able to play to performing delightfully, and even being enchanting!"

"He may have been referring more to *my* playing than yours," Mary said with a sly smile. At the surprise on her friend's face, she quickly added, "Seriously, Elizabeth and I were discussing how strong his interest in Miss Pinch might actually be."

"Oh, please permit me to triumph over her in the one way I may do so before introducing that subject!"

Elizabeth confessed, "Speaking for myself, I saw no particular regard in his attention to her." This was truly Lizzy's opinion, but seeing her young sister-in-law's disheartened look, she tried to sound as optimistic as possible.

Darcy, hearing the women talking and not wanting to be banished from the conversation, concluded that if he could not be permitted to join in on a discussion taking place between these three ladies, the world had taken a very strange turn indeed. With this object in mind, he entered the room and catching what his wife had just expressed, said: "Who is being referred to, may I ask?"

"We are talking of Mr. Thornburg, dear, and how strong his regard for Miss Pinch seems to be. Have you an observation on that head?" she replied, hoping his answer would not be more discouraging to Georgiana.

"They were together a great deal is all I can recall, but there was not that appearance between them that reveals an attachment," he admitted coolly, "at least, I saw nothing of the kind."

"Yes, that is what I was at the point of saying as well. She certainly is putting herself forward, always taking a place by his side, but I did not see any partiality from him."

Georgiana grumbled, "And why, pray tell, should he have to exert himself at all with her always coming to him? ... what man alive could possibly resist such a beautiful woman?"

Mary comforted her, "Attraction between a man and a woman is a very subjective human experience, Georgiana. Only consider—it is a commonly held opinion that of the Bennet girls, Jane is the most attractive. And yet despite her beauty, your brother was more strongly attracted to Elizabeth. So in the sphere of human relations, what is attractive to the eye is not always attractive to the heart."

"That may be for some men, but how many could resist when a beauty like her places herself within such an easy grasp?" Suddenly embarrassed by the look of sympathy on Elizabeth's face and the disquieted one of her brother, she broke off, "Besides, why do I care, and why are we even talking about this? He is nothing to me." And excusing herself, she went up to her room.

Elizabeth and Mary were now able to inform Darcy of their agreeing to watch the pair they had been discussing for any signs of a strong attachment at the evening party and were glad to have had his opinion on the subject. His response was with regard to his sister, "Does this mean she has developed an interest in Mr. Thornburg, Mary? Perhaps you can enlighten me on just what their relationship is."

"As I told Lizzy earlier, they have only just met and have been in company but two times. However, I will say that this is the first young man that Georgiana feels comfortable being with among all those we have met while together. It has to do, I believe, with the fact that they have music in common and he does not treat her as the other young men were doing. In consequence, he does not make her feel awkward by those assumed airs that men take up when seeking to recommend themselves to young ladies. Mr. Thornburg is, I would say, the first man—other than yourself, of course, Mr. Darcy—that she could be herself with."

"Well, if that is the case and he has seen her as she really is, the man would be a fool to pursue a shallow-minded pretty face instead. But he can do as he chooses. My concern is for Georgiana," Darcy stated emphatically.

"Please, my love," Elizabeth said soothingly, "don't take a dislike of the young man for being pursued by such a young lady. Remember, you yourself were the object of someone not very unlike Miss Pinch."

Despite all the observing being done and all the discussing being done, just how Van felt would have to wait till he revealed it himself. After all, it was further suggested that he may have no other interest than advancing his music career. And as many men driven by such motives, he may have no time to pursue a relationship. Mary concluded that men of that sort prefer not to have any distraction, as their passion is their art.

\* \* \* \* \*

Deciding enough time had passed for Georgiana to be calm and perhaps willing to talk with her, Mary headed to her room. As she approached the door to knock, she paused to listen first and see if there were any signs indicating what mood she would find her in, but heard nothing. Knocking softly and receiving no answer, she attempted striking louder, but still no response. She was at the point of turning away, thinking Georgiana may have fallen asleep, when the door opened. "Mary, I am so glad it is you! I was out on the balcony and could scarcely hear your knock," she said, motioning for her to enter.

Resuming her place out on the balcony, Georgiana said as she looked out over the roses, "I'm sorry for behaving like a silly girl earlier. Letting Mr. Thornburg trouble me so over—of all things—whatever his relationship with Miss Pinch is ... or might become. Why should I care? I barely know him! And as for her, why should I allow her maneuverings to have any effect on me? As if she is triumphing over me somehow! It is foolish, isn't it, Mary, for me to carry on this way? I can trust your judgement, and I want to know your opinion. I know you will see the value of my hearing from an honest companion, even if what has to be said may sting a bit."

"I will seek to be as valuable a friend to you as you were to me when I was recently in need of counsel." Collecting her thoughts, Mary went on kindly, "I would say you are reproaching yourself more out of what you are feeling than anything you have done. Your actions are beyond reproach and have not even slightly been foolish," adding light-heartedly, "or as my father was so accustomed to say, *silly.*"

"But why do I feel this way, as if I have exposed myself, or am contemplating some deed for which I know I will be sorry?" she importuned.

"Consider this, Georgiana," Mary urged. "Have you ever met a young man like Mr. Thornburg?" She shook her head no. "When you talk with him, are you made nervous, or do you begin to feel uncomfortable?" Again she shook her head. "Is it any wonder, then, that your heart is stirred at what might come of this? In one of the poems I've read, I believe it is *The Heart and the Rose*, there is a line that refers to the agitation that takes place in the heart when it first contemplates the idea of romantic love which states why the rose has thorns ... it is to remind us that the beauty of love is not without its potential for pain."

"Oh, Mary, to talk of love is ridiculous! I have no such feelings."

"I wasn't trying to suggest that you are in love, but every whirlwind begins with just a small stir in the wind. Is it to be imagined that my friend Georgiana Darcy will go through life without even so much as a stir? And why should not your heart feel a sense of tumult at the prospect, when the chance of even considering the prospect is spoiled by the appearance of someone such as Penelope Pinch? I would say you view her at this time, not so much as a rival for his affections, but as a rival for his attention."

"That is true. Tonight we could not have a simple conversation without her stepping to his side ... the nerve of that girl!" Having confided her own feelings and being encouraged by Mary's thoughtful remarks, not to mention that beautiful poem, Georgiana asked, "So what do you recommend I do?"

"First let me remind you, he is in the middle of his music career which at this time is taking wings, and he has been staying with the London Symphony conductor; so he is, it appears, on the brink of entering a whole new life. Therefore, even though he may be drawn to you or perhaps even Miss Pinch—he may have no desire to get involved with *anyone*. She may just be throwing herself at him as young ladies will often do with eligible young men, only to find he has no time for her. I recommend your doing nothing at all but going about your business with the library. He knows where to find you." Remembering something she felt might be valuable to Georgiana, she added, "And besides, Elizabeth related something that is pertinent to this subject."

"What was that?"

"She was talking about men in general ... actually it was in a letter she wrote me ... but she said that men often are more intrigued by a woman that is not so easily gotten, attributing it to men's love of sport. Therefore, you should definitely not put yourself forward as we see Miss Pinch doing, for he may find it a much greater enticement to go after you."

"Mary, we are talking about *me*. I could not put myself forward as Penelope Pinch does no matter how strong the inducement! Although I dearly would have loved to hear what he was going to reply to my pointing out the illegible way he had written out his music," she laughed. Calling to mind the look on Darcy's face earlier, she asked, "Did my brother have anything to say about all this? I have not made him uneasy, have I?"

"He is not uneasy for you, although I do believe he was on the point of going to have a sit-down with Mr. Thornburg until Lizzy calmed him down."

"Wait a minute—what was said? Was he really going to talk to him?" she asked anxiously. "Tell me, Mary—I can't believe you didn't mention this earlier!"

"No, he was not going anywhere, I was just overstating matters," Mary reassured her. "It irritated him that any young man would prefer some empty-headed—well, *shallow* is the word he used—young lady to his sister. But Lizzy reminded him that Mr. Thornburg was not responsible for which young ladies were trying to get his attention."

"My brother is a keen observer, though his observations do not take the same humorous turn that Elizabeth's do," Georgiana returned, much more calm now. "Well I suppose, as you say, I could do no better than just get about my business and let Mr. Thornburg do as he likes."

# Chapter Thirty-four

Next morning at the Dewey home, seeing the books all neatly separated inspired Mary and Alice to set their minds toward finding that workable system for cataloging the books, not allowing anything else to get in the way. Mary asked, "Should we try to discover a way of identifying the major divisions on the shelves or should we work on the cataloging of how the books are to be located?"

"Haven't we already resolved how the books are to be placed?" Alice replied with a bit of confusion.

"Yes, I quite forgot, it seems like days since we were working on this. Well then, we will simply organize our cataloging volume that is to be consulted for determining if a particular novel, essay, textbook, or other publication is here by getting busy alphabetizing the major sections."

"But Mary, such a volume is likely to be massive and weigh a great deal unless we divide it into smaller volumes."

"You're right, we may have to do that very thing. I'm sure it will become evident as it begins to take form. It seems what requires a decision now is how to identify the different sections of the library."

Georgiana, who was sitting at a desk looking over the various drawings they had done, wasn't paying any attention to their conversation. But looking up and noticing something was missing, she posed the question, "What has become of the library door?"

Alice answered, "They removed it so that the carvings would not be damaged."

"Oh, that makes perfect sense."

Mary turned toward them, exclaiming, "Wait—the carvings! That's the answer! That will do the trick if I am not much mistaken, *and* we can implement the use of color to make the sections easily seen, but the carvings will be in keeping with the elegance of the place!"

Georgiana and Alice had become accustomed to Mary expressing things in a way that made no sense at all to them, knowing that with a little patience all would be made clear. "Alright, Mary, now if you could inform us what *carvings* and *color* have to do with the answer to *what question*, we could join in your exuberance!"

"Instead of having whole sections of shelf space painted as we had once considered, we could have carvings made to identify the sections ... the area around the carvings would be painted forming a frame, if you will, with whatever colors we choose, so that from a distance the sections can be identified by the color ... but it will be the *carvings* that depict something to evoke the idea of the section," she explained enthusiastically.

"Yes, I see," cried Georgiana, "you're saying the music section could have music notes, or instruments, or something like that, and so on with the other sections."

Alice objected, "But wouldn't that mean the shelves themselves would remain dark, which painting them the different colors was to resolve?"

"Why don't we make the shelves out of a more natural light wood such as maple, instead of mahogany?" Mary offered, wanting to make sure Alice was involved in all the decision-making. "That is, unless you liked the idea of a multicolored library and would rather stick with that."

"No, not all, I think we were all struck with how strange that looked, at least on paper. Your suggestion of using lighter colored wood is definitely a fine solution to brightening up the area." With Alice expressing her pleasure at these ideas, they now simply needed to give the foreman directions on using maple for the shelves, determine what images would be appropriate to identify each section and the corresponding colors to be used, and find a wood carver who could meet their demands.

Arriving at this point was real cause for celebration, and they immediately had Georgiana fashion invitations for Lord Dewey and the Darcys to come to a luncheon the following day so they could inform them of their progress. Mary gave her directions on what to say, and with that in mind, Georgiana quickly sketched a library scene with the caption *The Breakthrough Lunch* written on it along with the request for them to attend. Alice had the manservant take them out for delivery at once, hoping her father did not already have things to attend to the next day. He came back with a reply from both parties, reporting that the requests were accepted and that all would be able to be present. In fact, the girls learned that the invitations were received with the utmost pleasure and amusement by their guests, who each later tried to pry some kind of hint out of them. They were close-lipped, however, determined to tell all their family members together at their little feast.

\* \* \* \* \*

Alice Dewey was so thrilled about all the wonderful things taking place that she could not settle herself that night. How thankful she was to her father for introducing these two lovely friends into her life! She kept going over the plans, imagining just how delightful her new library was going to look. Something, though, kept nagging at her, something was just *not quite right*. This kept her awake for several hours, driving her from her bed to walk out onto her balcony and look up at the starlit sky. Moving her eyes toward the beautiful Sugar Maple tree growing nearby, she began pondering, "It's curious that we call the pages of a book *leaves* since the pages are all bound together, and yet the leaves on a tree are all separate ... Well, if one is to be up at night, it is just as well that it be on such a lovely night as this ... I'm sure if I were Mary, some verse or something quite fitting would come to mind and enhance the moment." The night air combined with these musings brought on that sense of calm required to allow one to drift off into a blissful night's sleep, which is just what this contented young lady did.

The next morning as the girls gathered in preparation for the luncheon and each one was lost in her own thoughts, Alice spoke up: "Last night I couldn't drop off to sleep right away, so I stepped out onto the balcony. While I was admiring how the Sugar Maple's leaves seemed to shimmer in the night, a strange thought came to mind." Her two friends turned toward her with an amused look as if she were about to express some humorous anecdote, but she continued,

"It struck me, as things often do at such a time of night, that the pages of a book are called *leaves* and yet they are stuck together, but the leaves of a tree are all separated from one another. It made me wonder, whoever came up with the notion of calling the pages of a book *leaves?* I don't see the connection."

While Georgiana was considering how sensible a question this was to ponder, especially so late at night, Mary was brought to her feet, exclaiming, with hands to her head and eyes and mouth opened wide, "Alice, you're a genius!"

Georgiana retorted, "She simply came up with a question, Mary—she doesn't have the answer!"

"Oh yes she does!" Mary shot back excitedly.

Georgiana and Alice looked at one another in amazement, as Alice inquired, "I do?"

"Yes, my dear friend, you *do*," Mary said, still standing before her bewildered friends. "You see, you have come up with *the* alternative to the library guide being in book form. As we talked about yesterday, there is the problem of a book being too bulky. But now consider what is another big problem—that of making new entries! ... A book would sooner or later run out of pages for doing so, simply because the pages are held together as you pointed out, but the leaves of a tree are not, you see!"

The two girls did *not* see. "Well ... tell us more," coaxed Georgiana.

"Just consider whenever a new entry is suddenly needed—how is it to be put in its proper place? I mean, trying to maintain an alphabetic sequence, there would be markouts and scribbles in it everywhere. It would begin to look a mess!" Walking around the table, she continued, "Here's where Alice's brilliant observation comes in: what if we were to use individual cards, like the separate leaves of a tree, with the name of each publication on them, and then arrange it all in a lovely chest of drawers? That way any new book that comes into the library can be easily added in the proper alphabetical location."

"That's a superb idea, Mary! I had not thought of the other obstacle, and this plan of yours covers both of them nicely," Alice exclaimed, excited that all of that had come from her quiet considerations during the night.

Georgiana's feelings were quite the same, and she marveled at Mary's ability to find inspiration seemingly out of thin air. At that moment, though, another thought struck her, and laughing aloud she said, "We wouldn't want Van to be the one writing any of the new entries, for his scribbles would be illegible indeed!" They began to giggle together and the bond of closeness they had been developing was felt by all three girls, knowing they could express what was on their minds to each other without reserve.

Mary could not end this moment without proclaiming the inspiration Alice had about the leaves as the most useful of all their ideas they had had thus far. As the exhilaration of the moment began to wane and the girls were basking in the afterglow of satisfaction, there was time for contemplation. Mary could not help thinking, "How far dear Alice has grown out of her shell ... her journey is actually somewhat like my own ... it's wonderful to be spreading our wings like this together!"

Georgiana proclaimed, "Next time I have trouble going to sleep, I will be sure to report any thoughts I might have to Mary, to see what she can make of them! Although, I doubt my late night thoughts will prove to be half so brilliant as yours, Alice." Little did the two sisters realize just how deeply Miss Dewey was touched by this moment, nor how she wished these two friends would never have to leave.

\* \* \* \* \*

Before long, it was time for their guests to arrive. The Earl did have some things he was supposed to attend to this day, but he looked with such eager anticipation to hearing what this meeting was all about that he put everything else aside. The Darcys had no prior engagements and considered going early in order to help in the preparations, but thought better of it. Thus, as things turned out, their carriages came bringing them all at the same time. With the greetings aside and everyone comfortably situated at table, Mary addressed the small group, "We know each of you has been wondering why we would call this *The Breakthrough Lunch*. We're happy to say it is because we have made some major decisions with regard to the library that have thus far been sticking points. You've heard it said that *two heads are better than one*, but in this case it is *three heads are best!* We three feel that we can now proceed in a timely fashion in dealing with whatever problems might arise along the way." The next ten minutes was spent with the girls explaining the concept for the shelves and the carvings that would be chosen to identify each category of the library, even eliciting some suggestions for some of them from their guests. The whole party was pleased with what was decided upon.

"But I have saved the most significant breakthrough for last," Mary now said with a twinkle in her eye. Describing briefly the challenge of finding a workable system in which a directory could be consulted for finding a particular volume or ascertaining if it was even in the library had Lord Dewey, and Darcy in particular, acknowledging the need and usefulness for such a system. Darcy sat bolt upright, keenly anticipating what solution these blossoming, talented girls may have arrived at.

Excited that they could understand the importance of this, Mary went on, "We have determined that a *card index file system* will allow for the easiest growth of the library, with the addition of new books to be indexed in their proper place alphabetically." She proudly concluded, "We owe this last and most significant breakthrough to a bit of inspiration we got from Miss Alice Dewey, and I have therefore chosen to call it the *Dewey Index System*."

The two men were truly struck by the simplicity of the idea, seeing immediately how well it would work. Much praise was given to all the girls, but to Alice most especially. The shy young lady was overcome by all the attention she was receiving and felt the need for some clarification. "It is enough to be naming the system after me, but to give me all the credit is too much!" Looking at her friends, she asserted, "You know it is so! Please, may we not give credit where it is due?" Having gotten the attention of the table, she continued, "The truth is, I made some simple comment about the leaves of trees and it was *Mary's* extraordinary mind that extrapolated from that simple comment this most useful system."

Mary could not remain silent. "A writer once wrote, *'Creativity is what happens when the imagination receives a spark,'* and what Alice said was not just some off-handed remark about leaves; it was said in reference to books. My point is, her well-founded observation was the spark without which this index system would not exist."

His Lordship stood with a tear of happiness in his eye, exclaiming, "What did I tell you, Darcy? You see I was not exaggerating the good these two girls have done for this home!" He could barely finish with the words, "Girls, what tremendous pride I will take in having a library done over by you, Miss Mary Bennet and Miss Georgiana Darcy, and in using this new *Dewey Index System* which was inspired by my own dear sweet child."

# Chapter Thirty-five

Later that evening, Darcy, who had been seeking some time alone with his sister, found her sitting by herself in the drawing room. She looked up as he approached, smiling with pleasure at seeing him. The two of them had grown particularly close since their spending time together before Darcy had even become engaged to Elizabeth, and their mutual respect for one another's view of matters had grown as well. Therefore, it did not strike her as odd that he asked the following question; in fact, she had been expecting it to be brought up by him soon, albeit she still felt unsure how she would answer him. After a brief greeting, his question came: "Georgiana, may I inquire, just what is the nature of your interest in Mr. Thornburg?"

Maybe it was the directness of his eyes that caused her to momentarily hold back in answering, or perhaps it was his concerned tone of voice. Nonetheless, she knew the subject needed to be discussed and thinking about how Elizabeth loved to tease, she lightheartedly began this way: "My dear brother, there is no one I will develop an interest in without first having the approval of *Mary*, for she wouldn't have it any other way ... and if she deems a young man suitable, that would be an indication that I should then go to *you!*" Becoming a little more serious, she continued, "You can certainly trust that your approval will be what matters most to me. As you can see, with regard to young men, I am quite insulated from starting an imprudent relationship."

Darcy studied his young sister's face, briefly contemplating her answer. He had known this time of her life was coming and had tried to prepare himself for it as well. At this moment, he wished his parents could be here to see their lovely daughter and give her the advantage of their wisdom, but it was up to him to do the best he could now. With all the warmth he felt for her, he kindly replied, "I dare say Mary's rational manner is a good first line of defense, and as far as my own concern goes, you know I want only your happiness. But you may realize, I was asking very specifically about one young man in particular."

Reaching for his hand, she squeezed it, then rose from her seat in order to turn her face toward the opposite side of the room. Despite all her rehearsing for this moment, talking to Mary about this situation with Van was just so much easier. She believed Mary could comprehend this idea of not being sure what she was feeling better than Darcy could, not simply because she too was a female, but because they were of the same temperament, unlike her seemingly much more confident older brother. But, she thought, if she did not have to look at him, perhaps it would be easier to say, or at least to start. "Mr. Thornburg is a young man I have only met with on three occasions, and yet ... *I don't know*, it seems so strange for someone I am barely familiar with to be someone I think of so often. But our first encounter was so ... so ... well, it sounds ridiculous to say, but our first meeting was so *pleasant*, and as you know, for me to be in company with a young man and the experience be a pleasure is truly strange!" Having gotten those words out, she was now able to look at him again. "Mary says it is this fact that makes my always thinking of him such a natural thing."

Thankful that she had opened up her heart to him, Darcy did not hesitate to say, "I believe I understand your feelings. My initial introduction to Elizabeth was not quite the same, it is true, but it didn't take long before I could see she was a young lady that was unlike any other that I have ever met, and try as I might, I could not stop thinking of her. This, I assure you, was very strange for me as well, and it left me feeling confused, yet anxious to see her again."

Hearing Darcy express things this way made her realize that she had underestimated his ability to understand her feelings. Any doubt she had about releasing all her emotions melted away, and she began to express herself more freely, knowing he had been where she now found herself. "That is exactly how I feel, Brother! And to make things worse, each time I have seen him—that is, after that first time—there has been this other person, *Miss Penelope Pinch* ... and her presence has interfered with our getting better acquainted. Of course, I don't know if it is because he prefers *her* company to mine, or if her being with him so often is more her doing ... he is, after all, the sort of man that young ladies would clamor for," she finished, looking earnestly up at him.

"I have learned this much from my experience with Elizabeth: at this early stage in a relationship, it is often filled with such unknown factors as you are describing. With Elizabeth and myself, there was the added obstacle of Wickham's lies, and thankfully there is no such problem here." Darcy saw a shadow pass over his sister's face with the mention of his old adversary and wished he had not brought him up, but it was too late for that. He therefore patted her shoulder, giving her a sincere look of affection.

"That is true," she replied with a change of countenance, "but as Mary said, Mr. Thornburg may have no real desire to even enter into a relationship since his music career is about to blossom. So you see, it *is* more complicated, even without a scoundrel like George Wickham." It was painful for Georgiana to recall her association with that dishonorable man, but it was in the past and she was resolved to leave it there. So giving him no more consideration, she went on, "The fact is, I'm not sure if I would even like Mr. Thornburg so very much for anything to come of it, I just wish I could have the opportunity of getting better acquainted with him and then I would know for sure." Now smiling once again for his sake, she ended with, "Who knows what sort of things there might be about him I could not tolerate?"

Darcy laughed, glad to see she was able to make light of the situation. "I have spoken to his Lordship about his nephew, and he speaks very highly of him as a gentleman and assures me he would make a kind and loving husband. He also informed me of his being in no want of money, for as you can well imagine, the Deweys have wealth even beyond our family, and the Thornburgs are just as well situated. Consequently, he has no motive to choose to marry a rich girl." Quickly wanting to get past this unintentional reference to George Wickham once again, he said, "I mention this so that you need not add that to what is unknown about him and his reason for doing things, or not doing things, as the case may be." Knowing full well that the tumultuous feelings Georgiana was having about this young man could not be reasoned away, Darcy concluded by saying, "You have my earnest wish for happiness in whatever way it should come to you, Georgiana. Whether you join Mary in her endeavors or pursue something similar on your own, or if marriage turns out to be your choice, I have the utmost confidence in your good judgement. And as your most interested older brother, I will hasten to come at your beckoning if a serious attachment begins to form."

The two of them spent more time together that evening enjoying one another's company, Darcy relating to her news they had recently received from Charles and Jane Bingley, who were expecting to be home in a couple of months. Ere long, the time came for them to retire. "Elizabeth and I will be leaving tomorrow morning," Darcy said, and repeated what he had told his sister several times already: "We are both filled with pride at what you and Mary have been doing for Lord Dewey, and I know he could not be more pleased himself."

# Chapter Thirty-six

The work on the library window was coming to completion and the removal of all the old shelves was done. Now the room seemed to be twice as large. The enormity of what they were doing seemed to take their breath away, and the girls just stood there in the middle of this great openness to contemplate and try to visualize how the finished room would look.

"The window section looks incredible!" remarked Georgiana, breaking the silence. "Once the window seats are made, I cannot imagine a more inviting place to sit and read or just dream."

They walked about the room making steps around where the stairs would eventually land and considering what it would be like to have a balcony above that. Mary commented, "Only think, the balcony scene from Romeo and Juliet could be done here."

Alice said, "I never much cared for that story. I have seen enough of love being turned into tragedy in my own life, I suppose that's the reason why. I would hope love would make two people happy and those who cared about them would rejoice in their happiness."

Mary observed, "Yes, I can see your point. However, it seems to me that when it comes to love and happiness, the happiness does not come without some pain. There is one poet who put it this way ... *love is a pain that is endured for the sheer pleasure of it.*"

"But is finding love worth the pain one must endure?" Georgiana asked, feeling all the angst of her own situation.

Mary responded in her usual intellectual way: "We are, of course, talking of romantic love and not just love in general, for we, that is the three of us, are loved by others, and our love for each other is as real as any other. Although, *any* love will have its associated pain— only think of how each of us could relate some painful experience having to do with a family member! But it seems to me that romantic love is the most problematic. The ancient Greeks described it as *that which makes the rational man act irrationally,* and the Chinese had a saying, *love makes one look through the clouds,* meaning that a person's judgement is impaired by love." She finished with, "And it was Shakespeare himself, you may recall, who said, *The course of true love never did run smooth.*"

"I of all persons know the least about that kind of love," Alice put in, "but it makes no sense that two people who feel something for each other should find it so difficult to get together and be happy."

Georgiana replied somewhat gloomily, "Perhaps that is the lesson of Romeo and Juliet … the forces that conspire against love are sometimes too great for even love to conquer."

"Well, if that be the case, I like Romeo and Juliet even less than I did before."

A pall of sadness now settled upon Georgiana, urging her to go off on her own. She asked, "Would it bother either of you if I went to the music room to be alone for a bit?" They said it would not, and as she made her way there she was thinking of Romeo and Juliet. *"Kill yourself for love?* The concept *sounds* a little romantic—the idea of loving someone so much you could not go on living without them— but there seems to be something intrinsically wrong with the notion! … I would hope love for someone would make me want to *live* even if some tragedy should mean all that was left was the memory of that person."

Reaching the room and moving directly toward the piano, she sat down, not with the intention of playing something, but because it seemed like a good place to think of Van. She hit one note and then another, not concerning herself with the idea of a melody, but the sound of the piano gave voice to her thoughts, creating a sense of calm to her troubled mind. Deep in thought as she was, she was startled by someone saying, "Now you see, am I to be blamed if I concluded you could not play, when you sit at the instrument and that is what is heard?"

She turned, and though she had not heard what was said, she had recognized the voice, and exclaimed, "Mr. Thornburg!"

"Forgive me for coming upon you so suddenly, Miss Darcy, but I was returning the extra sheets of music that had been taken from my uncle's house by mistake."

"Oh, of course ... " Georgiana's melancholy thoughts were causing her some confusion, leaving her unsure of what to say, embarrassed to think Van may have heard what she had been thinking. Trying to shake off the mood, she asked, "But didn't you say something as you entered? I did not catch what was said."

"It was just an attempt at humor, nothing of any significance. I have obviously intruded when you wish to be alone, I see, since the other girls are not here with you. Let me place these on the table and I will trespass no longer."

"No, please, I did come here to be alone; however, if you have a moment, I would not object to some company." Georgiana did not want him to rush off, and therefore she quickly went on, "I know you must be very busy with the conductor. How are things progressing with your suite?"

"Things are moving along nicely, and I must say, the experience has been more than wonderful. He has asked if he could work *The Sun* suite into a piece for the full orchestra. It will, of course, be something that he wishes to have ready for next year, but it all depends on how quickly I finish the rest."

"Is he offering for you to play with them when it is finished?"

"He is," Van replied with satisfaction. "I'm not sure which brings me the most gratification, however—having my music taken up by the London symphony, or being allowed to play with them." Looking directly at her, he now changed the subject: "Really, though, enough of me. I must admit that I brought the sheet music myself in hopes that I would see you."

"Me!" she said with a gasp. She actually wanted to say something more, but his stated sentiment prevented anything further from reaching her vocal cords.

Taking a few steps closer to her, he said with concern at the look on her face, "Miss Darcy, I beg your pardon, I have no wish to make you uneasy."

This brief comment allowed her to collect herself and she was able to reply with the appearance of calmness, "No, no, not at all. It's just that ... " she paused, searching for something plausible to say, when an idea relieved her mind, allowing her to continue as follows,

"... your being in company with Conductor Wooddale ... honestly, the thought of your wanting to see me ..." pausing again, this time admiring his dark expressive eyes that were engaged with her own. Not wishing to sound as if she was making too much of his visit with her, considering what she had just said, she added disconcertedly, "... or anyone else, for that matter, is surprising ... I mean, given the fact that you are on the verge of being propelled into every musician's dream." She could not tell if she had come across as discombobulated to him as she sounded to herself, but if she had, he gave no indication of it.

"Indeed, that is so, but I do have time that I can call my own. And yet, every time I have had an opportunity to speak with *you* since our first encounter, we have been intruded upon. That has not set well with me, for I have so enjoyed our conversations, except for the fact that they have been too short." That disarming smile of his spread across his face as he said, "But more especially, I have been wanting to thank you for the advice you gave me about informing the gathering that night of the theme of the suite. That was kindness itself—and I should add, a most excellent recommendation, for many of the guests commented how the music captured the notion of the theme, just as you said they would."

"Thank you, and believe me," she smiled, "I am not trying to minimize your kind words, but if you recall, it was also I that made you decide not to relate the theme in the first place!"

"Be that as it may, I still feel a sense of indebtedness to you for trying so hard to speak to me in time for matters to be rectified. And I assure you, since becoming aware of how well you play, all the weight of your kind remarks about my playing have taken on greater meaning." Van could not help but add considerately, "Speaking of that, I must say, you took my foolish comments remarkably well all those times, considering your own playing is quite excellent."

"Again, I must thank you for the compliment, but how is someone that plays only as well as I do supposed to object to criticism, even if unfounded, by someone who plays as brilliantly as you?" Feeling more comfortable with him now, she teased, "Yes, I could have pointed out that you had not *really* heard me play ... yes, I could have pointed out that my clumsy attempt was because of *your* horrible scribbles that could not be read by anyone other than yourself ... but then even if I were to play better than I have ever played before, who could question your finding fault with my performance?"

He shrugged his shoulders, unpretentiously replying, "Regardless of how well I play, that could not in itself change the excellence of your own playing and that of Miss Bennet as well. I would be a pompous, inflated muttonhead were I to minimize it."

Georgiana viewed him with wonder at hearing him express himself that way, which cast her face in such a divinely lovely aspect that she positively glowed as she said, "And that is the other thing about you! How does someone as talented and so well connected remain so modest and humble? I would think someone like you would be so conceited it would be a torment to be with them for any length of time. It is no wonder that a young lady such as Miss Pinch is drawn to you." She didn't know if she mentioned Penelope Pinch by accident or if she did so purposely in order to see what his reaction would be.

Looking a little embarrassed, he replied, "To be sure, Miss Pinch is a beautiful young lady, and young ladies, it has been said, can prove to be a great distraction for the serious performer. In fact, I must admit I have been negligent in working on the rest of the movements of *The Sun* because I hear this *other* music in my head and have been spending time 'scribbling it down,' as you so rightly mentioned earlier." His tone changed as he went on, "Although, it is a piece of music that has come so naturally I scarcely need to look at the score to play it, for it flies from my mind to my fingers easily. I call it *Melody of the Heart,* and considering your wonderful ear for music, I would very much like to play it for you now." She agreed to listen, of course, with Van thanking her for her indulging him.

Georgiana sat down on the small sofa with mixed feelings. She certainly felt all the privilege of being the solitary audience for a new piece of music by such a rising star, but being asked to listen to music that had been inspired by Miss Pinch was difficult to take! The fact that *any* melody could be inspired by that woman just might make the music irksome. As Van positioned himself, she thought back to what she and the girls had been talking about: *"Just how much pain is to be involved in finding love ...?"*

Mary and Alice were at that moment leaving the library to find their friend and see how she was doing. Hearing music that had such a joyful tune, they were heartened and stepped lively, thinking they would find her much revived. Coming to the entrance of the room, they were astonished to see Georgiana sitting, not at the instrument, but on the sofa nearby it. Looking at one another, they asked simultaneously, "Who's playing that music?"

Stepping inside the room and spotting her cousin, Alice cried impulsively, "Van! We did not know you had come!" Creating a real sense of *déjà vu*, Van, being taken by surprise, attempted to stand and turn toward her in a display of gracefulness such as occurred when he met Georgiana, only to knock the piano bench over! "Oh, my, forgive me," exclaimed Alice, "I didn't mean to frighten you!"

Georgiana likewise stood up in very much the same manner, only she had nothing to knock over in rising so quickly! "Mary ... Alice!" she faltered sheepishly.

The two girls continued their progress from the door over to the piano, amused at the sight they were witnessing. Mary remarked, "We came to look in on you, Georgiana, to see how you were doing. When we heard the lovely music that had such an enchanting emotional quality to it, we believed it to be a sign that your spirits were much improved, but we had no idea you were not alone."

Georgiana, feeling embarrassed, although she did not know the reason why, declared in a fluster, "I *am* alone ... no, I mean ... I *was* alone when Mr. Thornburg came to return some sheet music." And Van, not raising his eyes as he reached down to upright the poor bench, mumbled apologetically, "This bench will soon forbid me to sit upon it."

Mary and Alice looked at them, both feeling this was an odd reaction from these two. Not knowing what to make of it, Mary concluded it would be best for her and Alice to leave as quickly as decorum would allow, expeditiously stating, "As I said, we came simply to check on you, Georgiana, and since you are in good company, we will return to our work in the library." Taking Alice by the arm, she left no doubt as to her intention of leaving them to enjoy each other's company without further interference, for something about their behavior, even though it was obviously innocent, still gave the impression that she and Alice had just intruded upon a private moment.

Georgiana, feeling the impulse to say something for fear her two friends would get the wrong idea, declared, "You need not leave! Mr. Thornburg was simply playing a new melody that he has been working on, that is all." After saying it that way, she wished it would not have sounded so unimportant to her. The reality was, her heart was being carried away with each note, as if Van were speaking sweet words of love to her, although she kept reminding herself that this melody was for someone else and he chose to play it for her only out of regard for her *'discriminating ear'* and not her heart.

Van added in a similar tone, "Yes, please feel free to remain here with Miss Darcy, for I must be getting back to the conductor's home to continue my work there." Then addressing his cousin, he politely said, "Alice, it is always good to see you, and Miss Bennet—a pleasure." Now only glancing toward Georgiana, he said, "Miss Darcy, how kind of you to listen to my simple little melody." Van now quickly turned to leave, while Georgiana attempted to say something but could not manage it because of the oppression of her heart. She was concerned that his manner indicated her comment about listening to his song had been construed as a lack of interest on her part, and this notion troubled her. It was too late to recover, however, and the impulse to move after him came on too slowly for any hope of detaining him, as he was disappearing through the door.

# Chapter Thirty-seven

After Van left, Georgiana most especially felt the need to be alone. "I'm sorry, but I have suddenly realized how tired I am ... if I could leave you two for a bit, I think it would do me a world of good to relax at home."

Alice responded understandingly, "Surely there is nothing so refreshing than being at one's own home."

Mary agreed, "These past few days have been quite taxing, nothing would be better than a good rest. Let me call for your carriage."

When she had departed, Alice discreetly remarked, "Did the two of them seem to act a little peculiar to you?"

"Yes. I don't know what we interrupted, but there was more going on than merely an idle moment of music and conversation." With a determined expression, she added, "If what I'm about to suggest sounds too much like a busybody, please just tell me." Alice leaned closer so as not to miss a word. "Do you know your cousin well enough to talk to him about Georgiana?"

"It depends. What might you want me to talk to him about?"

"Well, first we need to go talk to her and once we find out exactly what is going on, we might need to send you to your cousin." Alice became excited at the prospect of being involved in this little intrigue that was obviously in the cause of romance, so off to the Darcy residence they went.

Arriving there, they were informed that Georgiana was in the rose garden. Heading straight outside, they found her sitting on a bench, deep in thought. She was surprised to see them, exclaiming, "Alice—Mary! is everything alright? I just left you—has there been some strange development involving the library?"

Mary responded, "No, there is nothing new on that front. And I hope you will forgive us for coming when you wished for some rest and privacy, but we simply must speak to you." Taking a deep breath,

192

she continued, "If we are putting our noses where they are not wanted, only say the word and we will express nothing further and leave you to your privacy."

Unhesitatingly, she nodded, "I think I know what you are about to say. You want to know what was happening in the room with Mr. Thornburg and myself when you came in."

"Considering that we simply saw him playing the piano and you sitting nearby listening, the reaction of the two of you seemed to indicate there was more going on than what met the eye." Mary encouraged, "Would you like to talk about it?"

"Yes, I think so, because if I don't, I believe I will drive myself crazy going over matters in my own mind!" The girls sat down, preparing to listen empathetically, when Georgiana jumped up, saying, "I cannot begin with you two looking at me so intently ... please pardon me as I stand." The two now deliberately assumed a more relaxed posture, sitting back and trying not to appear so concerned.

Even so, Georgiana began by looking off at nothing in particular, pacing back and forth in front of them. She told them about Van's coming in shortly after she herself had and the reason he gave for coming, which was the same reason that they had heard from him. Next she related much of their conversation, even the part about him saying he was hoping to see her and how so many times their chances for talking together had ended too quickly. "Everything was going so well until he said how he had composed a song for Miss Pinch called *Melody of the Heart* ..." Here the girls could not keep their more relaxed posture any longer, nor could they maintain that calmer facial expression—in fact they could not help but exclaim, "He said he wrote the song for Miss Pinch? ... and the name of the song was *Melody of the Heart!!*"

"Well, he didn't exactly *say* he wrote it for her, but I had just mentioned her being drawn to him, then *he* talked about how *beautiful* she is and being distracted from working on his suite because he hears this other music in his head ..."

Alice interrupted, "But what happened next?"

"Yes, go on," Mary urged.

Astounded, she turned toward her friends with, *"What happened next?* What happened next was that you two walked in! And he had only just begun playing when I had to go and say *that* awful thing!" She flung her arms in frustration.

Alice now returned with confusion, "Wait a minute, I was there ... I didn't hear you say some awful thing."

"But I did! Don't you remember? I *said,"* drawing her words out dramatically, *"'You two don't have to leave, Mr. Thornburg is just playing a new song, that is all.'"* Rolling her eyes, she fretted, "Oh, how could I say '*that is all*' !!"

Alice was still confused. Looking back and forth at Mary and Georgiana, she asked, "And what is so awful about that?"

Georgiana was terribly frustrated. "I made it sound like I wasn't interested in hearing him play the song! Mary had just suggested that you two should leave and ... and ... well, I didn't know what to do, so I just said the first thing that came to my mind ... he came to me as a *friend*, to get my *opinion*, and now he thinks I'm not pleased with his song ... *or worse!"* Recalling Penelope Pinch, she bitterly complained, "And why *should* I be pleased with it since it was meant for someone else!" now lamenting, "in short, I ruined a lovely moment by being *stupid!* ... even though the moment didn't mean the same thing to him as it did to me."

Mary responded, "Georgiana, if he had written the song for Miss Pinch, why would he play it for you?"

"Because he thinks I am a good judge of music ... and I'm sure he wanted a woman's opinion before playing it for the *object* of his attention!"

"I do not wish to diminish what you consider to be his high regard for your observations," Mary protested, "but honestly, Georgiana, the idea that Van Thornburg would feel the need to play a piece of music for you that he intended for the ears of some other young lady—especially someone as dimwitted as Miss Pinch—to get an honest opinion of its merit, strains the imagination."

Still frustrated, Miss Darcy shook her head. "Since you were not there, Mary, and I was, you may have to defer to my impressions."

"Actually, you should more accurately have said I was not there the whole time, for if you remember, Alice and I did come into the room, and what we saw did make an impression."

Heaving a sigh, Georgiana replied, "Think what you will then, Mary, but even if you had caught a glimpse of something, certainly my last comment would decisively prevent him from any further thought in my direction ... and just as decisively give him all eyes for Miss Pinch, whom he described as *a beautiful a young lady that any man would hope to come across!*"

Mary and Alice not only saw but also heard heartache in their dear friend and both would have loved to be able to make it go away, but how could that be done? All at once Mary had a brilliant thought: "Hold on, all is not lost, Georgiana. I have an idea that may undo this little misunderstanding about his music and at the same time clarify your interest in Mr. Thornburg—I am correct in assuming that you would prefer to make things more clear to him, am I not?"

Georgiana replied sheepishly, "Well ... I would not want him to think I am not interested in his music ..."

"Yes, that is just as I was saying, but it will require some diligent effort on your part, and you will have to trust the poet's words: *He that is willing to risk nothing for love*—uh, excuse me, I meant *for music—should be prepared to have nothing of love*—that is, *music ...* So, are *you* willing to risk something for music?"

Georgiana sat down, intent on listening carefully.

# Chapter Thirty-eight

The next few days were filled with a flurry of activity, but Georgiana remained at home spending most of her time at her piano. Mary and Alice would come visit daily to have her observations on the symbolisms they were choosing to designate the major sections of the library. As one can only suppose, it required real creative thought to find imagery that would properly evoke each category's section, but their having made the most difficult decision of how to lay everything out now complete, this part was giving the girls a wonderful inventive challenge.

With the three of them working together again now on the *History* section, they determined to have an hourglass with wings between a representation of an Egyptian pyramid and the Clock Tower of London. Another decision made was that *Poetry* and *Music* would be placed together and divided within one section; therefore, they chose to depict this area with a hand and pen and musical notes as well as a short expression: *Poetry is the music of the mind.*

Now came the choosing of colors for each of the sections, and the girls began to see that this would be an even greater call for skill than they had supposed. Starting with *History,* they wondered, "What color comes to mind that makes you think of ancient times?" After any number of suggestions were offered and none unanimously agreed upon, Mary proposed, "Should not logic dictate what colors are to be chosen?"

Georgiana, looking at her friend incredulously, said, "And just how is logic going to help you find a color for history?"

"Well, I was thinking that since the sky has seen all that has happened on earth, *blue* would be a good choice." Her friends were amazed at how easy that was and praised her for such insightful imagination, only hoping that such logic would be just as helpful for the other sections.

Georgiana, feeling playful, thus defied her to do it again: "Alright, let's see what logic can do for our *'Poetry is the music of the mind'* section."

Mary's face broke out in a wide smile as she accepted the challenge, and after a moment's pause, she declared triumphantly, "Well, how about this for music and poetry—since they are designed to raise the passion for life and love, I think *red* or some variation of it would do nicely!" She was praised once again by the others, with Georgiana saying, as she bowed to her friend, "I acquiesce to the power of logic."

Alice, thrilled with this most interesting process, declared enthusiastically, "Let me see if I can use this concept to find a good color for *Science!*" Mary and Georgiana waited patiently as she rummaged her mind, and when nothing was found there, she began to look about herself hoping to come across a color that might do. "Oh, I know! What about the color of *dirt*, since scientists are always digging in the dirt to find things?"

The girls looked at their friend dubiously, which was enough for her to admit, "Alright, I'm going to need some help. What color comes to *your* mind when you think about science?" Alice had the most diverting look on her face, and what now began as a chuckle soon turned into laughter as the three girls considered her comment. When Georgiana repeated the question, that only served to make them laugh all the more. Alice blurted out, "My father will be shocked when he inquires why work on the library has stopped and I tell him it is because we could not find a color for science!" which led Mary to say, *"For want of a color* the great library at Dewey house was brought to a standstill!" ... It is a wonder, is it not, what good friends can find to laugh at when they're together!

After some time, the laughter finally stopped and Alice suggested the color *green,* since all agreed it seemed to be the most prominent color in nature—and what is science but the study of nature? In this way, but not always with this much tickling of the funny bone, steady progress was made on the library. The maple shelves were being brought in from the cabinet maker's shop, scaffolding was placed for the second floor shelves, and the girls got their first hint of what the library would look like, minus the stairs.

There was real excitement building with these developments, but there was still the situation with Georgiana and Van that gave Mary reason for concern, which tempered her emotion. Even though Georgiana kept up an appearance of happiness, his not coming around gave them all a sinking feeling. Still Mary would bolster her friend by reminding her how busy Mr. Thornburg must be trying to impress the conductor with a finished work. And even though Georgiana took courage from her friend, she couldn't help saying to herself, "I hope it is only the *conductor* he is trying to impress."

On those occasions, Mary would observe that look in Georgiana's eyes that said what her close companion was only thinking, and she would inquire, "How are things progressing on your end?"

"Not that well," would come the discouraged reply.

"Remember, the beauty and effect will lie in the sentiment." Mary, of course, was referring to their scheme that they hoped would undo the misunderstanding between Georgiana and Van Thornburg.

\* \* \* \* \*

The next day brought troubling news, that is, for our three friends. Lord Dewey informed Alice that he had heard the O'Learys would be leaving for Ireland on the following morning and that it had been reported that her cousin would be with them. This was told to his Lordship by a disinterested party who had the intention of bringing glad tidings, as they believed for Van to be presented there would certainly cause his musical reputation to grow more renowned. What is more, they hinted, nothing could be finer than for a well situated young man like Van to be nearing an attachment, especially with a rich beauty like Miss Penelope Pinch.

Upon hearing this, Alice made haste to find Mary, who was busy making notes about the card file system. Once she told her the news, the two of them went scurrying back to her father to inquire as to the certainty of this communication he had related. Not discerning their concern in the matter, he merely replied, "It is the custom of the O'Learys to make the journey there at this time of year. As to Van being in the party, my dear friend himself has made no secret of his wanting to take the young man with him. I'm sure you will recall how the subject was discussed as early as the party we had for Van, Alice." Smiling at the thought, he now said, "I suppose things have progressed between himself and Mr. O'Leary's niece! At least, that is how it was put to me and I have no reason to doubt that, considering how often they are seen together. He is, of course, an independent lad, being of age to do as he pleases, and he certainly is under no sense of obligation to seek my approval," he laughed. "He has his father and mother for such things as that."

Mary and Alice could do little more than look at each other with anxiety for Georgiana. Mary whispered to Alice, "We must go to her without delay. May we take our leave now?"

Alice, turning to her father, said directly, "You are right, Papa, and we appreciate your alerting us of this ... and ... we shall not be here for supper, for we must be off."

The Earl had grown accustomed to hearing his daughter and the girls talk about things he was ignorant of with a sense of urgency and therefore was not disturbed by this dialogue between the ladies. He knew if there was anything of real concern, they would not hesitate to come to him straightaway. It only did his heart good to see Alice so involved with these two fine young ladies. Hence, he wished them a good afternoon and returned to his own business.

Once the two got in the carriage, all that could be said between them were worried expressions for Georgiana, such as, "How will she take this news?" and "Poor dear girl." This, along with Alice constantly wringing her hands, made the trip seem to take forever, for they both wished to be by her side at that very moment. "There is no telling how such news might get about town, and we dare not wait for tomorrow to see our friend," she fretted.

Finally they were there, and going directly inside, they found her preparing to ring for supper. Her being glad to see them was a clear indication that she had not heard the news, for which they were grateful. As they headed for the dining room, however, Alice stopped Mary from proceeding further, whispering, "Should we perhaps allow her to enjoy this meal before telling her?"

"Yes, perhaps we should; after all even those about to be executed are allowed to enjoy one last meal," she replied pragmatically. And so, with somber faces they turned to advance the rest of the way toward the room.

Georgiana was saying, "As you can see, you are in time for supper, unless you have already eaten, that is. In which case, if you don't mind sitting here while I eat, I would greatly enjoy your company." The girls informed her they had not eaten, so Georgiana busied herself with the servants, making arrangements for them to join her. With the table now set for the three of them, she finally caught their downcast faces, and stated, "You two look as if something is wrong ... you look as if you bring bad news."

Mary looked first at Alice and then turned to Georgiana and said, "We might as well tell you now, otherwise you will keep asking—although, please let the record show we were trying to wait till after you had enjoyed this meal." Reluctantly, she went on, "Georgiana, we have just heard from Lord Dewey that Mr. Thornburg is to go with the O'Learys to Ireland tomorrow."

"That can't be!" Georgiana cried woefully. "There must be some kind of mistake! ... I mean, why would he leave the conductor for such an excursion? ... surely someone must be misinformed!"

"My father was quite certain of the information," Alice replied sadly. Trying to encourage Georgiana, however, she thought to say, "But perhaps no attachment has been made between Van and Miss Pinch—suppose he is simply seeking to get away for a change of scenery? He *is* still working on the rest of his suite ... is that not possible?" She looked hopefully toward Mary for support in this optimistic point of view.

"Alice is right, until something more certain is heard, there may at least be room for hope," Mary said, not sounding very convinced herself.

"Hope? Hope with no foundation is false hope—I will not grasp at straws, just because it might palliate for the moment!" Still tormenting herself, Georgiana carried on, *"Oh, why did I have to say those words!* Words spoken without thought can cause so much distress." She stopped herself and, rising from the table, began to walk the floor, while her two companions were at a loss for words. It had been their wish that their presence would offer some comfort, but that seemed not to be the case.

Georgiana halted, because with each step, her anxiety and sorrow were looking for release in words. "Did I not say to you, Mary, his beautiful music was meant for another? Why did I have to even consider that any man would choose me over Penelope Pinch?" She turned and walked to the window, much too angry with herself to cry. Suddenly, in a display of the Darcy family self-control, she turned back to her friends and declared, "No ... no! I will *not* be made to lament over something that was never mine—and I dare not call it love, for love is not so easily had nor so easily done away with."

Mary had come prepared to have a broken heart to help mend. Instead, seeing this reversal of attitude and wishing to encourage her friend's declared determination, Mary said, "Bravo, Georgiana! It is best to find out sooner rather than later that my advice to you about him was in error. Let me just add, if there would be any relief in venting some anger toward me, please feel free to aim your darts my direction."

At this, Georgiana did begin to cry, and rushing to Mary, she said through the sobs, "My dear sister Mary, I will never be angry at you for thinking I might be preferred by Mr. Thornburg!" Alice came to her side, stroking her on the shoulder until Georgiana reached her arm around to bring her into the embrace too, tearfully proclaiming, "What good friends I have ... look at the two of you, as distraught as myself over this matter."

After a few moments, Alice said of her cousin, "I am puzzled by these actions of his, but how much does anyone know of another person in matters such as these? I have no intention of being unrealistic, but do you think it is possible that in his spending more time with Miss Pinch, her true character would become known to him, thus putting an end to any feelings he might have for her?"

Georgiana said in reply, "No offense to you, dear Alice, but if he had not become aware of her true character within the first ten minutes of being with her, he must indeed be a muttonhead."

This brought on a much needed relief of laughter; it was so good to see Georgiana smile again. Nevertheless, the girls could not help but spend a little more time decrying the conduct of men and how so few are even worth knowing, much less raising the hopes of one's heart for. But alas, only so much can be said on any subject, *(that is, at least for one evening)*, and so with Georgiana being steadfastly unwavering in her resolve of not thinking about Van Thornburg from this time hence, the girls could talk of other things. Before it got too late, Alice sent around a note to her father saying that she would be staying the night with Miss Darcy.

\* \* \* \* \*

About midnight, they all began to feel hungry. It seems soothing broken hearts or railing against men—the two are so similar it is sometimes difficult to differentiate between them!—has a way of making girls' stomachs growl. And so to the kitchen they meandered, dressed in their sleeping gowns, trying not to wake the servants. This would have been more likely if they could have stopped making each other laugh, which required quite a bit of *shushing* from one another and that, to be honest, was just as loud as the giggling! Had they been dealing with a less experienced head cook than Mrs. Merryweather, there is a certain amount of possibility that they could have made their way into her domain unnoticed ...

"I wonder why the kitchen lamps have been left on?" Georgiana said as they walked into the room.

Alice ventured, "Perhaps the head cook was going to come back and inspect the cleanup of the kitchen and has fallen asleep instead."

"That is not likely. Mrs. Merryweather is the soul of reliability."

"Thank you for that, Miss Darcy." As those words were heard coming seemingly from out of thin air, the girls jumped and shrieked, trying to grab on to each other out of fright. Hearing the sweet laughter of the gentle old cook and spying her sitting in the corner, the girls now could not contain themselves and broke out into such amused laughter, it was a full five minutes before a sensible word could be spoken.

When everything died down, Mrs. Merryweather drew a long, satisfied breath. "Well, Miss Darcy, what can I get you and your friends this fine evening?" she asked, delighted to serve such a happy group of girls.

"We certainly did not intend to put you to any trouble, Mrs. Merryweather," she replied with concern for the late hour.

"Nonsense child, nothing could do my old heart more good than to see you and your friends enjoying yourselves. Now we have some bread and a good selection of cold meats; you three just sit down to table there and let me fetch it for you."

The friends were amazed at how quickly the cook had the table set with bread, meat, cheese, and even a nice selection of vegetables, as she said, "A meal without the color and fragrance of vegetables is not worth sitting to."

Georgiana loved Mrs. Merryweather and had often spent joyful times in the kitchen hearing her talk of years gone by and the lessons she had learned. Being raised without a father and a mother drew her to the kindly older woman, especially when she saw how much Darcy valued her. Thinking of times past now, she addressed her with, "Mrs. Merryweather, may I ask a personal question, like I use to when I was young?"

"My dear Miss Georgiana, as old as I am, you will always be young. Certainly, feel free to ask what it is you want to know," she answered, continuing to busy herself around the table.

"Did you ever have a young man break your heart?" Mary was a bit surprised at the question being asked of the cook, but Alice, who understood a world where faithful old servants made up that comfortable and familiar part of your life, was not.

Seeing the shadow of sadness overtake the young girl's expression, Mrs. Merryweather could tell the question was coming from her own sorrow. "Oh, have we come to that, my sweet child?" The old cook shook her head sympathetically. Ever since Mrs. Darcy died years ago, Mrs. Merryweather had felt a strong motherly concern for Fitzwilliam and Georgiana and loved them as if they were her own. Whatever they were going through, she proved to be a ready and willing sympathetic ear and shoulder for the young people. To be sure, she never forgot her position within the family, but she had proved her trustworthiness over and over throughout her years with the Darcys. Now with this inevitable part of her life facing Georgiana, the cook began with: "My father use to say, '*broken hearts are stepping stones on the road to real love.*'"

Georgiana quietly looked down, while Mary, who was taken with such a poetic way of looking at romance having gone wrong, spoke up, "May I ask ma'am, in your experience—how many stepping stones does it take before finding real love?"

"Well, I must say, Miss, Pa said that more to my older sister than to me. She was always getting carried away with any young man that would look at her more than once. As for me, I was the sort that kept busy, not bothering to have my head turned by the young lads. It wasn't till Pierce Merryweather tapped me on the shoulder and asked if he could sing me a tune that I had my first and only taste of love," she smiled, as if the event had happened only yesterday.

"So you never had a young man break your heart?" Georgiana asked mournfully.

"That, Miss Darcy, is so. But if you will allow me to say, first of all, any young man that has found his way into your heart and doesn't see what a treasure he has come into is not worth the regret," she replied, patting Georgiana's hand and impulsively giving her a quick hug. She went on, "I will tell you this from what I have seen in my life ... most of the time when a couple are romancing, there usually are some ups and downs and twists and turns that are very likely to make a girl, or a young man for that matter, feel as if their heart is breaking. In which case, not being in a hurry to think *all is lost* at the first sign of trouble might be wise. However, not knowing any of the particulars of your situation, my dear, I believe some other good advice on this matter worth mentioning is—a broken heart, like anything else that breaks, can heal if it's bandaged right and given enough time. All too often, young people go rushing from one heartbreak to another, looking for some way of dealing with the first, only to get hurt again because they weren't thinking right." Looking down at Georgiana's pretty, innocent face, she tenderly concluded, "It seems to me you're doing the right thing, gathering with good friends as I see here, for nothing would pain me half so much as to see our Miss Darcy in pain for too long."

Wiping a tear away, Georgiana thanked her dear motherly friend. Moments like this are ones that are never forgotten. After this bit of serious talk, though, the fun and laughter came back and the girls had as good a time as any of them remembered sneaking into the kitchen so late at night. When they had gone, Mrs. Merryweather, having taken note just what kind of friends Georgiana had now, felt a deep calm come over herself, as she was sure Miss Darcy was in good hands during this sensitive time.

# Chapter Thirty-nine

As they were admiring the progress that was being made in the library the next day, Mary and Alice were pleased to hear from Mr. Joseph, the cabinet maker, that things should be completed very soon. All the shelves would shortly be installed, sealed, and finished, and at the same time, the faux marble painting of the columns was to be done. The girls turned to each other, both drawing a deep breath of astonishment that all this was really happening! It was one thing to have talked of plans and seen them drawn out, but to now see those ideas become a reality was exhilarating. If only Georgiana was there at that very moment, the feeling would have been perfect.

She had not come with them this morning. Despite the happy way the evening had ended, Georgiana excused herself from being at their early breakfast and simply had her maidservant advise Mary that she would not be accompanying them today unless she felt up to it later in the afternoon. That was disappointing to the other two, but not so very surprising.

Before heading out to Dewey manor earlier, the two girls had breakfast at the Darcy residence, in hopes that Georgiana might change her mind and join them. Over their tea and toast, Alice confided to Mary that she just could not believe Van would really develop an attachment for Penelope Pinch. She related that as soon as she had risen that morning, she had written a note to him, inquiring as to whether what they had been told about his going away with the O'Learys was correct. They were just about to enter the carriage when the servant came back with an answer, and not handwritten as expected, because he was informed that Mr. Thornburg had left and was no longer at the conductor's home.

Mary could see how disturbed Alice was at this circumstance, but she knew their staying would not do either Alice or Georgiana any good. Therefore she suggested, "Let us continue with our ride to your home and get occupied with our work. It will take our minds off this business."

Following her lead, but shaking her head in perplexity, Alice could barely get the words out, "I can't believe it ... this is so unlike him. How could a girl as shallow and ... and ... well, she is just downright *mean!* Besides, she has nothing in common with him! How could he ... pardon me, *what* could he see in her? This makes no sense at all to me—I have to believe he has gone with them for his music career only, and I will not accept another explanation until it presents itself before my very eyes!"

Mary said consolingly, "There is no need for you to think less of him, Alice. That is, if he has formed an attachment to her. His love and kindness to you is not called into question. We would be fools to think Mr. Thornburg is the first person to have acted strangely in dealing with emotions of the heart, be it man or woman. It is just as you have said, we still do not really know how he feels about Miss Pinch, and what you have said about his going to Ireland with the O'Learys for his career is a plausible explanation. I suppose we could speculate all day long in order to come up with reasons that don't involve her, so it seems for Georgiana's sake, as well as our own sentiments, we should accept the fact that all we know is that he has gone. Would you not agree with me?"

"Yes, thank you, Mary, for being so level-headed," Alice said warmly. "And thank you for not thinking ill of my cousin Van over this horrid affair. It is no wonder that Georgiana cherishes your friendship and advice."

\* \* \* \* \*

Mr. Joseph had left and returned again with his men to start their work on the shelves and the painters were scheduled to arrive later. Before long, it was time for lunch, and as Alice and Mary began to move toward the dining room, they were pleasantly surprised to hear Georgiana calling out to them. She looked refreshed, all smiles as she asked, "How are things progressing? I see many workers are here today." They caught her up on everything over lunch, the three of them once again in a merry mood.

Now it seemed all the girls had to think about was focusing their attention on getting the library finished. There had been so much going on with the sorting of books, not to mention those emergencies of the heart, that they had quite forgotten they had yet to return to the shops for fabric, the desk, and everything else their list called for. Georgiana cheerfully remarked, "Let's get moving then, shall we? There is nothing like going on a shopping spree to get your mind off your troubles!"

The truthfulness of her words was felt immediately. It was a real pleasure for them to be out and about together again. Of course, aside from what was on the list already, there were also pillows for the window seats and all sorts of other wonderful decorations that just had to be bought. While in the furniture warehouse, Alice chose a group of very fine writing tables that she wanted for certain spots in the library, and Georgiana added some beautiful bronzes that looked very feminine and at the same time evoked a scholarly air. Mary showed her approval of their choices and arrangements were made for all the items to be delivered to the Dewey estate as soon as possible. All in all, it was a most profitable and enjoyable adventure.

Later that evening, someone brought up the fact that there were many books that dealt with the family history of the Deweys. Alice said, "I am of a mind that that these really should not be included among the other history books, but where else are they to go?"

Mary, of course, was giving this due deliberation when Georgiana said with some exuberance, "We should make a *centerpiece* that catches the eye as soon as one enters the room! It should be a beautiful stand-alone piece that is more than just another shelf, but rather is an ornately carved display that depicts the Dewey family crest."

The first to speak was Mary, who affirmed, "That of all things would be the crowning piece to our project! What an excellent suggestion, Georgiana."

"Yes, I love the idea as well, but we must make it a surprise for Father," Alice urged. "I am so grateful to him for allowing us to make all these changes to our family library, I would truly love to show him my appreciation in a special way."

"Certainly you would," cried Georgiana, "and you shall! Let us go immediately to speak with Mr. Joseph so he can start work on it right away. I'm sure he will be able to design a grand piece for you."

"What do you think of this as well, Alice? I'm thinking ahead to the day the piece is ready to put in its place—we could make arrangements for your father to be gone from home one way or another, and then we will have the display covered and forbid anyone to see it till the day of the unveiling of the Dewey library."

"Oh, Mary, Georgiana! ... these are perfect suggestions! I can't thank you enough, I would not have been able to dream up a more lovely idea by myself."

The excitement at this new plan guaranteed that no other concern was going to occupy their minds now, especially since everything having to do with the library was moving along so rapidly and no other changes would need to be made. Mary Bennet once again felt a deep contentment that her father had allowed her to set off in this endeavor that had led her here, not only to the reworking of such a fine library, but also to establishing such close friendships which she was certain would last their entire lives.

\* \* \* \* \*

To be honest, though, there were still times, mostly at the end of the day before retiring, that each of them had their own sad reflections about Van and Georgiana. Alice would think how much alike he and she are, and the thought of the two of them together seemed the most natural thing to her, not to mention how fondly she had begun to think about Georgiana being related to her should they marry. She lamented, "How many things am I to despise Penelope for? How I wish there would be no reason to think of her ever again, but if Van is serious about her and—heaven forbid!—*they* should marry, I will very likely not see much of him any more ... and how I will dread those occasions when I do."

Mary, instead, looked for something to be glad about in this matter concerning her dear friend and this young man who had very real qualities to be admired. She had seen his excellent character manifest itself during his speech before he performed for them all.

The general way he carried himself, displaying no sense of superiority, though he had good reason for thinking himself better than others, was another attractive aspect about him. "It takes a man of real strength of principle not to become egotistical when everyone around you is singing your praises. Considering how things have turned out, I am glad that they have spent so little time together, which prevented a strong attachment from forming ... and perhaps the thrill of being attracted to some special young man like Van may allow Georgiana at some later date to be more at ease in the company of other young men." Mary's analytical mind, however, would not allow for only one side being heard in this scenario. "On the other hand, the experience could very well have the opposite effect and create in her a barrier that only the most ardent and deserving young man could ever breech."

Last of all, there was Georgiana, who, during those times of idleness *(or what she would most definitely call weaker moments)*, would bemoan things turning out as they had. On those occasions, she would drift off into a world of having Van play lovely music for her, or perhaps even the two of them sitting together playing duets. She could picture herself accompanying him in his travels to those locales famous for their concert halls. She fancied herself whispered about as being *the most fortunate young lady* to have such a husband! How breathtaking to have Van stand before a large audience and say, *'This next piece was inspired by the most wonderful woman I have ever known, my own dear wife!'* To be sure, those periods of fanciful dreaming were most pleasurable for her. It was because these thoughts were so much to her liking, and even within the realm of possibility, that she would reproach herself to the point that there was no room left for soft regrets. This self-disciplining permitted her to go about her business without distraction and, in fact, with a steady purpose which made her friends marvel admiringly at her.

# Chapter Forty

Turning over the lists of books for the calligrapher to start making the index cards was another big step forward. There were, in fact, ten persons working on that project alone. Having counted the books as they were being separated, the number came to be a total of one thousand three hundred thirteen, although they did assume a margin for error. Nevertheless, the figure was close enough for Mr. Joseph to begin the design of the cabinet for housing the cards. The ladies asked that the files be accessible from a standing position so there would be no need of bending and stooping which, of course, would certainly be permitted in one's own home; however, when things are being made to your wish, it seems proper to request everything be to your liking. And the girls were very glad they did, for they could not have been more pleased with his design. Mr. Joseph suggested making a very large curved top and having the drawers made long enough for additional cards to be added at any time. Being the professional that he was, he also devised an additional element that was rather ingenious, which incorporated a way to easily expand for extra drawers should that become necessary.

Alice thought it would be nice if the card cabinet was placed near the sitting area for easy visibility during the day. "And wouldn't it be just the thing for offering some screening for anyone seated at the window in order to add to that sense of privacy which is most sought after when one is ensconced at a window seat!" she said with delight.

As the days rolled by, the Earl was growing more and more impressed at what was becoming of his library and any recollection of it being left in shambles by the girls scarcely entered his mind. He therefore collected them all together one day as the painting was being done on the columns and, with a sparkle in his eyes, began speaking to Mary and Georgiana: "My dears—I hope I am permitted to refer to you two in such a way, for you have become so to me ...." Including his daughter now, he went on, "What I see being done to this library is beyond anything I could have ever hoped! I dare say the Queen herself has not so fine a one—certainly not one that means half so much to its owner, I assure you! I very much want to say to you now what I know I will not be able to at its grand unveiling ... I believe you must know that I had such strong hopes for there developing a closeness between the two of you and my Alice, and I see that it is so. You three carry on as sisters and for this ..." his Lordship's tender heart was touched to the core and he had to struggle for composure. "Surely I need not hold my tears from you, as you have seen me in such an emotional state before! My gladness is overwhelming me and ... I thank the Great God above for such a blessing ... I speak more feelingly of this attachment between *the three of you* than what is being done to Dewey manor, for the beauty of your library is made insignificant by the beauty of what I see before me!" Turning to the two once again, he unabashedly affirmed, "Rejoice now, Miss Mary Bennet and Miss Georgiana Darcy, for you have wrought such a change to this family ... the like of which can never be repaid."

At that point, Alice could not contain her own feelings over his words without going to her father's side and taking his arm, looking up at him with such tender regard. Mary and Georgiana were likewise compelled to do the same, but would not permit themselves till the great man had been done with all he wanted to say. But holding his daughter in a warm embrace, he was no longer able to continue. Alice now extended her arm for them to come join in, and all gave way to their feelings. This house that had known so much of pain, sorrow, and isolation had experienced so dramatic an alteration that there could not be found in all the kingdom any place where love and friendship, true friendship, had worked its healing balm.

# Chapter Forty-one

As can be imagined, his Lordship was *very* curious at what the well-hidden object that held such a prominent place in his library could possibly be. Alice had approached her father the day the centerpiece was to be delivered in order to make sure things went as planned. She felt the direct approach was best and therefore said to him, "Father, a surprise for you is going to be delivered today and you mustn't, under any circumstances, come home until you receive word that it has been concealed."

Unaware that any such scheme was in the works, her father looked at her with amazement. A broad smile spread across his face as he replied, "Count on it, my dear, I will not approach home till I am given leave to do so by you." He went away as happy and filled with anticipation as any loving father could. But like any child who learns of a surprise, when he was sent for he came into his home so anxious to learn what it was that the girls just had to have a bit of fun with him. They led him by the hand, directing that he shut his eyes until they reached the library, whereupon they opened the door, revealing this very large object covered so securely that not even a hint of what it was could be ascertained even by its shape. As he began to make his way toward it, he was halted by Mary's words: "Not quite yet, I'm afraid, Lord Dewey."

Turning to them, he playfully roared, "You mean to tell me that I am to be tormented by the knowledge that right here, under my very roof, is a surprise for me that I cannot open right away? When then?"

"Not till the grand unveiling, when all your good friends have gathered about you."

"And what is to prevent me from coming into my own library whenever I wish, say at some early hour, to have a look?" he laughed.

Georgiana, taking him by the arm and directing him out of the library, returned ever so sweetly, "The ruined happiness of your three girls, I believe, is restraint enough, would you not say, sir?"

"Indeed, I would! However, I may just move this grand unveiling event to this very evening to keep myself from having to wait, for I am all in suspense," and he could be heard chuckling all the way down the hall.

* * * * *

There was only a few days before Lord Dewey's curiosity would be satisfied, as everything was running quite smoothly. All the shelves were finished, the books were being placed in their proper places, the desks had arrived and been fussed over, the curtains were hung, and the entire room was being cleaned and polished to perfection, so there was very little left to do but check everything once, twice or three times! With an air of exhilaration, it was determined that the grand library revealing could take place the following week and invitations could be sent out now.

Alice's dear father realized what a special occasion this was to be and truly was as ecstatic about the whole affair as any of them were. For that reason, he directed the young ladies be taken to the finest dressmaker in all of London. Mr. Perkins was a short, handsome older man who had been serving Lord Dewey for decades, but had never worked with Alice. When she was younger, her mother had taken her to her own favorite seamstress, who always complained about the little girl as much as her mother had. Because of that, the Earl enlisted a kind older woman to come to their home regularly to fit his daughter, but since there were three to be cared for with this event, he felt it best to send them to Mr. Perkins. Therefore, off to the dressmaker's they went, a fine shop where could be found all manner of silks, muslins, poplins, linens, lace, gloves and more in the latest style and fashion.

They were shown into a lovely private sitting room to await their fittings. Mary, who was somewhat ill at ease but realized the necessity of the ordeal, could not help making light of the situation, not unlike her father would have done. A moment after sitting down, she took a sideways look at the others and quipped, "What does one wear to a library opening?"

Georgiana, with a straight face, replied with an affectedly grand and solemn tone, "Why, the latest fashion for libraries, dear madam, is book dust upon one's garments."

It was helpful for young Miss Dewey to hear the two of them carrying on this way, for she actually was *more* than just ill at ease here. Alice had been made to appear the fashionable little girl so many times by her mother, who would then despise her for not looking the part no matter how fine the attire, that she had grown to actually fear being measured and fitted for new dresses. This was just the relief she needed, and laughing at this comic representation, she joyfully joined in by giving them more fodder. "But what sort of shoes are we to wear ... is there not some protocol for that? Let us not commit a shoe fashion *faux pas* for our own event!"

Mary lilted, "I believe one does not wear shoes to a library grand opening, for when one reads, one wants to be as comfortable as one can possibly be."

"Oh, certainly," cried Alice, "neither does one fix up their hair for the same reason! And if you and Georgiana would be so kind as to tell me how you did your hair the first time I was to meet you at the shops, that would do for us all."

This recollection was too much and they began laughing merrily at the idea. Considering they *were* in the finest dress shop in London, though they were in their own private fitting room, this outburst that could be heard about the whole place was a bit unladylike, but they were enjoying themselves. As soon as she got control of herself, Georgiana, rising and again assuming her pompous air, declared, "This is why young ladies of fashion are not permitted to come into the shops unattended, for you invariably act so unfashionably." This, of course, did nothing to make the young ladies act more fashionably, that is, until the dressmaker came into the room!

As was his custom, Mr. Perkins came in first to interview the girls before getting measurements, for this assisted him in determining what type of material and style he would use. Upon hearing what the occasion for which they were seeking a dress was, he asked for more details, such as what colors they might be interested in—would they like to all be in the same color or did they have a personal preference? The girls said that didn't matter and spoke of how colorful the room was, even finding themselves telling him about the day they chose colors for the history, music and science sections, for Mr. Perkins was adept at drawing his clients out. Ere long, he began to make mental notes from their conversation and presently stepped back, striking a thoughtful pose and mumbling, "But what does one wear for a library unveiling?" This caused the girls to start giggling again, and looking at each other was certainly not helpful in their efforts to compose themselves! The tailor, however, was quite accustomed to dealing with young girls excited to the point of being silly, and took it all in stride.

"Please rise, ladies," he directed. This was enough to call the girls to order as they took to their feet quickly, as if they were soldiers in a regiment. He now began to look them over carefully, asking that they turn around slowly, and then directed each in her turn to walk across the room. With a discerning eye, he questioned, "May I ask if I am correct in assuming that none of you young ladies are partial to wearing ornate dresses such as are often seen?" They all declared that their taste did not run in that direction. "Yes, it is easily seen that you are the sort who carry your finest adornment upon your souls. You are most to be praised," he approved warmly, "and it is an honor for me that you have come to my establishment to have your dresses made for this grand event for Lord Dewey. His instructions are that I give you three young ladies all my attention so that your gowns will be to your liking and ready in time for your special occasion. To that end, please, will you trust me to design something befitting each of you individually that will not make you feel uncomfortable, but will suit you perfectly—will you trust me to please you and fit your taste?"

They peered at one another first with a look that said *'should we?'* and then all began to nod their heads in agreement. So they gave him leave, stating they would gladly trust him. Their measurements were then taken and as they walked away, each one wondered what he would design for herself and the others. Alice quietly observed, "It seems my father will not be the only one to have a surprise to unveil."

# Chapter Forty-two

After the passage of two days, the girls were called in for a fitting. They entered the shop with a nervous excitement, wondering if Mr. Perkins had indeed captured a style that would suit them individually. It was decided that each one should try her dress on separately so that the other two could be free to look and give their opinions. Mary said she would go first, thinking it was highly unlikely he would have created anything that she would object to wearing, for she determined regardless of its appearance she was going to look as if she were pleased. After all, such things as gowns and feminine accessories were not what held her greatest interest. How pleasantly surprised she was, then, to see the beautiful blue dress set out for her, simple and yet quite lovely. Once it was on and she looked at herself in the mirror, there was no need to force herself to be pleased. Stepping out to her friends with a feeling that was new for her, Mary Bennet looked more lovely than they had ever seen her. The girls gasped and began to clap their hands. "Oh my, what a splendid vision you are, Mary!" they cried as she glided gracefully about the room, not speaking, just being carried away in the feeling of beauty that seems to make you walk on air. Mr. Perkins, who was present for the fitting, recognized that look and walk, realizing he had captured Mary's comeliness just as he had hoped. He now explained that he chose the color for each girl's dress from the details they had given him, and since Mary had picked blue for history, blue was her color.

Who should try on the next dress was met with a brief discussion, but Georgiana put an end to it by popping up, saying, "Let me go." As she was about to enter the dressing room, she turned with a look of a child about to open a present and quickly disappeared. Of the three girls, Miss Darcy was most comfortable in this setting, but even she was not quite prepared for what awaited her. Recalling that she had been the one to mention to Mr. Perkins about the music and poetry section, she understood why he had chosen this beautiful shade of red for her lovely gown. How did he know it was one of her favorite colors? Immediately, she grabbed it, exclaiming, "This is splendid—beyond anything I could have imagined!" And though Georgiana did not have a vain bone in her body, she was finding it difficult to pull away from the mirrors as she looked herself over from head to toe.

Mary finally called out, "If you would stop admiring yourself and allow *us* the pleasure, Miss Darcy ..."

At this, Georgiana stepped out and now it was her turn to be praised. She was, to be sure, more accustomed to wearing fine clothes than Mary Bennet and, really, even more than Alice Dewey, who was more her equal in wealth but who had kept herself away from occasions for public exhibition. Yet at this moment, Georgiana Darcy felt more elegant than she ever had before. It was such an honor to have the great pleasure of being tailored by someone with such a fine eye for fitting fashion to the individual as Mr. Perkins.

Wasting no more time on herself, Georgiana, who could hardly wait to see what he had done for Alice, reached out to her, and pulling her to her feet declared, "Come, dear Alice, it is your turn now!" As soon as the words were out of her mouth, however, she saw the look on her friend's face and knew something was wrong. "Oh, my, what is it?" she asked.

Alice suddenly had all those old feelings come flooding back—how many times had her mother compared her to all the other little girls, chastising her severely for not looking as pretty as they did? She knew there was no chance that she would look as beautiful as Mary and Georgiana did now and declared she absolutely could not even think of trying on her dress. Seeing her agitation, Mr. Perkins discreetly excused himself, taking the attendants with him.

Unaware of what was going through her mind, Georgiana pressed her, "But Alice, why ever not?"

Starting to cry now, Alice stammered, "Of course the two of you look lovely ... charming ... just *splendid* ... in your new gowns ... but ... look at *me* by comparison! Nothing could possibly help me to look anywhere near as attractive as I have just witnessed with you."

Mary, knowing all about the uncomfortable anxiety of comparison, called for the young lady's attention, "Come, come, Alice, if you and I are to be prevented from putting on pretty things because someone more attractive is to be found in the room, we dare not show our faces out and about at all." She paused here to look at Georgiana with genuine appreciation, for Miss Darcy was lovely but had never made Mary feel any less pretty than herself, even though Mary knew that wasn't the case. Turning back, she continued, "No one who cares, or matters anyway, will be comparing you to anyone else. Certainly Georgiana and I will not. You may not know this, but I have come from a family of four other sisters who are renowned for their beauty, and yet look at me—I say, let the beauties of the world have their looks and give me a happy heart and good friends such as you and Georgiana! What say you to that? Let us all three put our noses up in the air to all the *Miss Pinches* that are to be found, for we shall be proud of who and what we are!"

This inspirational speech dried Alice's tears, and taking her friends' hands, she drew further strength from them as they all rose in unison. Mr. Perkins was called for and stepping forward, he gently coaxed her, "Please Miss Dewey, would you do me the honor of trying on what I have labored to create *just for you?*" Taking a deep breath, Alice allowed herself to be led over to the dressing room, anxious now to see what awaited her behind the curtain.

With her being attended to by his staff, Mr. Perkins came to Mary with the words: "Miss Bennet, please permit me to say, if it be *so* that your sisters possess such beauty as you describe, you have been doubly blessed, for from among all the women who have ever come through my shop, I would tell everyone, yours is the rarest beauty to be found. You are a lovely young lady whose confident and steadfast qualities shine forth as a wonderful ray of sun. To show my gratitude for what you have done to encourage Miss Dewey, may I be so bold as to offer to make a hat to compliment your dress, one that I hope will remind you of my admiration of your spirit?" Mary was quite astonished at his kind speech, and with a bit of shyness expressed as heartfelt an appreciation as she could muster, declaring herself in great anticipation for his most generous gift.

At that moment, Alice could be heard giving way to what might best be described as a faint scream. Mary and Georgiana, not knowing how to interpret the sound, called out to her, "Is everything alright, Alice?" and waited as they held their breath. When Miss Dewey stepped out from behind the curtain, both of her friends gasped in awe. Standing before them in a most becoming green gown, Alice Dewey was the picture of loveliness. Modestly she acknowledged, "I am actually stunning, am I not? ... Mr. Perkins has performed a miracle!"

"You certainly are," Georgian cried immediately, "*stunning* is positively the correct word for how you look!"

Mary, who found herself still reeling from everything that had taken place in this fantastic wonderland, was rendered speechless for a few moments. "I believe we shall all be walking on air at our grand event ... you are a picture of perfection in your *science green gown,* dear Alice!"

They all broke out in big smiles, realizing Mr. Perkins had chosen the right color for Alice, whose deep green eyes matched the shade of her gown, not to mention he had remembered that she was the one who chose green as the color for science. Standing together for a few moments in silence, Georgiana now broke their reverie with, "The library will not be noticed, dear Alice, when you enter looking as you do."

\* \* \* \* \*

As can be imagined, all the girls could talk of as they were leaving the dressmaker's was their new dresses ... that is, until Alice cried out in astonishment, "Is that Van?"

The others turned to look but saw nothing of him. "Was it him?" asked Georgiana anxiously.

"I didn't have a good look, but I really think it *was.*"

Mary asked, "Where did you think you saw him? Should we go have a closer look to see if it was truly him?"

Georgiana didn't know whether she was inclined to go or if she would rather not. Alice, though, said, "Yes, I'm going," and she proceeded to march across the street in pursuit. Mary followed right behind her, and with somewhat reluctant eagerness, Georgiana did likewise, all the while saying it would not be him. "Which way did he go? Did he go into a shop?" they all wondered as they were gathered together looking about themselves.

Mary directed, "Alice, you go into this shop, I'll go up the street this way, and Georgiana you go up the street that way."

Georgiana objected, "I will not! What do I care if he did go in this shop or up the street one direction or another?" She was feeling confused about what to make of all this, and her Darcy pride suddenly rearing up, she could not go running around trying to find him. However, before Mary or Alice could make a reply, a familiar voice was heard asking, "Whom is it two of you are seeking while one of you does not care?"

"Van!" Alice cried happily. "It *was* you! I was certain I spied you from the other side of the road, so we came over to see if I was correct, and I'm so glad I was!"

"Since I am here, it may very well have been me that you saw, cousin, but perchance it was only someone who looked like me and it was just a happy accident that I also was here," he laughed. "But I understand *one* of you did not seem too keen on determining if it was me, is that not so, Miss Darcy?"

"I had no wish of being sent on a wild goose chase is all," she protested, not able to look directly at him, "since it was understood you were in Ireland with the O'Learys."

Van, who had been smiling broadly, now looked at her with a quizzical expression, saying, "I've been *where* ... with *whom?*"

The three girls now looked at one another with his same expression, as Alice responded, "We were told that you left with the O'Learys for Ireland. I even sent a note to the conductor's home and they sent word that you were no longer there. Were we given incorrect information?"

"Well, yes, I had left his home, but I did *not* leave with the O'Learys. I went to our country home to be alone and concentrate on finishing *The Sun* suite. I was too distracted here in London."

Georgiana was rendered speechless at what she was hearing and did not know in what light to take what he was saying, since he was not specific as to what had been causing his distraction. She tried to think of a way to ask something that might give her a clue, but it was Mary who asked, "Your being here now—does that mean you have finished it?"

At this very moment, the Earl himself approached the young people, for he had come to see how the girls liked their dresses. Discovering Van in the group, he gleefully declared, "Van, my boy! I did not know the O'Learys had returned from Ireland ... or did you come back alone?" Not waiting for an answer, he continued, "Well, no matter, you are in time for the grand unveiling of the library, and believe me, it is really something to see!" Then addressing the girls, he went on, "I came to inquire if the dresses were to your liking. How did you find them? Were you pleased?"

As Alice began to praise Mr. Perkins, his Lordship interrupted, "Wait, what is all this, our standing around out here? Shall we not go home and continue our discussion there instead of in the street? Let us head for the carriages."

It was determined best to do just that. However, Van had to decline, for he said he had an appointment to attend to. He was informed of the day of the grand unveiling, and promising to be there, he bid them farewell and walked away.

# Chapter Forty-three

At the Dewey home, his Lordship had a surprise for Mary and Georgiana. He knew that not only they but also their brother and sister would very much want to be together for the upcoming special event, so he privately arranged that Darcy and Elizabeth arrive at his home while the girls were away getting fitted for their dresses. During the time they were waiting for the Earl and the young ladies to return home, the Darcys made a tour of the work that was done on the library and were in amazement at the transformation they saw. Of course, they wondered what could possibly be hidden there in the middle of the room; however, no one was allowed to guess what was under wraps, and whenever the girls were with them over the next few days, they made sure no accidental slip of expression on their own part would give away even the slightest hint.

When at last the others arrived, the joyous reunion gave way to happy talk mixed with pronouncements of praise for all three girls, reflecting how they all felt. Georgiana was as happy as the rest, but she had reason to be distracted. She could not stop thinking about Van and the fact that he had not gone to Ireland! Mary would very often take notice of her and knew exactly what she was thinking; the truth is, she could not help wondering about the same thing since their chance encounter with him. She began looking for an appropriate time to get Georgiana away to talk about it, certain that her friend would be incapable of settling her mind without being able to express her feelings. No such opportunity came, however, and she had no alternative but to wait until later when they were back at the Darcy home. Ere long, after a very pleasant visit together, they said goodnight to the Deweys and took their leave.

Before she could find time to be alone with Georgiana, however, there was another surprise waiting for Mary, because this was a day for surprises both large and small. Elizabeth had been wanting to do something special for her sister, so she brought a present she deemed appropriate for Mary. This particular item had sent her shopping for a few weeks until she found it. Of course, as is usually the case, half the fun for Lizzy was in finding her gift and wrapping it up with the most beautiful linen cloth that Mary would also be able to use in her sewing basket, for there truly is more happiness in giving than receiving, as is said. As soon as possible, Lizzy discreetly pulled Mary aside and asked that she follow her to her room.

"What is it, Lizzy? Has something happened at home?" Mary asked, unsure of why Elizabeth would want to see her alone.

"Oh, no, all is well. Father and Mother send you their love … I just wanted to have you to myself for a few moments so I could give you something," she replied with a smile. Going directly to her bedside table, she picked up the neatly wrapped gift, and handing it to her sister, said simply, "This is for you."

Mary looked at her with astonishment, reaching her hand out and saying, "For me?" Being prodded by Elizabeth to open it, she sat down on the bed and carefully undid the ribbon. What she found was a book with the unusual and intriguing title, *Sense and Sensibility*. Elizabeth explained, "It is a new story I have been hearing a bit about, but I haven't read it yet myself. I know you are not much for novels, Mary, but the title seemed perfect for you, regardless of whether the story is much to your liking. It is reported to be quite good, though, and the author is a woman, no less, whose name is Jane Austen."

"We've been so busy lately with our work on the library, I haven't even been able to do much reading myself, as odd as that may sound. If the story lives up to the title, I'm sure it will be entertaining. And thank you so very much for thinking of me like this. I shall treasure it, dear Lizzy."

"I hope every time you see it you will remember my sentiments, that of all the Bennet girls, you have proved to be the one that has shown the greatest *'sense and sensibility.'* And having seen what you have accomplished at the Earl's home, I wish I could have found a book titled *Sense, Sensibility, and Ability!* With his Lordship's permission, I must bring Father to see what all you have done."

Even though Mary was anxious to talk with Georgiana about Van, the time she now spent with Elizabeth was some of the most pleasurable two hours she had ever had. These two Bennet sisters were truly forming a steadfast relationship that would continue to grow the more they were together.

\* \* \* \* \*

There was no need for Mary to go find Georgiana now, because *she* came to Mary's room after Elizabeth left. "Mary, what does it mean, that Van did not go with the O'Learys? And how could such confusion have come about? ... and what did he mean there was too much distraction in London? I had just gotten used to the idea that he would be with Miss Pinch and now this ..." Georgiana said, jumping right into her thoughts as if Mary had been thinking them with her. "Could there be anything more distracting for me the day before the library is to be seen by all? And I looked so lovely in that dress from Mr. Perkins; now I will be so nervous I am sure I will look ridiculous ... as you know, there is nothing quite so frightful as a lady in an elegant gown looking nervous ...." Continuing without taking a breath, "I speak feelingly, you know, for that has been my lot for most of my life ... and just when I believed I had developed some pluck, he has to come and create all this confusion!"

Mary sat listening with the greatest patience. Georgiana, who had been pacing about the room while giving vent, finally observed her friend sporting that gentle expression of calmness while the room was full of emotional chaos. She stopped her pacing and venting, and taking a position in front of her with hands on her hips, looked straight at her friend. After but a moment of Mary saying nothing, Georgiana finally cried, "Well, have you nothing to say?"

Smiling with eyebrows and shoulders raised in a quizzical gesture, Mary declared, "I did not know you were through talking."

"Very funny! Seriously, Mary, what do you make of all of this?"

Mary, her countenance taking on all the real concern she felt for her friend, replied, "Well, on the one hand I am tempted to think if he was sincerely interested in Miss Pinch, the temptation of being with her while at the same time giving his name and reputation wider circulation would have been too much to pass up. And if we look at it from that point of view, we might with good reason conclude his attachment to her is not very strong." Changing her tone contemplatively, she went on, "But on the other hand, he may very well have been thinking that to abandon Conductor Wooddale simply to chase a young lady to Ireland could have been viewed as career suicide and therefore he was not willing to take the risk." Contemplating that point, she concluded, "If we take *that* particular way of viewing his actions, his not going to Ireland may tell us little of how he feels about Miss Pinch, since such reasoning could be understood even by someone as weak headed as her."

"Mary!" Georgiana exclaimed, pursing her lips, "that was no help at all—I'm left exactly where I was!"

"My dear Georgiana, if I had stated that his actions declare you have no rival in the person of Miss Pinch, that would not have voided the possibility of my more rational explanations even if they had gone unsaid."

"I know that's true, Mary, but something inside of me didn't want to hear a sensible accounting of his actions. I wanted to hear ... oh! you know what I wanted to hear!" she said, exasperated. Then raising her head with a look that suggested she remembered something that might throw a different light on the subject, she added, "Well, what do you think he meant about being distracted? With the O'Learys gone, why would he feel distracted here?"

Mary shook her head, replying compassionately, "Georgiana, I will not say something just because it might make you feel better for now, and I know you really don't want me to either. I will admit there is at least room for hope, but please don't get your hopes up too high, because there may be a logical explanation for his statement that has nothing to do with Miss Pinch or any other female."

Georgiana sighed and sat down on the bed beside her friend. "You're right, Mary, I will be calm now. Thank you for bringing me to my senses. Now, what is this logical explanation you have?"

"Only think, with regard to Van's being distracted—here we are in the middle of The Season and one can only imagine what Conductor

Wooddale's home is like. You know how they celebrate after a performance, and I'm sure his home is very likely not a quiet place with all that going on. Is there any wonder why Mr. Thornburg would seek the solitude of the country?"

"So *that* is the distraction you think he was talking about?"

"You want to know if I think *you* could have been the distraction he was referring to," Mary acknowledged. "It is possible, of course, but it seems to me the distraction he referred to was something he evidently could get away from, which he did by going to the country."

Georgiana, looking a bit put out, said, "Why, Mary? Why could not I be the distraction he meant?"

"Because, dear Georgiana, if you are in his heart and his head, as you are suggesting—*or hoping*—he would not get away from your being a distraction simply by getting further away from you. And if it was you he was thinking of, why would he not come to his uncle's home more often, even under the guise of some other stated reason?" Seeing her friend's downcast face, Mary said earnestly, "Please understand, I am not trying to sound definitive, but it just seems to me he went away to concentrate on finishing *The Sun* suite because of all the activity at the conductor's home."

Georgiana reached right over to hug Mary. "I am so glad I have a friend like you! I can be so insensible, and instead of belittling me or making me feel stupid, you're forever just kindly reasoning with me. You are so smart, I love you so!"

She got up to take her leave, but before even making it to the door, Mary threw one last statement at her, "You do realize this is all conjecture ... I could be totally wrong and *you* might be right."

"Yes, of course I do, but I still feel better and I still think you're smart ..."

"And yes, I know, you still love me," Mary grinned.

"I wasn't going to say that."

"Goodnight, Georgiana. Oh ... one more thing."

"What's that?" she said over her shoulder, out in the hall by now.

"You better start practicing again."

Miss Darcy came rushing back, sticking her head around the door, looking concerned. "Oh, no! You're right!" Stepping back in the room, she shut the door again, with Mary smiling and looking quite mischievous.

"You did say that he had composed a song... what was the name of it?"

*"Melody of the Heart,"* Georgiana said ardently.

"Oh, yes, that was it."

Georgiana declared, "Mary, don't tease me like that."

# Chapter Forty-four

The day for the grand unveiling of the library dawned as any other day. The three girls were up early, however, each one privately considering how this important day would end. At the Dewey estate, Alice and Mary were already anxiously looking about the library and checking the index cards. Mary said to Alice, half-joking, "Georgiana should be here with us now so that our anxiety can be divided by three instead of two. Where is she?"

"Here I am, as you can see. And I assure you, I didn't have to be present to have my share of the worry," came the familiar voice from the direction of the library door. Moving quickly across the room, the friends came together, feeling all the excitement of the approaching event. As if they had rehearsed it, they individually drew a deep breath on cue, each with her share of nerves. Impulsively, each girl took the others' hands, forming a ring of solidarity, steadying one another in this way as they shared this moment of pride, respect, and a closeness that comes from laboring in unison and accomplishing something truly remarkable. For Alice Dewey, this was especially sweet and in her heart she cherished this moment, hoping her days of isolation had come to an end.

They proceeded to take a position at the entrance of the library to take in a panoramic view of it. Alice said, "I still can't believe all this was done for me. I never tire of walking in here."

"Well, it is an expression of how much your father loves you," Georgiana replied.

Mary added, "And it is befitting such a home as this. But I must say Alice, your contribution toward a real workable system of cataloging and indexing the books was genius. You have every reason to feel that you did every bit as much as either of us on your library."

"All I know is, if Papa had not chosen you two, my life would still be very lonely and I would never have been able to contribute to a library remodel."

Georgiana, afraid Alice's thoughts about her lonely days might continue, said with a bright air, "Alright, enough of this ... this is not the day for sad reflections ... it is a day for celebrating our friendship and this grand library," and with heightened excitement, she finished with, "which we three dreamed up and accomplished ourselves!"

In hearty agreement with those sentiments, the happy young ladies moved over to the window seats, considering how superb the idea of adding these had been. And, of course, such a last inspection would not be complete without going up to the balcony and taking in the view from there one last time while the moment still belonged just to them. But the hour had come to get dressed, so they left the library to prepare for the big event of the day.

\* \* \* \* \*

As promised, Lord Dewey had invited many guests, including all those that had been there at the dinner in honor of Darcy, which was in a way the beginning of this project. Darcy and Elizabeth were busily engaging every guest as they arrived, very pleased to see such a nice crowd forming. Among the guests were two that were a complete surprise to Mary, for despite Elizabeth having mentioned that she hoped they could come, Mary had no idea that Mr. Bennet and his wife had been able to make the journey there after all, for they had arrived only this morning.

"Papa, Mama! How wonderful to see you here," Mary greeted them with a kiss. "I had hoped it was possible that you would come, but knowing your aversion to town and Mama's to traveling, I dared not expect it."

Mr. Bennet said, in a tone that would have raised the eyebrows of any of his acquaintance, "Your letters keeping me informed of how things were progressing with your time here, my child, created a great curiosity in me that would not permit me to miss this for the world."

"You are too kind, Father. Thank you for giving yourself the trouble of coming, for even though I say it myself, words could not do justice to what we have done here on the library."

Mrs. Bennet had, through the course of all this time, been kept in the dark as to what Mary was really doing in London, for Mr. Bennet saw no need to fluster her poor nerves. She consequently was at a loss to understand this exchange between father and daughter. In fact, she was under the impression that the only reason they had been invited to this grand estate was because of Mr. Darcy, and therefore was somewhat surprised to even see Mary at the party. "Mary, what are you doing here? ... oh, of course, you're here with Georgiana Darcy ... " she began. Nevertheless, she did grasp one thing about their conversation and with agitation, she remonstrated, "However did you find time to have anything to do in his Lordship's *library* during The Season? Oh, *what am I saying*—knowing to whom we are speaking, I am sure you have kept yourself locked away in some dusty old library instead of spending your time in more worthwhile pursuits that would lead you to becoming a wife! Well, now that I am here, I may still manage to do something for you this very evening, if you will but ..." she was interrupted by her husband directing her attention to Lizzy who wanted to introduce someone to them. This was not absolutely true on Lizzy's part, but it was the best way to spare Mary the rest of the speech—or anyone else close enough to hear for that matter, for Mrs. Bennet always spoke in a gathering as if the person to whom she was speaking was on the other side of the room and was the only one who could hear her.

Mr. Bennet said comfortingly to Mary, "You know your mother means well, but I will do my part to check her, and to that end I have enlisted Lizzy's assistance. I'm sure between the two of us we can keep her occupied." Mary thanked her father again and moved on to some other guests that had just entered.

Right behind them came the O'Learys, who had returned only yesterday from Ireland. As one can imagine, it might be suspected that their niece had something to do with their early return. Georgiana saw them come through the door, and the sight of Miss Pinch made her glad his Lordship had arranged for them to have their dresses made by Mr. Perkins. Everyone who had arrived thus far had been praising the loveliness of the three ladies, allowing that it was quite unlikely that anything about the library could compare with them.

The Earl, calling for everyone's attention, informed the party, "I know there is great interest in seeing the library now that it is complete, but the grand unveiling will not take place until after dinner. Believe me when I say, no one is more excited than I, for the young ladies have a special surprise for me that has been placed there under covers waiting for this very day!" he said jovially. "Now as things are best experienced on a full stomach, let us go to table."

Mrs. Bennet asked her husband in wonderment, as the group moved into the dining room, "What is he talking about? What could Mary have done for the Earl's library that could honestly be referred to as a grand unveiling?"

"Judging from what his Lordship has just said, it would appear we will have to wait till after we have eaten," Mr. Bennet replied flatly, directing his wife to move on. This was a sufficient answer for her, however much she was at a loss to understand all the excitement about this library which was the main topic of conversation among the guests. For Mrs. Bennet, the Earl's home was grand and the evening gathering was likewise grand, and this was enough to make understanding what was being talked about of little matter to her.

\* \* \* \* \*

Alice's cousin had not yet come, for Conductor Wooddale had been detained and Van would not think of making him enter his uncle's home alone later than was expected. The soup had been poured when they finally arrived and his Lordship, in as friendly and hospitable a manner as ever, welcomed them to come join the festivities. They were seated by the head of the table to the consternation of Miss Pinch, who was now doubly troubled about the fact that she was sitting at quite a distance from Van, as well as the irritating reality of how beautiful Georgiana Darcy looked this evening. It seems Mr. Thornburg's declining to go with them to Ireland had created in Penelope visions of her losing any grip she may have had on him, and she was determined to make up for lost time this very night.

There was excited talk at table about the balcony which had been heard would be part of the addition, but the notion of the whole wall being converted into a window was met with mixed feelings. It seems the idea of a library having such an open, airy feel is quite a novel concept given the fact that most libraries are looked upon as a quiet, subdued place of refuge and solace, so most of the guests were simply going to reserve judgement till seeing it. There was also plenty of discussion about a rumor of some new way of cataloging the books, of which no specifics were known since this was to be part of the unveiling. All in all, the girls were quite satisfied at the level of anticipation, for they felt certain that no matter how ambitious anyone's imagination might be, the reality would not fail to impress.

With dinner over and Lord Dewey and the girls leading the way, the excitement of this gathering of friends had reached its peak. Stopping at the entrance of the library, he turned to the group and declared ceremonially, "Before throwing open the doors, I will now turn over this tour to the capable hands of Miss Mary Bennet."

Amiably stepping forward, Mary said, "Thank you so much, Lord Dewey. I do not wish to needlessly prolong everyone's anticipation, as you have informed the group of your already being held in suspense for several days now over one special part of the library, and everyone is here to see it all." Turning to address the guests, she went on, "Our surprise for the Earl has been well covered in order to *keep* it a surprise, and it was deemed appropriate that we should first allow a half hour for you all to walk about the library, exploring as you will, and then we shall make the presentation to his Lordship." Standing before this prestigious crowd, at ease and confident, Elizabeth and her father could not have been more proud of their Mary. Mrs. Bennet was dumbfounded, and even Mr. Darcy was quite amazed. Mary looked at her two companions with eyes sparkling as she said, "So without further ado … it is my great pleasure to invite you into the newly remodeled library for Miss Alice Dewey."

The doors were opened wide as Mary, Georgiana, and Alice moved aside, permitting everyone to enter. From their position just outside the door, they stood arm in arm for several minutes, looking on with a satisfaction mingled with suspense. Their satisfaction was increased and suspense ended as they heard exclamations of approval and astonishment coming from the guests. With heartfelt joy, they quietly congratulated one another, moving beyond the entrance to take their places among their friends. The room, albeit quite large, was barely able to hold the expressions of praise that could be heard, words such as *magnificent, superb, splendid,* and *more wonderful than imagined.* There were even those that declared it a *masterpiece of design,* which term seemed to be most appropriate to the gathering, for it soon was on the lips of everyone.

Mrs. Bennet, who continued in astonishment at seeing her daughter commanding the attention of such a gathering with exceptional grace, could hardly be restrained from approaching her middle daughter as soon as could be. Her husband was inclined much the same way, for he was gratified that persons of rank were paying such rapt attention to a *Bennet* from Meryton! As they made their way across the room, the lady remarked to her husband, "Mr. Bennet, I am quite at a loss for words ... our *Mary* is responsible for all of this?"

He replied good-humoredly, "I doubt seriously if our Mary wielded a hammer or any other such instrument, my dear. But according to the Earl, she is very much responsible and he holds our girl in the highest regard. He told me so himself and, I must say, could hardly contain his praise of her."

"Well, his Lordship's praise is all well and good, but having a husband would be a great deal better," his wife said unrelentingly, never forgetting her duty as matriarch of the family, which was to try to make a good match for all her daughters. All such issues aside, they were both rich in their compliments to Mary herself, for which she was pleasantly surprised.

At that moment, Mrs. Randall, who had received an invitation from Georgiana and Mary, approached the girls to give them her personal raptures at what they had accomplished. Addressing Mary with a proud smile, she said, "It seems, my dear, that even though my friend Margaret James had no children, her spirit lives on in *you*. This library is such an accomplishment, more astounding than I had imagined from the notes on your progress I received from you both! I am quite delighted to be here; you were very kind in allowing me to share in this joyous occasion."

Mary replied sincerely, "Mrs. Randall, we're so glad you are here! You must know, hearing of Margaret James certainly has been a source of strength and inspiration for me, and since you so poignantly shared your friend's life experience with us and our visits with you have been a highlight of our time here in London, we just *had* to invite you, for this event would not have been complete without you."

"You are a dear sweet girl and I can see you have found an outlet that you obviously excel at, Mary. I am glad your pursuits have not met with the same overwhelming obstacles as Margaret's course did. I know that, had she been alive today, she would have been cheering the loudest at what you have accomplished here."

Modestly, Mary replied, "Now, Mrs. Randall, you have gone a bit too far in giving me so much credit for this magnificent library. Without my two friends, what you see would not have been possible."

Georgiana, grasping Mrs. Randall's arm, protested, "Now, Mary, *Alice and I* would say that without your drive and motivation, what we see here would not even exist! So for our part, we know all too well how much credit you deserve."

Alice likewise said it was so, and after a few more compliments, Mrs. Randall excused herself to indulge in the comfort of the window seats while the girls took in the gratifying vista of the party, who were all marveling at the beauty that was to be found. The men declared to Lord Dewey how the overall impact upon entering the room was almost overwhelming, and the ladies admired how even the little details such as the carvings, the fine fabrics and the color scheme all worked together with the grandeur of the marble columns of the library.

# Chapter Forty-five

The half hour had passed and the three girls took a position upon the stairs that led up to the balcony, calling for everyone to gather around. Taking the lead once again, Mary began, "I know everyone is quite anxious to see what is under this cover, and his Lordship in particular. But if I may delay *just a moment longer* and call your attention to this magnificent filing cabinet." Walking over to it, she continued, "This in many ways is the real masterpiece of the library. Those of you who love books, as Miss Dewey and I do, may have at many times in your visits to a library been struck with what a great difficulty often arises in finding a particular book among those containing so many as this one does. How does one know if the book is even to be found upon the shelves?" Pausing momentarily to let that question penetrate, Mary went on, "Well, this *file cabinet* holds the answer. You will notice the corresponding colors on the drawers to those on the shelves ... this system permits a person to search first for a book here in the cabinet to verify if it is here and then, of course, where it can be located on the shelves. We call this the *Dewey Index System*, for it was inspired by Miss Dewey herself. You can imagine what a time saver this is and how it is the heart of this truly well thought out library! As you can see, what we have here is, not just a wonderfully remodeled room, but the best organized library, I dare say, in the Kingdom."

This explanation was needed, for many were questioning what this filing cabinet was all about, and now with this understanding, expressions of approval and praise for such an innovation were heard. Van was so proud of his cousin he could not restrain himself, exclaiming, "Well done, Alice! Bravo, indeed!" which was taken up by many as they all applauded Miss Dewey.

Waiting for the guests to quiet down again, Mary continued, "Now if I may take everyone back and put an end to Lord Dewey's suspense ..." Joining the other girls again on the stairs, Mary informed them all that what was about to be revealed was the idea of Alice and Georgiana and, therefore, she would now permit Miss Darcy to take over.

Looking about the group of friendly faces, Georgiana noticed that Miss Pinch was still by Van's side as she had been since the exodus from the dining room, but she took courage from what Mary had said to Alice when trying on their dresses, recalling her words about *'letting all the beauties have their looks, whereas we will take pride in who and what we are.'* After this brief reflection, she looked at Alice's father with a smile and began, "Lord Dewey, if *I* could now tax your patience *just a little bit longer ...*"

The Earl let out one of his hearty laughs and said, "I have not found waiting to be lacking any pleasure, my dear Miss Darcy."

Georgiana went on, "Thank you, sir ... Miss Mary Bennet has been so modest and generous in ascribing all the credit to Miss Dewey and myself, as if she has only stood by watching. However, Miss Dewey joins me in saying, if it were not for Miss Bennet we would not now be here in this fine new library. *She* was the one that initiated this whole project. *She* began the idea of cataloging the books in some orderly fashion ... It would not be an exaggeration to say *her* determined spirit truly led the way for any contribution that Miss Dewey and I had in this splendid and functional library. So please join me in giving Miss Mary Bennet the plaudits she so richly deserves."

After the applause ended, Georgiana said to his lordship, "May I thank you again for your patience, sir." Once more came his hearty laugh, but now his excitement was heightened knowing the anticipation was almost over! "We believe you will find this long wait we have put you through has been well worth it! Let me explain ... as you know, there are among these many volumes some very important books on your family history. Miss Dewey felt it was not proper that those treasures be placed among the other books of history, for it seemed only right that these special family books have their own *special place* to occupy! And where better than *the* most prominent position in the library? So, in honor of your Lordship and in recognition of your excellent family name, we present to you ..." and with those words, the covers were removed.

What was seen literally took everyone's breath away. A magnificent mahogany cabinet which, by virtue of being the only dark piece of furniture in the room, would surely attract the eye of anyone upon first entering, but the beauty of it would surely draw attention regardless. The cabinet was oval in shape and placed so that it was lengthwise as seen from the door of the library. Atop the piece was the Dewey crest, which has one dragon on its shield, symbolizing valor and protection. The expert sculptor had formed, from one large piece of mahogany, *two* dragons standing almost two feet high holding the family crest, with its suit of armor's helmet sitting above the shield, its single dragon carved in relief. The family name was also done in relief upon the decorative ribbon work running across the bottom and up the sides as a border, in the same manner all crests have. The artist had even carved both sides so the crest could be read from either side.

Spontaneous applause broke out as everyone exclaimed what a marvelous finishing touch this intricately carved masterpiece was to Lord Dewey's fine new library. The group called for a speech from his Lordship, but he declared himself too overwhelmed for it, which he was. But even if he could have found his voice, this kind humble father did not wish to detract from the rightfully earned attention and praise that was due these three young ladies, and most particularly his dear young daughter.

\* \* \* \* \*

After spending a little more time exploring and examining the library, the party was taken to the concert hall where it was announced that Mr. Thornburg intended to play. Taking a stand before the instrument, Van addressed those gathered, "When we were last together, at the start of this project that has been so gloriously brought to a finish tonight, I did not play. However, that night we did hear a most excellent performance by Miss Darcy and Miss Bennet, and since this evening is really as much about them as it is my cousin's new library, I would be honored to play this evening ... if Miss Darcy will join me in a duet."

Georgiana was all amazement and turned first to Mary and then to Alice as she was taken aback by his request. Mary rose so as to bring her to her feet and urge her on, and Alice followed her lead. Darcy, throwing off all reserve, began to clap and exclaim *"splendid idea!"* and, of course, Elizabeth joined her husband in cheering her on. This created a response from the crowd of friends for Georgiana to join him at the piano, for after discovering all the marvels of the new library, some splendid music seemed just the way to end the evening. The whole group began to clap, *that is*, except Miss Pinch.

Graciously thanking them all, Georgiana took a seat at the piano, whereas Van continued standing, commenting about what was to be played: "I have recently completed this piece and have yet to play it for anyone, so if you will, please indulge me in trying it here with you." An air of excitement came over the crowd at hearing that.

As he was spreading out the music, he could be seen saying something to Miss Darcy, speaking loud enough only for her to hear. "I said no one has heard this, which is not completely true. This is the piece I had started playing for you when we were interrupted and I was not permitted to finish. Since it seems that is always the case with us and to prevent you from leaving without hearing the whole of it, I decided to make it a duet." Smiling that disarming smile, he continued, "And since you play so very well, I have no doubt of your doing an excellent job of it even though this is the first time you have seen it. Oh, and I should mention," he laughed, "lest you be concerned you might have to struggle with my scribbles, when you saw me in town I was having the music written out properly so it could be easily read. I also changed something else about it, but alas," he said, eyeing the crowd, "if we do not start playing we may lose our audience ... which may not be such a bad thing ...."

Georgiana's smile kept increasing, as did the gleam in her eye, with each word he expressed. Near the piano, Miss Pinch sat watching the two of them with disdain and would not allow herself to be passed over any longer. Van having declined her invitation to Ireland could be explained away in some manner that still left her feeling capable of alluring him, but seeing him talking in this cozy way with Georgiana was too much! Penelope leaned over and informed her uncle that she was not well and wished to leave, which she did as hurriedly as she could before the music started. Her uncle was of a mind to take her out, but the idea that Van was going to play a new piece of music was too strong a draw for him, so without compunction, he turned the removal of his niece over to the competent care of his trusted servant.

When at last an attempt was made by the duo to begin, there was a false start to their playing. Van had begun but Georgiana was prevented—in fact, she reached out for his hand, which brought the music to a stop. Only then had she taken a look at the title ... *Melody of the Heart: Georgiana's Song.* Seeing her name there required her to display great self-control so as not to ask what it meant, at the very least. She was, rather, more inclined to give out an exclamation of joy, that being her first impulse. For Van, holding back the satisfaction of finally letting his feelings be known to the girl he admired was also a display of great self-command that the two sitting at the instrument alone could admire. It was, all things considered, an exhibition of composure in as heroic a fashion as a pair of young people who have just revealed their feelings to each other ever had to do, for they were before a group of onlookers that were ignorant of what was happening between them. But contain, or *restrain,* themselves they did, and had their audience been aware of what they been witnessing, they surely would have taken to their feet and applauded this young couple's strength of self-composure! Lacking in this knowledge, however, the audience began to rustle and shift about out of concern for Georgiana, and some began to whisper that she must be overcome with nerves to be playing with someone as accomplished as Mr. Thornburg. Darcy was about to suggest that Elizabeth go up to see if all was well with her.

Van, realizing what was happening, though, now stood again and said to the party, "I must apologize. I had placed the sheet ill for Miss Darcy to be able to see it well. After all, please remember this is the first time she has seen this piece of music." He reshuffled the sheets in an effort to look convincing and placed them just as they were before. This was not lost on Mary, but it was sufficient for Georgiana to gather herself and begin to concentrate on playing.

The group could not have been more pleased at the lilting melody that was being played on Georgiana's more complex high and middle side, whereas Van's deeper tones simulated what was clearly the human heart—from simply *beating* to *racing with excitement*—going through the whole range of emotion. Surprise registered on the faces of some that Van was playing the more simple side while his partner played the more difficult, but the audience was unaware that what made the piece more challenging for her to play was not the complexity. Van had written it with her playing a duet with him in mind, and the changes in tempo and melody were marked on the page, but there were also extra notes, such as: *Our first meeting, The second time we met, Thinking of her,* and finally, *What to say to her.* Most distracting, indeed!

When they stopped, Van grasped her hand and took her to the side of the piano as they took a bow. *"Perfectly charming, what a lovely piece of music! How well it sounded as a duet,"* the crowd expressed along with their applause. As it turned out, it was a good thing indeed that Miss Pinch had gone, for if the mere sight of Georgiana joining Van at the piano was too much for her, seeing them hand in hand before everyone, being so applauded, would have surely driven her out of the room!

* * * * *

Everything had been declared a success by one and all. As the party began to break up and move out of the concert hall into the vestibule, Mary wandered over to the piano, suspecting something about the music that had been played. Spying the sheet music, she flipped through the pages and caught the title, which had not been given to the group, not to mention all Van's little notations. Smiling at this, she knew just what she had to do.

# Chapter Forty-six

Mary first approached Alice and taking her by the hand declared, "Come, we have something to do," and said nothing more. She had a determined look and her friend's face was registering suspenseful wonderment as they approached Georgiana, who was talking to her brother and Elizabeth. Mary said, as abruptly as only a family member can do without being thought too rude, "Excuse us, if you will, but we have need of your sister, Mr. Darcy," and she walked away with both girls in tow.

Lizzy, laughing at Darcy's shock over Mary's impertinence, teased, "Are you longing for the days when older brothers were more interesting than anything friends might offer, my dear?"

Not slowing down to hear his answer, Mary continued her mission with Alice still wearing that quizzical look, now joined in the same expression by Georgiana who, though asking, received no answer as to what was going on. Miss Darcy's mind began to race with possibilities when she noticed they were marching across the room toward Van and his uncle, engaged in conversation with the Bennets and the conductor, who was the only non-family member that had not yet left the event. The gentlemen turned as the girls arrived by their side, Lord Dewey again giving compliments on how enchanting the evening had been and Conductor Wooddale declaring, as he had once done when the project was in its beginning stages, that the girls must come see what could be done with his own library. Mary now permitted herself a smile and said, "It has been enchanting indeed, sir; and, Maestro, it would be a great pleasure to look at your library. However, if you will please excuse us, we are here to summon Mr. Thornburg to the family room ... with your permission, of course, Lord Dewey."

"But, of course!" the great man bellowed. "I am quite certain my nephew would prefer to exchange his present company for you three lovely ladies, is that not so, Van?" he added, giving his approval in as loud a manner as he was accustomed to do when he was in a merry mood, for tonight he was in the highest of moods.

Mary, having gathered all the participants of her scheme, led the group away. They headed straight for the smaller music room, where Georgiana and Van had first met. The piano here is not quite as grand as the one found in the concert hall, but is still as fine an instrument as one could wish for to carry out what Mary had started.

Continuing in her role as director of the troop, the resolute Miss Bennet gave directions as to where everyone was to be seated. She said to Georgiana, "You, Miss Darcy, take your place at the piano." Georgiana began to understand what this was all about and offered a mild objection, to which Mary said, "Have you worked and practiced for nothing?"

As she was still hesitating, Alice, who also grasped what Mary was doing, added, "Yes, Georgiana, you simply must do it!" With this further encouragement, she took her seat at the piano.

Van was wholly engrossed by the proceedings playing out before him, realizing he was the only person present who did not know what the bustle was leading up to. He asked enthusiastically, "And me, Miss Bennet, where am I to be positioned?"

"If you will take a seat here near the piano, that will do nicely. And Alice," she added, "if you would be so kind, please take this seat behind your cousin." Thrilled to be there, his anticipation for whatever was about to take place growing, Van eagerly followed the directions and sat down.

Mary, still standing by the piano with everyone in their place, turned to Van, cleared her throat, and putting on a great air, said, "Mr. Thornburg, let me invite you to sit back, relax, and listen to a tale ... Once upon a time in a room very much like this room, there was a boy and a girl enjoying a moment of quiet conversation and music. Coming upon our two main characters—quite unaware, of course, and quite unintentionally, I should add—were two interlopers. Yes, much could be said about the close bond existing between our heroine and these two unexpected intruders, but this tale is not about that! No, no, this is a story of what took place between the leading boy, or *man*, and our leading girl, or *lady*. As our protagonist was in the middle of playing a new piece of music to the delight of the fair lady, it was then that her very innocent companions came upon them. That interruption led to a certain exchange of words, brief though they were, and unfortunately that dialog—it was feared by our leading lady—was liable for misconstruction from the point of view of our leading man ... "

A thought came to her mind, causing Mary to stop to explain: "Let me just insert here that, as any good story has, so does our story have an *antagonist* (let us not use the word *villain*) to our heroine. This *adversary*, possessed of a cunning charm that belied her stunning beauty, was making overtures to the hero, attempting to whisk him away with her, far from our sweet maiden, with promises of fame and fortune—and with the added inducement of having *her own lovely self* by his side always."

That being made known, she continued, "Now let me pick our story back up where I left off ... the aforementioned fear of misunderstanding was compounded with the subsequent sudden departure of our leading man. What was our dear leading lady to think? Had he succumbed to the arts and allurements that had been dangled before him by that *other person?* Well might a less brave and courageous damsel have given in to feelings of despair and hopelessness ... but our heroine, true to her noble nature, gathered strength around her two faithful companions and valiantly pressed on, trusting that *character which is most to be admired is character which has been tested by adversity!*"

Pausing dramatically, looking wistfully toward the window, Mary shook that expression off and went on, "Now, lest you grow weary of this little tale, let me assure you it *is* coming to an end ... Our fair maiden had taken it upon herself to correct any misunderstanding our hero might have gotten from those words spoken in haste—those *thoughtless* words given when they had been intruded upon by her good companions—and to that end, she composed a melody of her own. This is why we, all the players of this little saga, are once again gathered where it all began!"

Van had been listening with the greatest interest and was very much amused with Mary's antics in relating her story. She now concluded by saying, "If you have kept up with this narrative, sir, the piece of music our heroine—otherwise known as *Miss Darcy*—is about to play will make more sense to you. If you have not, I am sure you will still want to hear it anyway and any further explanation can be made more clearly afterward. The piece of music is titled ..." then pausing for effect ...

Georgiana quickly interrupted, "Mary, I can give him the title, if you please." Mary turned toward her and with bow, took her seat next to Alice. Georgiana now continued, "Thank you, my dear friend, for that most imaginative introduction, but truly, Mr. Thornburg, let me speak plainly *before* rather than *after* I play ... You see, as Mary so ingeniously pointed out, I feared you had mistaken my meaning when I said to the girls on the day to which she was referring, that 'you were only playing a new piece of music' and then finished with—*'that is all!'* I worried those words were taken by you to mean that what you were playing was of little interest to me and, of course, that was *not* the case! So, it just seemed that one way to show my real feelings about that day was to write down a little tune of my own." Looking at him earnestly, she confessed, "I had hoped to be able to play it for you when next I saw you, but as was said, you had suddenly left town. Now, however, thanks to my very determined friend, who is in every way a sister to me, I am able to play it for you. It is titled *A Day Remembered* ... I tried to incorporate some of what I heard you play that day, as much as I could recall." Her voice quivering a little, she finished with, "Well ... here it is ... *A Day Remembered,*" and she began to play.

It was a very short piece, only a little more than two minutes long, and of course, compared to anything Van would compose, it was simple. But to him, nothing could have been more lovely. When she was done, Mary and Alice sat in silence waiting for his reaction; Georgiana could not even lift her eyes from the piano keys. Van, whose tender emotions had been touched with each note she played, sat in quiet admiration and satisfaction, thinking how impressive this piece was, laughing at himself inwardly for supposing she was just a beginner. He was so grateful for their chance meeting on that *day remembered,* a day he certainly would never forget. Leaving off his reverie, he now broke the silence as he stood and began clapping, unabashedly proclaiming, "Excellent! If I only had a rose to throw to the performer!" Mary and Alice now joined in the applause.

"I am quite certain, Mr. Thornburg," said the lovely young pianist when they stopped, "you could greatly improve it."

"That, Miss Darcy, is *impossible*. I will not have a note changed, or added to, or taken away. It is *perfect*, because it was a day to be remembered .. in fact, it has been in my thoughts constantly, even as this day will prove to be."

"That is all well and good," Mary broke in, "and how pleased we are that all the misunderstandings have been dispelled." She now rose and headed toward the piano, "But it has been some days since I myself have sat at the instrument, and therefore let me play a waltz for you two, so you will have something other to do than just stand there looking at each other! And besides, a dance is all that is needed to make this evening complete."

"What a splendid suggestion, Miss Bennet," Van grinned.

Georgiana *eagerly* gave up the bench, and Van *eagerly* extended his hand to her. As the pair began to dance, the rest of the family, having heard the sound of music and clapping, decided to join the young people. Seeing Van and Georgiana dancing, Darcy turned to Elizabeth, "Would the most beautiful lady in the room also care to dance?"

"Well, Mr. Darcy, I dare say you are *tolerable enough to tempt me* into dancing," she laughed.

Conductor Wooddale addressed Alice, "Miss Dewey, would you favor me with a dance?" And would you believe it—even Mr. Bennet took his wife's hand and joined them!

This intimate impromptu ball was indeed the way to make this special evening complete. It went on far longer than anyone could have anticipated, and when the dancing broke up, all present were happy, content in a way that can only come with the feeling of friendship and family. Of course, added to that, there was also the joy of a budding romance that had finally been allowed to be kissed by the light of the sun, now that the clouds that kept it hidden had parted.

# Chapter Forty-seven

Slowly everyone assembled outside to await the carriages. Van and Conductor Wooddale were at the point of entering theirs when Van stopped and said, "Maestro, would you mind terribly if I made you wait for just a moment as I speak with Miss Darcy? There is something I forgot to say to her."

"Heavens no, dear lad, go and take your leave properly, for I'm sure it could not have been done with all of us about you two."

Van smiled with gratitude and a bit of embarrassment at the conductor knowing so well what he was doing. Approaching Georgiana, who was standing with the others, he said, "Miss Darcy, may I have a word before I am off?" The two of them walked over toward the carriage but halted before reaching it. "I wanted to say again how pleased I was with your melody, *A Day Remembered.*" Smiling down at her lovely face, he continued, "And now that the truth is known about my whereabouts when I had gone missing, may I call on you when the conductor allows me time to do so?"

Georgiana was thrilled but kept a composed demeanor, though all the delight of new love danced in the glow on her cheeks and the sparkle in her eyes as she modestly replied, "Yes, of course, that would be quite nice ... I will be in anticipation of seeing you again."

Van's heart leapt for joy, his voice now taking on a tender note as he said, "I'm sorry, I mustn't keep the Maestro waiting." He took a step away but was forced back to her by the impulse to add, "You should understand, now that I have your permission to come, I am very likely to do so often." All Georgiana could manage at hearing this was a blush and a nod that left Van in no doubt of how she felt about this prospect; with that he reluctantly turned and walked away, taking one last look back at her before entering the carriage.

The two of them, each caught up in this romantic bubble that had enveloped them, were oblivious to the eyes of those that loved them, who were looking their direction as inconspicuously as possible, of course. The conductor, on the other hand, was simply sitting back, his eyes closed with the sound of the evening's music playing again in his head, knowing full well what scene was playing out on the pavement, which was the reason for the very large smile he was sporting. For as is true of almost all musicians, he harbored a soul that was very much inclined toward that feeling of excitement that is associated with the mystery of love. Naturally, he also had a certain anticipation of what lovely music would be born from Van giving voice to those tender feelings of the heart, knowing those very feelings have been responsible for so many exquisite melodies throughout the ages.

As the carriage pulled away and Georgiana was still standing where she and Van had just said goodbye, Mary and Alice went directly to her. Taking her by the hand, and with more eagerness on the subject of love and romance than she would otherwise have, his cousin asked simply, "Well? What did he say?"

Her cheeks, flushed with that color that only the hint of love can give, Georgiana turned to respond, but spying her brother along with the others still gathered some twenty or thirty feet away, she hesitated. They were looking at her with expressive faces that left no doubt what they were thinking, and she heard Mr. Bennet remark casually, "It appears, Mr. Darcy, that the yellow iris is beginning to show its color."

Before he could reply, Mrs. Bennet exclaimed, *"The yellow iris is beginning to show its color?* Whatever could you be talking about?"

"My dear, if you would spend just half your time *reading* about love as you do trying to get the world to *fall* in love, you might know that the yellow iris is considered *the flame of love.* Be that as it may, I must confess, young love is a sight to behold as it lifts its pedals toward the warmth of the sun."

"Father! What a romantic you are!" Lizzy cried, sliding her arm into her husband's, looking up at Darcy with that same blush of first love that seemed was being carried through the air just like the sweet scent of the jasmine. Looking over at her parents, Elizabeth saw that Mrs. Bennet took her husband's hand, drawing nearer to him, showing that the yellow iris could still bloom even after twenty years of marriage!

"Your father has always had a way with words, Lizzy, and when he was courting me, he simply swept me off my feet with them," said Mrs. Bennet, who despite all her nonsensical ways, felt a respect for her husband that she didn't often show; and she was well aware that he truly loved her.

Meanwhile, seeing that Georgiana had become aware of their watching her, Darcy quietly urged the group to look away. They all quickly did so, making a rather pathetic attempt at seeming nonchalant! Of course, this only served to make her blush all the more. Her two companions, however, did not see what was happening in that direction, for they were both focused on Miss Darcy.

"Come, Georgiana, will you not tell us what was said?" Alice prodded.

"Yes, of course, only allow me first to catch my breath." All this attention was sending our heroine into a bit of confusion!

"From what I've been told, losing one's breath while only standing and talking to an attractive young man is a sure sign of the female heart having been sent aflutter," Mary observed with a smile.

"Oh, Mary, don't tease me ... it's the cool night air that must have affected me, that's all," she replied sheepishly. Mary and Alice looked at this excuse with suspicion, assuming a posture that showed they were determined to wait as long as necessary for an answer to the question that had been put to her.

What an unconventional group of observers the Earl, Darcy, Elizabeth, and the Bennets made as they stood looking curiously on, trying to go unnoticed! They were each struck with how peculiar the scene before them was, as Mary and Alice were looking intently at Georgiana, who was obviously saying nothing. Finally, she broke out into a broad smile, assuring them, "You know I am going to tell you, but it's hard to find the words."

Mary quipped, "Hard to find the words! We are waiting to hear the words Mr. Thornburg spoke to you not five minutes ago ... how did you lose those words? He said he wanted to speak to you when you were over *there*, and then the two of you walked to right *here*, and then something was *said*—so now all you have to do is tell us what that something was!"

"Oh, Mary, must you always be so logical?" Georgiana laughed. Growing a little shy about relating their conversation, however, she continued, "I don't want more to be made of what was said than … than what was said."

Alice said feelingly, "Oh Georgiana, we are just so excited for you! Will you not trust us to be directed by your own cautiousness?"

"You are quite right, Alice." Then taking on an expressionless attitude, lowering her voice, she spoke rather quickly, "He just asked if he could be permitted to call on me, that is all … You see, it was nothing."

The curiosity of our unconventional group of observers was now raised higher when Alice and Mary became animated with excitement, while Georgiana, for whom this outbreak of delight was apparently directed, remained as still and calm as possible. Unknown to them, however, she was struggling to suppress that sense of joy that was threatening to break forth across her face. Lord Dewey, seeing no need to continue on the sidelines completely ignorant of what the commotion was all about, suggested, "Should we not step inside and allow the girls to finish their little conference without us looking on? I have a surprise of my own for them that has to do with the library and I must see if it has been attended to." They all agreed and headed back inside, each privately planning just how they were going to find out what that *little conference* was all about!

## Chapter Forty-eight

When the small celebration the three girls were having calmed down, Alice's countenance took on a look of sadness; indeed a glimmer of moonlight could be seen on the tear that streamed down her face as she turned away, trying to hide her emotions. Noticing this change of expression and the tear, though, Georgiana said with concern, "Alice, whatever is the matter?"

Miss Dewey had managed to chase away her melancholy thought every time it came to mind as the project was coming to an end, but now it was impossible to brush aside. "I'm very sorry, it's nothing ... pay no attention to me and this turn in my mood."

"We most certainly will not!" Mary and Georgiana cried together. Each took her by the hand, imploring her to relate what it was that suddenly made her so sad.

"Oh dear, how horrid and selfish it will make me sound," she muttered.

Georgiana said with great empathy, "Anything that has affected you this much is of the greatest concern to us, surely you know that. Please, what is it that is weighing on you?" Searching her mind for a reason for this change of attitude and not finding one, Georgiana's heart gave way to her own insecurities and she began to wonder if Alice now had misgivings about Van showing attentions to her after all, fearing that may be the case.

As we are well aware, that was not it at all. Drawing a deep breath, Alice answered, "Yes, of course, you have both been so very kind and I have grown so attached to you ..." At this point she paused, trying not to cry, and having fought back the tears, she continued, "but with the library finished, I fear this will be the end of it ... and ... I will never see you again." Those words having actually been spoken, she began sobbing.

Mary and Georgiana, in a flush of emotion, embraced their good friend, declaring each in her turn, "Dear sweet Alice, nothing of the sort could possibly happen! We will come see you and you will come see us. This is only the end of our working on your library; now we will be able to see each other for the sheer enjoyment of it."

Alice looked up at hearing this, repeating softly, *"For the sheer enjoyment of it'* ... you really do enjoy my company, don't you?"

Squeezing her firmly, her two companions exclaimed in unison, "Indeed we do, dear friend!"

The sense of celebration returned and Alice's tears were now falling for the happiness she felt as she observed, "When Papa proposed the idea of making over the library those many months ago, I had no idea it would end with so much more than just a new library."

"You're quite right, *far more,*" Mary replied, "for if you are of a mind and your father does not object to you joining us in our next project, Conductor Wooddale has asked that I go and see what can be done to his library. You certainly were a big help in remodeling your own." Looking curiously at Georgiana, she continued, "Well, I say join *us,* but I suppose *you* may have some other matters to tend to. However, come to think of it, since it will involve working at the conductor's home, it may prove to be quite convenient ... might it not, Georgiana?"

These three girls carried on for a while out of *sheer enjoyment,* laughing and teasing at the convenience of that proposition. The feeling of satisfaction at another such undertaking was discussed, as well as a bit more talk on how the evening had gone and quotes of the praises that were heard. They were especially delighted at the great pleasure of his Lordship, merrily recalling how he had quipped that *'his library just might end up in shambles.'* But as everyone is aware, all good things do come to an end and the night was bidding them to disperse. They walked away to inform the others that they were now *really* ready to go, expecting to see them still outside nearby. Not finding them, however, they guessed the group must have moved back indoors and they headed that direction to find them.

Coming upon them in the foyer, Alice felt it her duty to address Georgiana's brother who, although she had known him for some time, was still somewhat intimidating to her. "Forgive us, Mr. Darcy, for having detained your leaving," she said politely, "but the excitement of the evening is our excuse, of course."

"It is perfectly understandable, and no apology is needed," Darcy replied calmly, remembering all he knew about Alice, not to mention all that Elizabeth had taught him about how to relate to young ladies!

His Lordship, who had left the Darcys and Bennets to see about the preparations he had earlier mentioned, now returned. Seeing the girls there with them, he called, "You have come inside, that is excellent timing! If you will follow me, I have something to surprise *you* with!" Leading the way back to the library, he stopped just outside the door. "I had intended to show this to you tomorrow, but the present moment seems to beckon that I do so now." Smiling, obviously elated to reveal his own surprise that he had hidden so well from the girls, the kind old gentleman went on, "Higgins has just put this up in honor of the two dear angels that came into this home and brought a blessing, the like of which my sweetest dreams could only imagine. Forever more—as long as this house stands—the names of Mary Bennet and Georgiana Darcy will be a part of it."

Darcy, Elizabeth and her parents wondered at Lord Dewey speaking in such a way about Mary and Georgiana. Yes, the work on the library did, without question, exceed all expectations, but what could he mean by it? They could only conclude that the great man was eccentric with regard to his home, since they were ignorant of the deeper meaning of his words and all he had let the two girls in on about his daughter those months ago. Stepping inside, he now directed their attention toward the top of the door, revealing a plaque beautifully carved with roses and this inscription: *In gratitude to Miss Mary Bennet and Miss Georgiana Darcy.*

Without hesitation, the young ladies went to his side, embracing him as each in their turn declared, "Lord Dewey, sir, how kind and generous this is of you, and so totally unexpected! However were you able to hide it from us?" Alice happily joined them, the four of them sharing their special relationship that had started slowly and was now a permanent bond. The effusions of the moment were as one might expect …

Mrs. Bennet was beside herself with awe that Mary, her own daughter of whom she thought *her* greatest achievement would be to find a man who would marry her—this very daughter was having her name placed perpetually for all to see in an Earl's grand home! Mr. Bennet, who had similar reflections, could not keep himself from a chuckle at the notion, saying to himself, "My girl being honored in this way, and by an Earl no less .... I would not trade this middle child of mine for ten sons!"

Elizabeth turned to Darcy, remarking, "It seems the Darcy and Bennet names are to be forever coupled in more ways than one," to which her husband replied, "Yes, and I am as proud of this pairing of the names as I am ecstatic about the first."

After all the many things that had occurred on this momentous night, there could not have been found a happier group nor a more perfect end to an evening than this one.

# Chapter Forty-nine

Back at the Darcy residence, everyone had retired to their own apartment when Mary heard a soft knock at her door. She had been too excited to fall asleep, and reaching the door, she opened it to find Georgiana, who began, "Are you exceedingly sleepy, Mary? If so, I will not disturb you."

"No, do come in. I'm glad you have come, but before you tell me what your reason is, I must say something before it gets shoved aside ... it wasn't until I was alone thinking over our event that I realized I neglected to properly thank you for all your kind words about the project, and particularly regarding myself tonight. Your praise really touched my heart."

As they took a seat next to the fire, Georgiana said, "I hope you know I wasn't just trying to be polite. I meant every word of it! That's really what I have come to say to you; there has been so much happening I have not been able to tell you how thankful I am for your letting me be a part of the work on the library, and even more so in helping dear Alice. If it were not for you and your efforts to reach out for your aspirations, I would still be dreading each dinner invitation and ball—I would have some time ago run out of excuses to avoid the lavish, insincere attempts from those suitors bent on wooing me, when they were really more interested in being connected to the Darcy name than they are in me as a person!" This was said with some feeling, but changing from those reflections, she smiled, going on: "And besides ... I would never have met Van."

"I take it, then, you are pleased with the attentions of Mr. Thornburg?"

"It has been so different with him, Mary. He never made me feel nervous ... maybe it had something to do with the fact that I didn't know we were going to meet, since I just stumbled upon him that auspicious day," she laughed. "But, on our first meeting he was so embarrassed because he was rather *clumsy,* knocking over the piano bench, and even falling himself, so I had to do most of the talking. Of course, we were able to talk about his music, but honestly, I think it had more to do with the way he looked at me."

"The way he looked at you?"

"Yes ... he just looked at me as if I were a *person,* not like he was trying to measure my comparative worth in relation to my brother's fortune."

"Ah, I can see why you would appreciate that. I will say this for him, Georgiana: he shows good taste in preferring you over Miss Pinch. It seems most men pander to their vanity when it comes to choosing a young lady and would make their choice based purely on physical and monetary considerations. You, of course, understand I mean no slight on your looks, but Miss Pinch has that kind of beauty that can make men easily overlook her having less fortune. But then, Penelope Pinch also comes with a great fortune."

Georgiana laughed, "I think my value went up in Mr. Thornburg's eyes when he discovered I could play—he seems to prefer that to fortune *and* beauty."

"Men can easily make their preferences when they have their own independent means, certainly; we have that example in your brother choosing my sister. But I will not sit here and sound as if I am demeaning your own beauty and charms when it is clear Mr. Thornburg values these as he should," Mary assured her. "And the fact that he has been so kind to Alice all these years speaks volumes about his being an amiable, loving person who is more interested in character than the pretensions of beauty."

This sort of praise and banter carried on for a few minutes more, after which Georgiana changed the subject. "As much fun as it is to talk of Mr. Thornburg, I did want to ask what you think of your continuing to work on libraries. Is this going to satisfy you, do you think—is it what you were looking for?"

"I may very well have come across something I would not have otherwise thought I could do, much less know that there might be a demand for. But I suppose when someone like Lord Dewey has anything such as this done, it has a way of creating a demand whether there is a real need or not. However, in answer to your question, working in some of the finest homes and making over the libraries within them, at present, is a prospect I find quite stimulating. This makes perfect sense, because that is the wonder of books ... they can take us to places we want to be, they can match our mood when we are down and want to cry, and they can be our companion in pain or lift us up out of our doldrums and bring us out into the hopeful light of the sun. So all things considered, I would say things are looking bright for both of us."

\* \* \* \* \*

The sun *was* shining for Mary and Georgiana. When they began this endeavor together, they were like two birds for whom the sun was beckoning they seek a way to take flight and feel the warmth of its caress. Trusting in their sense of purpose and their convictions, they set out looking for the clouds to part and had found their way to that promising brilliance of the sun.

What a distance our Mary has come ... the middle child that had lived in the shadow of her sisters. Her love for books and learning, contrary to what many may have assumed, proved to be the ray of light that would lead her out into the full brightness of day. Indeed, she now has her own verse to add to the poem of the aristocrat:

> *Mary Bennet I might be ...*
> *The middle child—not much was thought of me.*
> *Open, oh door; let me free.*
> *And I will let the world see*
> *That **the sun also shines for me**.*

~~~~~ THE END ~~~~~

*Noe and Cindy*

# NOE'S NOTES

This writing has been, in some ways, an attempt to give a voice to those people in families that are so often ignored—the middle child. You could say my feelings about this subject were personal, because the individual for whom I have the greatest respect and high opinion of, my dear wife, is a middle child like Mary Bennet.

The more I thought about how amazing my good wife is, therefore, the more I considered what potential there must be in the fictitious character Mary Bennet, who had the tenacity to study diligently and read extensively, something she did for the sole purpose of bettering herself. And this in the face of a family of siblings each pursuing, in one way or the other, the pleasures and advantages to be found at the time. In addition to this, she had the will to excel at the piano by constant practice, even without the stated advice of someone like Lady Catherine; it seems she received no encouragement from anyone in the family for that matter. I asked myself, why would Mary not improve with the passage of time? Certainly seeing the events in her family's life would have undoubtedly caused her to think seriously about what she wanted to do with her own life.

There is also Georgiana Darcy, who is described as being so very shy in **Pride & Prejudice** she could sometimes barely speak. My Cindy is not now, nor has she ever been, like that, even though she did consider herself to be shy when she was younger. How splendid we can find these quiet persons to be if we just take the time and patience to talk with them, bringing their inner beauty out into the light.

I hope after writing this book about Mary and Georgiana that I am permitted to be on a first name basis with these two young ladies, because I certainly feel I am well acquainted with them now. And the idea that these two girls were left hidden in the shadows, as I often feel my wife is, created in me a determination to bring their characters to light, just as I will speak from the rooftops about my wonderful dear wife.

In the writing team of *Noe and Cindy*, I have the imagination to come up with a story, but she has the genius and touch that makes what I write worth reading. She had at the beginning only wanted to be listed as the editor, but because she contributes so much more, I have finally convinced her that she should be put down as co-author.

## About the quotes

Our book has many quotes throughout its pages; it seems only right some explanation be given. Mary, of course, is known for quoting or moralizing in **Pride and Prejudice,** so there needed to be plenty of quotes for her to spread around. Since she's older and more mature than she was in **P&P**, we wanted to make her less annoying about doing that than she may have seemed then, and hopefully we succeeded in that. Most of the quotes are made up by me, and those that are attributed to famous persons like Shakespeare and John Heywood are from them. Coming up with some pithy saying or poem at the right moment was one of the most fun things about writing the book.

## About the cover art

In reading advice about self-publishing, one of the strongest suggestions that's always given is to have the cover done by a qualified expert. As I look at the artwork of many of those so-called professionally done covers, my impression is *cookie cutter.* It appears that most authors go to the very same person for their cover art, or maybe all these pros went to the same school. It reminds me of Andy Warhol and his Campbell soup can art when you go to the bookstore these days.

I do all the work on our book, and Cindy then scans that into the computer and plays around with it. After that, we choose the one we like best. I'll be the first to admit I would never be described as a great artist, but the covers are a rendition of what *I think* best captures the spirit of my books. I prefer that much more than having a marketing person try to place my book into some category that therefore should have this or that look about it, in *their opinion.*

I have a couple of nieces that are exceptional artists and I may one day ask them to help me on a cover. If I do, they will of course be credited, but until then, I love creating the cover art as much as I enjoy writing the story. It isn't just about control of my books and their finished look … there is just a deep satisfaction in knowing that everything about our books is really *ours.*

# CINDY'S NOTES

I love this book. I love how Noe really cares about women, and *me* in particular, of course! He has always been a defender of women, always able to understand and sympathize with us … well, as far as a man can, that is. I think it is a *real man* that loves what most guys call "chick lit" or "chick flicks" and will read those books or watch the movies and actually enjoy them, not being afraid to admit it either. I mean, when you think about it, there's a whole lot of men involved in the making of those books and movies, and I'm proud that Noe is one of them.

When I suggested a few years ago that he write the **Pride & Prejudice** story from Darcy's point of view, I knew he could do it. He did have to do several drafts and even update the book after we published it; it was tough staying within the confines of someone else's story. We absolutely did not want to change anything about Jane Austen's telling from Elizabeth's point of view, so we diligently consulted **P&P** to make sure we were keeping on track. There are many people who have written Austen fan fiction, and that being our thing too, we have kept an eye on what's going on in the field, including reading some of them that I have enjoyed. However, I don't understand, or appreciate for that matter, the way some authors have changed Jane Austen's superb characters into sex-crazed villains or stupid people no one would want to meet … and yet it sells anyway. It's a testament to how much people love **Pride & Prejudice**, I suppose. We would never do that to these characters, and given the fact that all of Jane Austen's books are loved around the world, I think it's safe to say everyone likes the characters and things they do as they are portrayed by her. I was curious to see how Noe would develop Darcy's character, what *Noe* would feel was important to tell that **P&P** didn't, and I was very pleased with the result. If you don't have *Mr Darcy falls in love* yet, you should get it—I think you'll like it too.

Noe and I love to read. I guess I must have read a thousand books when I was a kid, but unfortunately I don't have the memory Noe has, so I can pick up a book I've read before and find it new all over again! Noe has a great memory but didn't read much as a kid; he's found that pleasure as an adult. This hasn't kept him from reading what might be considered "kid's books" though—one of his favorites is *Anne of Green Gables*. But

Noe was *always* a storyteller, and I'm really glad he decided to write them out for all to enjoy.

## The Sun Shines

Now about this middle child book! It's sweet that Noe thought of me in relation to writing this book about Mary Bennet. We both come from big families; he's a middle child too, actually, and even more in the middle than I am, since I'm next-to-last and he's right in the middle. Both of us had parents that were not partial, though, and for the time we grew up and the things our families went through, our parents did a good job raising us both. It's got to be hard having so many little personalities to mold, but it's not hard to love all your kids if you really try. That being said, it is possible to get lost in the crowd or compared unfairly sometimes, so we parents should never forget that each child is a separate person that needs our help to find the sun shining on them individually.

Mary Bennet being such an avid reader and not being talked about much in **P&P** gave us an interesting character to write about. Noe wanted her to be able to go out and grow as an individual, to put all that reading she'd done to good use. But what would be her interest, what would she do? The two of us got to talking about libraries and somehow wound our way to the cataloging of books by means of the *Dewey Decimal System*. Well, as fiction goes, we let Mary come up with a similar system, but we didn't want to use the same name for it so as not to mess with history. Therefore, Mary meets a man named *Dewey* who not only has a large library that needs work but also has a daughter that needs a friend, and together they come up with the *Dewey Index System*. That's the idea in a nutshell and Noe went with that to make this wonderful story about three girls bonding, blossoming and finding their own sunshine.

## Do-it-yourself

Noe and I make a great team. We've been married over 35 years and have been self-employed for almost that entire time. I had the privilege of homeschooling our only son. Noe has always done just about all the maintenance on everything for us, from plumbing to cutting our hair! He's a wood artist too, makes all kinds of wood stuff like earrings, barrettes, silhouettes, lettering, puzzles, statuettes and more—does all the patterns for them also.

So … we self-publish! That's been a really nice project all on its own. When you're used to doing things yourself, there's nothing like the feeling of accomplishment you get when you finish your work and can step back and take a good look at it. Then when other people praise your work, that's a super great feeling! Self-publishing is not too hard, it's the marketing we aren't real great at … so please, tell everyone you know about our books! Word-of-mouth advertising is the best anyway.

I also keep at Noe to do his own cover art. I think he's very good and love that he can draw the concept he has in mind; he doesn't feel as confident about it as I do. But he does agree that far too many covers look the same these days. If one book cuts off everyone's heads, the next one does too! What's with that, anyway? Well, to each his own, as they say, and we just hope our cover art intrigues enough people to pick the book up and take a look.

## The Editor
Do I qualify to be an editor? I don't have any letters following my name, but maybe I should add LECt after mine. After all, *Life Experience Counts too,* doesn't it? Seriously, I'm sure you can think of a few people who are good at what they do even though they never got a degree. Well, I think I do a fair job of editing our books … I can at least say I know that sometimes it is proper to say *"you and me"* instead of *"you and I"* … one of my major pet peeves! However, I do make mistakes, but we really try to comb through and find them all. Hopefully, we have, and if not, I apologize. And as you can see, I like to italicize words frequently, not to mention using dashes and *dot dot dots!*

You may have noticed there is one word I spelled a certain way that some would consider incorrect, but I reserve the right to keep the spelling I use: *judgement* instead of *judgment.* Dictionaries admit to both choices as being fine even though judgment is mostly preferred. Nevertheless, there are other words that could be pointed to in this argument, such as *encouragement, engagement, arrangement,* and more. And online discussions show lots of people prefer the same spelling I do, if only because *it just looks better* to us.

# Thank you

Last of all, but very important to both of us, we would like to say thank you for reading our books. It's kind of incredible to know that something we wrote is in the hands of someone way on the other side of the earth, and especially nice to hear what they thought of it. We hope you'll submit a review for us on Amazon, Goodreads, Barnes & Nobles, or wherever you are able, so that others can decide whether they'd like to read our books as well. It means a lot, so once again, thank you!

It is also our sincere wish that you, just like Mary, are able to say:

## The Sun Also Shines for me.

Made in the USA
San Bernardino, CA
03 June 2017